ARCANE SCHOLAR

FAE ACADEMIA

KATHY HAAN

ISBN 979-8-9855077-9-9 (eBook)

ISBN 978-1-960256-05-8 (paperback)

ISBN 978-1-960256-18-8 (hardback)

First edition May 2023

Book cover design by Leo Burk and Kathy Haan

Published by Thousand Lives Press, LLC

Edited by Fervent Ink

To my beloved Leo, you've given me the gift of life twice over: once when I gave birth to you as a teen mom overcoming addiction, and again every day since, as you and your siblings have been my reason to stay clean and fight for a better future.

Addiction is a monster that feeds on love, until it consumes everything in its path.

— KATHY HAAN

PREFACE

This book dives deep into drug addiction. If you are sensitive to this topic or other adult themes, please proceed with caution.

CHAPTER ONE

ROSE

The woods are eerily silent, as though the entire universe has ceased to take a breath. Tendrils of fear uncoil within me, snaking up from the depths of my being, threatening to throttle me. One thought consumes me.

We're the bad guys.

All it took was one moment of vulnerability—an earth-shattering accusation—and now the only world I've known seems to be unraveling before my eyes.

The scent of damp earth saturates my nostrils, making me acutely aware of my surroundings. My heart thuds against my ribcage, a wild and unsteady rhythm that echoes the pace of my thoughts. It's all so surreal—the darkness of the woods, the incessant buzzing of insects, and the oppressive stillness that envelopes everything around me.

For a moment, I feel as though I've been transported into a nightmare, a place where nothing is as it seems. Somewhere danger lurks around every corner. I pinch myself, hoping to wake up, but the sensation is all too real. I'm here, in the heart of the Witches' Woods, and I have never felt more alone.

My family's fault.

Theo's arms wrap around me, his warmth a beacon of comfort

amidst the chaos swallowing me whole. "I won't let anything bad happen to you, Rose," he promises, his voice like a lifeline.

But it's more than that. It's everyone. My friends, my family. If the secret gets out that we have a royal baby, the repercussions could be devastating. With such low birth rates amongst the fae—though it's on the rise—kidnapping is a very real threat, especially for a royal. And if the unhinged dean of my university gets to my family before I do, no matter how complicit we are in the events that have led to this?

I've got to stop her.

The words Kieran has just spewed toward me echo in my head, filling me with a dread I can't shake. His expression is filled with devastation and rage, the seafoam green of his eyes darkening as they bore into mine. *It wasn't enough that you took my parents from me, but you had to take my best friends, too?*

He hates me, and he has every right to. My family's actions during the war cost him everything. Now he holds the power to tear my world apart, and I'm not sure there's anything I can do to stop him.

My heart thunders in my chest as the crushing weight of our dire predicament slams into me like a crashing wave. Panic starts to ripple through my veins, consuming me with an urgent sense of dread. We need to make sure my sister, Baby Bee, is safe. We can't waste another second.

Casting Kieran one last lingering look, I see the pain etched on his face, his eyes gleaming with tears. I whisper, "I'm sorry," before turning toward my soul-bonded mate, Theo. "We need to sift to my home now," I say, my voice trembling with urgency.

Theo nods, understanding the gravity of the situation. Whispering to him, I describe my family home that's nestled at the top of a mountain pass, so he knows where to bring us. I haven't learned how to teleport yet.

With a sudden, nauseating jolt, we're enveloped by the familiar sensation of sifting, the world around us blurring as we teleport to our destination.

As we reappear, the breathtaking beauty of my family's alabaster home greets us. Nestled between two Rift Pass peaks, the bone-white walls contrast against the vibrant green of the surrounding landscape. The sound of running water echoes throughout the house, soothing despite the urgency of our situation.

My gaze is drawn to the clear floors, through which we can see the river running beneath our feet. Large silver fish with translucent fins swim past, their graceful movements mesmerizing. The breathtaking view of the Sea of Triune stretches out before us on the South side of the house, while the back side offers a snow-covered valley far below.

Before we can take in the rest of the surroundings, the weight of the truth crashes down on me. Dean Fallgren knows about Baby Bee, and she must be seeking revenge for her own loss. Kieran's mom—also Dean Fallgren's daughter—is dead.

One daughter for another.

The thought is almost too much to bear, and my breath comes in short, panicked gasps. I feel Theo's hand on my back, rubbing slow circles in an attempt to soothe me.

"We'll get through this, Rose," he whispers, strength lacing his voice, bolstering me where I have none. "Together."

His reassurance is a balm to my frayed nerves, and I cling to it, though my entire body still trembles. I feel like I'm drowning.

As we search for Baby Bee, I call out the names of my family members, my voice ringing through the silent halls of our home, shrill and so unlike my own. The house feels empty, devoid of the warmth and love that usually permeates the air. Why is it so quiet? My heart thrashes in my chest with the possibility that the dean could still be lurking somewhere, waiting for the right moment to strike.

I know we have silent alarms set up to trigger if someone without our blood sifts here. Very few people outside of the family know about this place. After the artifact went missing—the one that enables its bearer to control our family—we'd devised a spell that alerts the household when there's an intruder, but it can't be heard by those teleporting in. It casts a silencing bubble over us, so there could be a whole party going on in the next room, and we'd never hear a peep. And because I sifted here with Theo, I won't know if the alarm has been activated. It needs to be reset each time. Does this mean that Dean Fallgren didn't trip it? Or that she did, and my family is hurt?

The shadows that have been lurking just beyond the edges of my world seem to be closing in, and I can't help but wonder if it's already too late. Has the darkness finally come to claim us all? As fear coils in my gut, I know one thing with chilling certainty: our lives will never be the same again.

Standing inside my family home in the mountains of Rexuna, it's more like a wilderness day spa than a castle, with a waterfall running underneath the see-through floor that spills over the side of a mountain, and white, stone-carved walls. The tranquil sound of the water offers no comfort as my pulse thunders with worry for Baby Bee.

"Mom! Dad!" I call out, the sound frantic as I search the room for any sign of my baby sister or my parents.

Theo stays close, his hand resting protectively on the small of my back as we make our way through the house. The echo of our footsteps reverberates through the spacious halls, heightening my unease.

My parents emerge from an adjoining room, their faces etched with concern. The sight of my mother and my seven fathers makes my knees buckle, and Theo supports me with an arm around my waist.

All eight pairs of eyes shift from me to Theo, their gazes narrowing with suspicion. They've never met him before, and it's only natural for them to be cautious of a stranger in their home. Do they suspect he's controlling me with the missing artifact?

"Rose, who is this?" my father, Oz, asks, his voice guarded as he holds out a cautious hand to shield Mom.

"I'll explain that in a second," I choke out. "But first, where's Baby Bee?" My voice is tinged with hysteria, causing them to pause.

Auguste takes a small step forward, his vampire eyes locked on me as his instincts kick in. He's been head of our security since long before they ever came to the fae realm. "The strength of a kingdom?"

Right. Our secret phrase, the one we came up with that'll let them know I'm not being controlled by the missing bracelet. "Lies in the bonds of family."

They each relax, approaching me with an easy familiarity.

"Wait!" I try to sound calm, even as my nerves threaten to shatter. "Where's Bee?"

"We got her into the safe room as soon as the alarm tripped," Gideon says, nodding toward Finn, who disappears behind them, presumably to get Bee now that they know it's safe.

My anxiety coils inside me, tightening until my chest aches like I've been punched. "I have to see her!" I cry out in desperation. Until I'm sure she's safe, every breath will be a struggle.

I tear away from my parents and race down the hallway, heading for our family's hidden entrance between the kitchen and stairwell. My fingers trace the secret rune that opens the panel, which shimmers before fading away. I lunge through it, sprinting down the stairs and across the basement floor with only one thought on my mind: I need to make sure Bee is okay.

I skid around the final corner, letting out a breathless gasp when I spot Bee in her crib. She smiles wide at me, wriggling her little body against side rails as if trying to reach me. My heart leaps with joy and my worries disappear. Bee is safe. For now.

"What's going on?" Mom calls out behind me, but I'm too focused on reaching into the crib, needing to hold her, to anchor myself to the fact she's okay.

My knees collapse beneath me, tears streaming down my face, as relief courses through me at having her safe in my arms. I press my tear-stained cheeks against hers as she babbles happily in my ear. I cradle her to my chest, trembling as I rock back and forth.

"Rose?" Finn's voice startles me, and I meet his eyes, feeling the weight of betrayal slide under my skin. "Dean Fallgren has to be the one behind it all," I gasp between sobs. "Kieran is her grandson. His parents were killed because of our war—and they hate our family as a result."

I see the moment the gravity of the situation registers on each of my parents' faces. The dean is the one who teleported me to this very house when Mom was in labor. She knows both about Baby Bee and how to get here.

We led our enemy right into our home.

In a broken voice, I relay what happened in the woods, and Auguste barks out rapid-fire instructions to each member of the family. Within moments, my dads fall into their roles, preparing for battle against an unforgiving foe.

Theo stands on the stairs, hesitant as he explains what he knows to Gideon, who stops in his tracks.

"And who the fuck are you?"

"Dad, this is Theo," I explain, trying to keep my voice calm. "He's—"

My words are cut off by a terrifying screech that shreds through the air like a razor blade. A chill of dread runs down my spine and I whirl around, sprinting toward the kids' bedroom in the basement where Mom's agonizing screams cascade from the walls.

"Novaleigh!" She shrieks my other little sister's name with guttural panic.

"What?!" Oz tears through the room, searching for something unknown, his fingers clawing at his hair.

"Where is Nova?" My legs buckle beneath me as I lean against the doorframe, my lungs constricting in terror. "Where is she?!"

Grimm's hands dig into my shoulders like a vice, radiating magical energy that attempts to quell my rising panic. "Where is Kieran now?" His voice rumbles with power.

"We left him in the woods, but he's probably back at the dorms now. His room is next door to mine," I explain.

Penn slams his fist against the fingerprint pad next to our cache of weapons and magic-inhibiting cuffs. "I've been waiting to get my hands on this little fucker."

"I'm coming with you." Casimir reaches for a pair of cuffs and slides them into his back pocket. "Grimm, you're with us."

"We'll search the property for Nova." Gideon turns the display on for all our security feeds, illuminating the whole room with its glow. His movements are swift and smooth, a master of his craft as his eyes rapidly scan the display, taking in every detail for any sign of movement. He barely blinks as he searches for my sister.

As my parents prepare to search and confront Kieran, a mixture of dread and determination wells up inside me. We must find Novaleigh and bring her home, safely.

My parents exchange a look—fear flickering in their eyes, but beneath it, a stubborn defiance. Without a word, we all know the same truth: whatever comes next, we'll face it together.

Theo watches from the stairs, clearly unsure of his role in all of this, desperate to do something but not wanting to get in the way. Our eyes meet for a moment, and I give him a small nod of gratitude for helping me get here.

With a deep breath, I gather my courage and step forward to join my family, ready to do whatever it takes to protect those I love.

We all run up the stairs, ready to scour the property as Casimir, Penn, and Grimm sift to the Bedlam Academy campus on the continent of Academia.

Mom's voice is hysterical as she calls out for Nova.

Sensing an opportunity to help, Theo's eyes meet mine again. "Rose, I can shift into my griffin form and get an aerial view of the property. I might be able to find Nova faster."

I nod, and he leads me to the deck. The wind whips around us as Theo closes his eyes, concentrating. In seconds, his body transforms into a majestic golden griffin. The sun catches on his feathered wings, casting a shimmering glow on the snow-covered ground below.

He spreads his wings wide, and with a powerful leap, takes flight, his strong wings beating against the frigid air. He soars high above the property, his keen eyes scanning the landscape below for any sign of my sister.

CHAPTER TWO

THEO

The scent of pine greets me as I rise higher into the sky; the world below me begins to transform into a vast mosaic of snow and forest, with the stark contrast between the white and dark making it easier for me to spot any disturbances. The cold air rushes around me, its icy bite sinking into my golden feathers, but I'm undeterred.

I allow my senses to adjust to my griffin form, focusing my keen vision on the landscape below, searching for any hint of Novaleigh. It's vital I find her quickly, and my heart hammers in my chest as I scan the property below, hoping for a glimpse of her.

I circle the property, allowing the wind currents to guide me effortlessly through the sky. The biting air buffets me as I glide over the mountain pass, the view beneath me becomes a wonderland of snow-capped trees and hidden trails. The snowy landscape, beautiful and serene, belies the danger that my newfound family faces.

Continuing my search, I become hyper-aware of the sounds around me—the wind rustling the branches of the trees, the distant roar of the waterfall, and the almost imperceptible crunching of snow beneath the feet of the family members searching for Novaleigh.

With each pass, my determination to find her grows stronger. I focus intently on the ground below, using my enhanced vision to spot any movement or tracks that might lead me to her.

Eyes keen on the glittering landscape, I sweep over the woods, my eyes catch a small flash of movement near the base of a tree. My heart leaps with hope, and I quickly swoop down for a closer look.

There, huddled against the snow-covered trunk, I find Novaleigh, her wide eyes filled with wonder and her cheeks rosy from the cold. She's cradling a tiny, snow-covered creature in her arms. A snowfurl, a native fae creature that resembles a cross between a rabbit and a fawn, with iridescent fur and curling, delicate horns.

She must've been off chasing this little beast. My body sags with the immense relief at finding her safe, and I can't help but let out a triumphant call that pierces the sky. It reverberates through the forest, cracking the air in an unmistakable caw of victory that also signals to the others my discovery.

I lower my massive body, carefully approaching her to avoid scaring her further. With my gentlest caw, I use my magic to reassure her that everything is okay, and that I'm there to help. Novaleigh, awed by the beautiful griffin before her, reaches out to pet me.

Allowing her to sink her fingers into my feathers, without a doubt, I know this is her. Her aura is the same brilliant blue as her sister's, though I get a sense of reckless wonder beneath it all, even more than Rose.

I carefully scoop her up in my massive talons, ensuring her safety as I prepare to take to the skies again. With Novaleigh secure, I leap into the air, my powerful wings lifting us both as I soar back toward the house, eager to reunite her with our family.

Approaching the property, I angle my wings to slow my descent, ensuring a smooth and gentle landing on the expansive deck. The relief of having found Novaleigh safe and sound courses through my veins, fueling my every movement.

As soon as my talons touch the wooden surface, I gently set her down, making sure she's steady on her feet before I begin to shift back into my fae form. The transformation is smooth and fluid, the once-golden feathers of my griffin form seamlessly melding back into my skin, leaving me standing in front of her in my fae state.

Novaleigh gazes up at me with awe and admiration, her eyes wide and sparkling with wonder. Though I may be an outsider in this family, the desire to protect and care for them has become a part of me.

With a shy smile, Novaleigh reaches out and tentatively takes my hand, her fingers small and cold from her time spent in the snow. I give her hand a reassuring squeeze, promising her that she's safe now and that everything will be okay.

As we step inside the house, the rest of the family converges upon us, their relief palpable as they see Novaleigh safe in my grasp. Rose rushes to her sister's side, wrapping her arms around her and holding her close, her eyes brimming with tears of relief and gratitude.

My gaze meets Rose's, and we share a moment of understanding, the bond between us only growing stronger in the face of it all. In that instant, it's clear that I'm no longer just a stranger who'd wandered into their lives but a part of this family, united by love and a fierce determination to protect one another.

Relief sweetens the air, and Rose's parents each take their turns ensuring Nova's unharmed, needing to inspect for themselves. She holds up the little snowfurl, her eyes bright with excitement.

"Look at what I found!" She squeals, hugging it to her chest. "Can I keep him, Mom?"

"Sweetheart, the beauty of nature is that it cannot be tamed or controlled, and to cage a wild creature is to deny its true purpose and destiny." Her mom runs a hand over the animal's back. "You can admire it and work to keep it safe and free, but a wild beast belongs to no one, except to the earth and sky. I know you already love this little fella, but the true wonder of nature is in its diversity and unpredictability, not in our ability to shape it to our will."

"Sorry, pumpkin." Oz puts a comforting hand on her shoulder. "It isn't meant to be a pet to be kept, but a spirit to be respected."

Nova frowns, shedding tears as she puts the snowfurl down. It curls around her ankle, making little mewling noises as it tries to get her to pick it up again. It gets more insistent as she cries harder.

High King Finn steps forward, wincing as he takes in the scene. "It'll do no good to tell it to go away. It's already bonded."

"What do you mean?" Gideon crouches so he's at the same level as Nova.

"It's imprinted on her," I breathe. "Snowfurls are spirit-bound, sent by the gods to keep special fae safe. This is the greatest gift one could ever receive from the council, aside from maybe a soul-bonded mate."

The king spins on me. "You're a griffin—I'm guessing that's how you know this, and thank you for finding our daughter—but who the hell are you?"

～

Rose

"THIS IS THEO," I explain, trying to sound calm even as my nerves threaten to shatter. "My soul-bonded mate."

My parents exchange a worried glance before Finn steps forward to take my hand. He's my mom's soul-bonded mate, so he should have a good idea of where we're coming from. "Are you sure?" he asks gently, his expression softening with sympathy. "You're so young, and this kind of bond can be overwhelming."

"Positive," I reply firmly, allowing him to embrace me. When mom recovers from her shock, she joins him.

"I want a soul-bonded mate." Novaleigh sighs, like a fairytale princess in a movie. It's that lovey-dovey, forlorn kind of sigh that tells you she's probably romanticizing every piece of it in her head.

Next, Mom pulls Theo in for a hug. He beams under her affection, relief softening the expression on his face that he isn't about to be thrown off the side of the mountain. Not that it'd kill him. He's got wings.

But my dads are creative. They probably would've tied him to a boulder at the top of the waterfall and pushed him over it, just to give him a little scare.

We gather together in the living room, the sound of rushing water from the waterfall roaring like a beast through the open balcony doors. The transparent floor beneath our feet trembles with every step we take, and embedded floor lights casts a dazzling glow that bounces off the smooth, stone walls, illuminating our faces with an eerie brilliance.

"What are you guys going to do with Kieran?"

"I vote we just kill the little prick." Gideon leans back in his recliner, cleaning his fingernail with a dagger.

"Language!" Mom scolds him, earning her an affectionate grin after Gideon leans over to give Baby Bee a kiss on the head.

It's funny, because Mom swears like a sailor, too.

"He's got a point." Oz stretches, causing Theo to shift nervously in his seat beside me.

I cast a worried glance his way, wincing at the stricken look on his face.

Doesn't everyone's parents casually talk about murder before bed?

No?

Just mine?

Novaleigh leans against me affectionately, eyes trained on Theo as she runs her fingers through the fur of the little beast on her lap. I elbow her a little, and her cheeks turn scarlet as she grumbles at me. She's already got a crush on my boyfriend, Mekhi, and now it seems she thinks Theo is cute, too.

Not that I blame her.

He flashes her a grin, damn near lighting up the whole place with his golden aura, and it's then I notice he's glamored his tattoos. Right now, his skin only appears tanned.

As a professor, he's used to doing that on campus, but I guess we never really talked about how half of my parents have their own tattoos. Mom and Finn even have their soul-bonded tattoo covering their arms and necks.

Will Theo and I get them, too? The thought of it stirs something sweet in my chest.

Dragging my eyes away from his dark hair and gilded eyes, I feel my own cheeks flush. I'm still getting used to the fact that this man is mine.

Forever. They all are.

"We should let Bennett and Mekhi know." I turn to Oz, and he nods while I get in touch with Jax and Deakan.

I pull out my own phone and send them a quick message, letting them know that we're safe and filling them in on the situation. I ask them to join us as soon as possible. "Jax and Deakan are on their way, too."

As I put my phone away, my mother speaks up. "We need to ward the house again. Just in case."

"Agreed." Finn runs a hand through his hair.

My parents stand before me, tightly woven ropes of energy shooting from their hands to create an invisible wall around our house.

I feel the weight of despair pressing against my chest like a boulder as I watch the edges of the life I know dissolve into nothingness. The last vestiges of my childhood claw at the air in vain, desperately attempting to keep the world I know afloat.

But as I look around the room at some of the people who matter most to me—my family, Theo, and my other mates who will soon arrive—I know that I have to find the strength to face what's coming.

And I've got to protect them, no matter the cost.

WE GATHER around the dining table, my parents sharing their knowledge of the school's administration, what we know of the Fallgrens, and possible motives for the threats against us. Theo chimes in, earning suspicion from my dads.

Now that I've got several mates, my parents seem more receptive to including me in making decisions.

The sound of the front door opening and closing alerts us to the arrival of Jax and Deakan. Relief eases my taut shoulders as I see their familiar faces. Jax, tall and broad-shouldered, exudes a confident air. His curly brown hair is swept back, accentuating the striking blue eyes that ensnared me long before I knew he was mine. He's dressed casually but with an undeniable elegance that speaks to his wealthy dragon lineage, and his mere presence commands attention.

Deakan, my lion with sun-streaked blond hair that falls effortlessly around his face, offers a bright and laid-back vibe. His eyes, like molten amber, seem to radiate warmth, making everyone around him feel at ease. His athletic build and easy smile give him the aura of a friendly, approachable guy-next-door.

I choose my words carefully when I tell them what happened with Kieran. After all, he's their best friend. The looks on their faces are those of absolute heartbreak.

"Are we sure Kieran is in on this?" Jax sinks into the seat across from me after giving me a kiss on the head, earning the stink eye from a few of my fathers. "I just . . ." he buries his head in his hands. "Gods."

I scoot my chair back and come around the table to stand behind him, running my fingers through his hair. "We can't be sure yet, but everything points to him being involved in some way."

Deakan sighs. "I hate to say it, but *if* he is involved, it could be dangerous to confront him directly. He's a serpent."

Jax's agony radiates off him like the dark tendrils of a haunting mist. When he looks at my parents, his tear-stained cheeks nearly bring me to my knees. His broken words fracture the air around us as he says, "I have to talk to him. He . . . he's troubled, but he's our best friend. If he knew what his grandma was doing, there's no way he would've . . ." His voice is so tortured and despairing that it shreds away at my heart until I'm left with nothing but aching sorrow.

"I'm sure we'll get it all sorted," I whisper, running my fingers through his curls. "They'll bring him in for questioning. Dean Fallgren, too."

A piercing sound fills the air, vibrating through our bodies like a shockwave as the perimeter alarm erupts into an infernal wail. So *this* is what the alarm sounds like. We gather around the live camera feed with bated breath, waiting to see what could have caused such a disturbance.

Two guys wearing hooded sweaters pop through a portal, and through the grainy picture in the dark, I can tell right away who they are. I barrel for the door, my bare feet slapping on the glass floor as Theo calls after me.

The portal set off the alarm, not the people who stepped through it.

I throw the front door open, tackling the first one to enter. As my twin, he looks a lot like me, only he has curly hair and much darker skin on account of Oz being his biological father. "I'm so glad you guys are alright."

"Can't. Breathe," Bennett wheezes, and I chuckle and let him go before doing the same to Mekhi.

As Mekhi picks me up and spins me around, I take in his strong yet gentle presence. His dark hair, slightly tousled, adds a touch of rebelliousness to his demeanor. A charming, crooked smile graces his lips, emphasizing his handsome features. His tanned skin highlights his toned physique. As he tightens his arms around me, I can't help but appreciate the sense of security his embrace brings.

"You're okay." He tightens his arms around me.

"Yeah, I'm okay."

When he sets me down, I tug him inside, and introduce him to Theo.

As a witch, Mekhi isn't as enormous as a fae, but he's pretty built after spending so much time training with my family. We took him in over a year ago after he came to Bedlam.

He stands tall and proud amongst the rest of my family, commanding respect as if he's always belonged. His regal features are as handsome as any of our kind, and though we haven't mated yet, I can feel the eventuality of it all. His eyes captivate me, and I let out a deep longing that I hope he can feel too.

"Hey." Theo shakes Mekhi's hand. "Thanks for keeping her safe when I couldn't be there."

"Anything for her." Mekhi's eyes soften as they find mine.

Nova peeks out from behind me and rests her head on my shoulder. "Hey, Khi."

"How's my favorite Luna fae?" Mekhi pulls her in for a hug and she giggles when her little creature crawls up her to weave itself around her neck. "Been practicing with any of the throwing knives I made? And who is this?"

"My new friend, but Mom says I have to go to bed." She pouts. "She took my knives away after Pierce let me use him as target practice after supper."

Pierce is our family's personal guard, though now he's just like one of our own.

Mekhi chuckles. "How else are you going to grow tall and strong like Rose and Bennett if you don't get some sleep?"

She sighs. "Fine."

Novaleigh trots upstairs, Mom following closely behind her with Baby Bee on her hip.

WE SPEND the next hour brainstorming, going over different scenarios and possible outcomes. It's a daunting task, but we all know that we need to be prepared for anything.

As the night stretches on, I can feel the exhaustion creeping up on me. My mates exchange looks, silently communicating their concern for my well-being. I smile, because they think I don't notice, and lean into them.

"I'm okay," I tell them as a yawn wracks my body. "Just tired." Glancing at my phone, I see that it's already past two.

"Why don't you all head to bed? Auguste and I can continue researching," Oz says. They're the only two vampires in this house and don't need sleep. And while fae don't need as many hours as humans do, we still need to recharge.

"You sure, Dad?" I reach for my mug of coffee, frowning when I find it empty.

Theo nudges his mug over to me, and I beam at him when I find his full. "Thank you." I take a sip to test it before emptying it down the hatch. "Okay, I'm ready for bed."

Mekhi chuckles at the bemused expression on Theo's face. "You should see what she does with pineapple and pizza."

"What do you do with pineapple and pizza?" Deakan, who has never turned down a meal in his life—though you couldn't tell from his rock-hard abs—is always down to try my crazy food combinations.

I shrug. "Pineapple and Canadian bacon go together on pizza. It's delicious."

Gideon shoves back from the table. "I can't listen to this blasphemy."

"Dad!" I laugh. "It's so good! Ask Mom." It feels good to joke around with the family, though under it all, I can sense the unease censuring our words. I've found a way to use humor to help me cope with my trauma, otherwise I'd crumble, especially after everything we've been through.

Exhaustion seeps into my bones from the stress of everything. Anxiety still stirs in my chest over the huge ordeal with Kieran and his grandmother.

Gideon turns to face me, a repulsed look marring his features, though not hiding his deep-set dimples. "You know I was born in Italy, right?"

"Doesn't count if you haven't lived there in hundreds of years," Oz adds, his brow cocked.

Another yawn sneaks up on me, and I stretch my arms above my head, feeling the pull of muscles from the impromptu lovemaking session Theo and I had in his office earlier tonight that spurred this whole ordeal—Kieran finding us and later confronting us.

"You." Auguste gestures to me. "Head to bed. We'll clean up."

"You sure?" I ask. Though I'm not sure I can actually sleep. Not when my other dads are out looking for Kieran and his grandma.

Oz and Auguste are already busy collecting mugs and bringing them into the kitchen before Mom can respond, "Go."

I give everyone hugs and pause on the stairs when Gideon calls out to me. "Alone."

I whip around, scoffing. "Dad, I'm mated."

"Pity she'll be widowed so young." Oz turns to Gideon, frowning.

Deakan makes a choked sound, somewhere between a laugh and a cough. "I don't mean to be a pain, but do you all remember what happened the last time I was kept from her?"

If the memory wasn't so terrible, I'd grin at how brave he's being. Seven royal dads are intimidating.

But I can't. It was one of the worst days of my life.

When Deakan and I first mated, he thought I was rejecting him when I didn't come back to the dorms, but it was only because I hadn't realized when I had bitten him, that I'd solidified the mating bond. He went feral, and while he doesn't recall—and we haven't told him—his lion jumped through a window, with Jax in the way.

It had killed Jax, and I'd been arrested for his murder.

My dads seem to register the way my expression shutters, because they relent. Cautious feet climb the stairs behind me, and I lead my men down to my bedroom.

"Rose!" Mom shouts from downstairs, and I freeze before turning toward the stairs. "Your dads just called—they've got him!"

Relief sinks in my chest as she makes an appearance on the landing. "What about his grandma?"

"Not yet," she frowns, hugging her middle. "They're holding him for questioning until morning."

Jax and Deakan step forward, anxiety pouring off them, but she reassures them. "No harm will come to Kieran until we've had a chance to interrogate him."

"Thank you," Jax chokes out, bracing himself against the wall.

She smiles at him, nodding before she goes back downstairs.

Deakan claps Jax on the shoulder. "They're good people," he reminds Jax. "He'll be okay until we get this all sorted out."

I take Jax's hand, leading him back to my room.

We file in, and I wince when I spot my twin-XL bed along the wall.

"Oh, I guess I didn't think this far ahead." I shut the door, making sure to lock it.

Mekhi places his hand over mine on the lock. "Hold up."

I step back, and he disappears down the hallway for a few minutes before he returns carrying his much larger bed he grabbed from his room. He lives here, when not at college, because our family took him in over a year ago when his uncle died.

"How is it fair they let you get a big bed, and they give me a small one?" I pout.

"Calculated move on their part, I imagine." Deakan chuckles.

"Double standards," I scoff, stepping aside while he hauls it inside the room.

"Here." He tosses it on the floor before dragging mine onto the floor next to it and slides them together. "All better."

"Good idea."

I cross to my closet, searching for something I can lend Jax, Deakan, and Theo to wear to bed, but come up empty-handed. Poking my head back out of the closet, I make to tell them I don't have anything, but they're already tugging their shirts off, and my mouth dries up, and the sound that comes out is less of a coherent word and more of a squeak.

Their heads snap up, each wearing identical expressions of amusement.

"What's wrong, Rose?" Deakan grins.

"I-uh," I stammer, my eyes darting around the room before gesturing wildly to the obscene picture they make, standing there half-naked in my bedroom.

"What is it?" Theo raises a brow, enjoying watching me squirm.

I disappear into the closet, shutting the door so I can compose myself. Taking several deep breaths, I pull my shirt over my head and change into pajamas I find in the bottom of my drawer.

By the time I step out, the guys are lounging in various spots around my room, still amused as they take in my frazzled state.

"Theo?" I approach him, gesturing my finger in a circle to indicate the whole room. "Can you put up a silencing bubble?" Since he'd reached maturity six years ago, he's the oldest and most versed in magic amongst us, so these little things come easy for him.

"Already did." He pulls me into his arms. "I was just really enjoying watching you try to keep your hormones under control. And I already sealed the two beds together."

I swat at him playfully. "You're a terrible influence on them all. Aren't you supposed to be the mature, distinguished professor?"

He raises a brow at me, and the look in his golden eyes tells me he's up to no good. "Who says I can't have a little fun every now and then?"

Images of him bending me over his desk earlier tonight have me weak in the knees. But if I didn't roll my eyes, I wouldn't be me. A smile tugs at my lips. "Just don't corrupt them too much." I press a kiss to his cheek, pausing at his ear. "Sir," I add as I push off him and saunter towards the bed.

The chuckle that rolls through Theo's chest sends a flood of heat through me as I plop onto the mattress on the floor.

I reach over to grab the pillows, arranging them at the head of it.

"Why do you have so many pillows?" Theo remarks, taking in the six king-sized pillows and three body pillows I've arranged.

I shrug. "Since I was a kid, I always said I was going to grow up to have lots of mates like my mom. Guess I was just practicing."

Theo shakes his head as he takes a seat next to me, his hand reaching down to caress my thigh.

The others scramble for the bed, diving onto the mattress in an attempt to get close to me.

"I think we'll have to set up rotations to keep it fair." I use the scrunchy on my wrist to put my long brown hair into a messy bun.

"Jax has used up all his turns." Deakan hauls me out of my spot and brings me onto his side.

I laugh as Theo captures me, lifting me over Deakan's head and onto his side again. "Fine, but as soul bond, I think I have—"

"Okay, okay, guys." I sit up. "First night, Theo and Deakan sleep on either side of me. Tomorrow, it's Jax and Mekhi."

"But Mekhi isn't even your ma—" Deakan begins.

"Don't you dare finish that sentence," I warn, venom in my voice. "Just because Mekhi and I haven't mated—yet—doesn't mean you can treat him as though he's less than. I've loved this man for over a year. That's a whole year longer than I've loved you. Understood?"

Regret flashes in Deakan's eyes. "You're right, I'm sorry."

"New bonds are a little emotional." Theo places a reassuring hand on my arm. "Deakan's beast might still be feeling territorial after everything that happened."

"Sorry." I give Deakan a kiss on the lips, lingering long enough so his beast settles down a bit. "I shouldn't have raised my voice at you."

"I'd hardly call that raising your voice." He twines his fingers in my hair. He seems to consider his words for a bit. "But hold up a minute. Did you say you love me?"

A grin crosses my face. "I do."

Tears well in his eyes. "I love you, too."

Climbing over Deakan, I crawl into Jax's lap, wrapping my arms around his neck. "I love you." I kiss him, lingering on his lips. "And you." I turn to Mekhi, who's sitting next to us. "I love you, too."

Mekhi gives me a small smile, his dark eyes locking with mine. "I love you most."

I shake my head, chuckling softly as I crawl back over to my spot.

As I lay down, my thoughts turn back to the broken man we'd left in the woods. As if sensing my overwhelm, Theo gently pulls me toward him, making sure I'm comfortably tucked into his side.

Deakan slides in closer behind me, wrapping his strong arms around me, effectively sandwiching me between their warmth. Being between them helps ease the ache in my chest over worrying about Kieran.

With a flick of my wrist, I use magic to switch off the light and turn the fan on, hoping for some relief from the heat enveloping me.

However, the combined body heat of my two companions quickly becomes too much. With a small sigh, I decide to strip down to just my underwear, seeking a bit more comfort in the sweltering situation.

Deakan lets out a playful groan, the vibrations tickling my skin. "Your dads are going to kill me," he murmurs, his lips gently brushing against my neck as he speaks. The sensation sends shivers down my spine, and he adds with a mischievous grin, "But I'll die happy."

I laugh, feeling his breath stir the hair against my neck. The intimacy of our position, combined with the light banter, brings a sense of contentment and closeness between us, helping ease the stress of the night.

Deakan traces small circles on my hip, kneading my flesh every few minutes to soothe me. Soon, a soft blue glow illuminates the room, and the rest of the men groan, too, knowing it's basically a giant bat signal advertising just how aroused I am.

Luna fae only glow when we're aroused, hurting, healing, or when we are under the moon. And with the drapes shut and my arousal perfuming the air, it's easy to guess which one it is.

Theo's hand grazes my thigh as he shifts closer to me. A whisper of, "I have an idea," brushes against my ear, and I feel a wave of chills cascade throughout my body.

I turn to face him, intrigued. With Theo, there's never a dull moment because he was made for me, and knows me better than anyone at my most fundamental level. "And what might that be?" I whisper back, tracing my fingers along the defined muscles of his chest.

Theo grins before he murmurs his idea in my ear. I can feel my heart racing with excitement as I nod my agreement and lay on my stomach.

We need this distraction.

He slides out of bed, planting a soft kiss on my lips before heading over to my nightstand. He pulls out a small bottle of oil and makes his way back to the bed.

Deakan, Mekhi, and Jax watch with interest as Theo pours a small amount of the oil into his hands, heating it up with his magic. I can feel my skin flush with anticipation as he gently rubs the oil onto my shoulders, his fingers massaging out any tension that had built up during the day. His touch is slow and deliberate, each motion calculated to elicit a moan from my lips.

As he works his way down my back, his hands trail lower until they reach the waistband of my panties. I can't help but arch my back, silently begging for more.

Theo chuckles, dipping his fingers underneath the fabric, teasing me until I'm writhing beneath his touch.

Deakan leans over me, his lips ghosting over my ear. "Can I take these off?" he asks in a husky voice, his hand slipping down to my hip.

I nod, my breath hitching in my throat as Deakan slides my baby blue underwear down my legs, exposing me completely to the eager eyes of my mates. Mekhi crawls up next to me, his hand trailing up my thigh as he leans in to plant a kiss on my lips.

Theo's large hands bracket my hips, and he hoists me until my ass is in the air, bared to the room.

Jax comes up behind me, his hand running over my exposed back as he leans in close to my ear. "You're so beautiful," he whispers, his voice thick with desire.

I shiver in anticipation as Theo pours more oil onto his hands, rubbing it over my skin until I'm coated in the slick substance. Deakan's lips are on my neck now, nipping and kissing the sensitive skin there as Mekhi's fingers trail over my stomach.

Theo takes a deep breath before easing two fingers inside of me, a low moan escaping my lips. His fingers move in a slow and steady rhythm, drawing out pleasure unlike anything I've ever felt before. The feeling of my mates' hot bodies radiating warmth over me is comforting, but the knowledge that they're getting excited by watching Theo's hand disappear inside of me almost pushes me over the edge.

"God, baby," Deakan moans into my hair, "you look amazing. Can't wait to have you coming all over our cocks."

I push back, riding Theo's hand until I'm practically seated in his lap. Jax reaches for my clit, dragging a low keening sound out of me as my orgasm rockets through my body.

Theo's hot breath whispers against my neck as I come down from the high, and a moment of clarity strikes me.

"Condoms. Tell me one of you brought condoms," I beg as Theo drags his fingers out of me and bands his arm around my waist.

The room quiets as they all exchange looks.

"Do you have any in your drawer?" Mekhi asks me.

"Now why would I have condoms in my drawer? My dads would've murdered you if they found any, whether or not we'd even been intimate."

"Isn't there a spell you can do to prevent pregnancy?" Jax looks at Theo over my shoulder. "Or that one tea?"

"There is, but I don't know it. I didn't think I'd be meeting my soul-bonded mate anytime soon."

Griffins save themselves for their soul bonds, and some people wait thousands of years to find theirs.

"If she got pregnant now, I'm pretty sure each of her dads would kill us. Her mom might, too." Deakan huffs. "Can you imagine? Going to college with your own kid?"

Fae mature within eighteen to twenty-four months of age, and inherit their parents' intelligence. And at full maturity, they attend university, with the physiological bodies of twenty-five-year-old humans. The thing that non-fae folk struggle to comprehend, is that this supercharged aging process from birth to full maturity actually only takes two years to complete.

The sudden change in conversation has a sobering effect on me, extinguishing the fiery desire that had consumed me just moments before. The blue glow emanating from my skin slowly fades away as my libido retreats, making way for a more subdued atmosphere. Carefully, I slide off Theo's lap, gently tugging at his arm to guide him down to the mattress alongside me.

As we lay there, the darkness envelops us, allowing for a moment of quiet reflection. The gentle hum of the fan in the background seems to underscore our measured breaths, creating a soothing symphony that fills the room. In this calm and peaceful space, we find solace, connecting not through touch, but through our shared presence in the stillness.

"I think I have a breeding kink," Mekhi calls out, earning chuckles from the others and a groan from me.

"Don't you dare," I whine, burying my face against Theo's chest. It rumbles with his barely contained laughter, and I grumble, flopping over so I can rest my head on Deakan's instead.

"I heard kinks are hereditary," Theo muses, causing everyone else to groan. "Makes sense, though."

"I don't know, Rose." Deakan's chest purrs with deep contentment, his beast sated to have me in his arms. "What Mekhi says has merit. Watching my come spill out of your pussy, only to shove it back in, sounds kind of hot."

"I'm with Mekhi on this, too." Jax props himself on his elbow so he can see over Mekhi. His eyelids are at half-mast, and a grin plasters his face. "You'd take it so well."

This is dangerous territory. "The first one who can learn—and apply—that birth control spell can be the first to come in me." I hitch my leg over Deakan, settling in.

The room is silent, kind of like a calm before a storm, and then everyone erupts into absolute chaos as they lunge for their phones. I'm left on the mattress by myself, giggling like an idiot as I watch them hunt my room for ingredients while referencing their phones.

The whispering of disagreements lulls me into a heavy slumber, dragging me down into the murky depths of dreamland. I drift off with a contented smile on my face.

CHAPTER THREE

ROSE

id-morning, a knock at my bedroom door wakes me, but I can't move. Can hardly breathe. For two seconds, I panic, until deep purring rumbles against my chest. Somehow, I've ended up under Deakan, his body draped over me like a blanket made from solid concrete.

"Rose?" Mom's voice calls through the door. "Breakfast is ready if you're hungry!"

Deakan sits up right away, his beast attuned to any and all phrases about food, hunger, or sustenance. Out of all my guys, he eats the most, and never seems sated.

"Be down soon." I rub sleep out of my eyes and take in the state of the room.

Theo must've had the foresight to remove the silencing bubble before he fell asleep last night because she responds for me not to take too long.

There are ingredients everywhere. Cauldrons, crystal balls, candles, and all forms of ritualistic paraphernalia are laid out on and around my desk, the hardwood floor littered with herbs, powders, and liquids. My closet door is hanging open, and everything inside is out of place.

"What did you guys do to my room?" I breathe, climbing to my feet so I can stalk across my bedroom. "My parents are going to kill me."

Masses of ingredients are spread across every surface in a rainbow of colors that would make a painter cry. I spot some of these in my room, but most are still in the bathroom or spread along the windowsill.

The air is filled with the scents of incense, spun sugar, and potpourri. It's overpowering and makes my nose itch.

Everyone but Deakan is asleep, but they're all *covered* in it. In the harsh light of day, he takes in the scene before us, eyes wide.

"Pretty sure everyone's beasts took over last night." He chuckles. "But none of us figured it out before we passed out."

"Remind me not to issue a challenge like that again." I wince, bending over to pick up a ruined pair of . . . "Are these my panties?"

Soft snores saw their way from the nest of sheets and half-naked bodies.

Another knock sounds at the door, firmer this time. And *loud*. "Rose," Oz calls from the other side of it. "Time to get up!"

My stomach lunges into my chest when the doorknob wiggles, and he curses, finding it locked.

"Why is this locked? Rose?"

"We'll be out in a minute!" I scramble to wake them all up.

Theo is the first to sit up, eyes huge as he sees the destruction of my room. Immediately, he begins to repair it with magic. The clothes file themselves away into my closet, the chair rights itself, and the others join in once they get a good look at what happened.

By the time I've finished getting dressed, my room is spotless again, and the mattress is back on the bed. The guys are also dressed and lined up against the walls, looking a little guilty.

"Sorry," Theo is the first to say, and the others echo the sentiment.

"*Beasts*, the whole lot of you." I shake my head. "Breakfast is ready. Let's not keep them waiting any longer, okay?"

～

"SO, THEO, ARE YOU A STUDENT?" Mom asks as she passes him the platter of French toast.

I stiffen, and it catches the eagle eyes of my fathers.

"Professor of Astrology, actually." He meets her curious stare.

The room erupts in chaos, and I drop my fork, gripping the table as every one of my dads tries to speak at once, and Mom stands, trying to calm them down.

"Rose is an adult." She stares her mates down as they all quiet. Though it might be the knife she has in her hand that sends a better message as she levels it at each one of them before gesturing wildly. "Would you rather she brings home some frat boy from Earth who's just going to break her heart?"

They begrudgingly shake their heads, and Mekhi leans over, whispering to Theo, "They did this to me, too. It gets better. Just give it time."

"I need to stab something." Gideon shoves back from his chair, and Mom scowls after him as he stalks out of the room.

"Sorry. It isn't about you." She winces, placing her hand on Theo's shoulder. "They're just barbarians. I can't take them anywhere."

Theo only chuckles, casting an affectionate glance at me. "I'm a griffin. You're not going to find a more territorial order than mine. I imagine I'll be the same way when we have children."

Jax and Deakan chime in with a resounding, 'yep.'

Mekhi has a smug look, no doubt at the mention of putting a baby in me someday.

My attention catches on Bennett, sitting across from me. He's scowling as he takes in the scene. As my twin, he's protective of me, too.

The sound of Auguste's phone chiming with a notification breaks the momentary silence, and he retrieves it from his pocket. His face lights up with a grin as he reads the message. "It's Bellamy. Kieran is awake now."

Bellamy, my mom's first boyfriend when she was first turned into a fae, is also her current suitor, and he leads one of the royal guard units.

"Where do they have him?" I ask, my curiosity piqued as I sit up straighter in my chair. Our family, being the royal family of Bedlam, has several castles across the kingdom, but we don't have a place to interrogate people here at our mountain home.

My dads exchange glances and push their chairs back from the table, mischievous grins stretching across their faces.

"Mom?" I turn to her for an explanation, as my fathers and Bennett begin to sift out of the room.

She frowns, adjusting Baby Bee who's nursing at her chest. "The dungeon at Convectus Castle," she sighs, her voice filled with a mixture of relief and concern. "It's where they take all traitors before going to Bedlam Penitentiary."

THE FAMILY QUARTERS at Convectus Castle, where we currently stand, are a testament to the warmth and love that the castle's inhabitants hold dear, despite the horrors of the dungeon many stories below our feet. Luxurious furnishings and intricate tapestries line the walls, and the golden glow from a grand chandelier casts a cozy light throughout the room.

Deep-set windows framed by cascading curtains look out onto the serene castle grounds, as though it can't feel the unease in me. In all of us. From this vantage point, I can see the impressive stone walls, adorned with soft green moss and entwined with ivy, reaching up to meet the clear sky. The vibrant green leaves of the treetops within the walls sway gently in the breeze, and the calming scent of lavender from the gardens below fills the air.

Or at least it should be calming. My stomach is a pit of dread, knowing that no matter the outcome, my mates will likely have been betrayed by their best friend. I just can't see another way to justify Kieran's involvement. I cling to the little sliver of hope that there might be a small misunderstanding when I turn to my fathers.

"Dad, there's a reason he despises our family. Keeping him in the dungeon will only reinforce his negative perceptions of us," I say, wrapping my arms around myself as a feeling of anxiety settles in my stomach.

"We aren't hurting him—yet. We just want to talk to him," Penn reassures me, a grin on his face. He leans against the back wall, shrouded in shadows, appearing like an avenging angel bathed in the flickering torchlight. Despite being my father, with his dragon fae nature, he's not someone I would want to cross.

"I'd like to talk to him first," Jax interjects, stepping forward. "Kieran has been my best friend since we were kids."

Bennett narrows his eyes, crossing his arms as he blocks the cell door. "And how do we know you're not conspiring against our family?"

"Can we not do this again?" I plead. "Mom and our dads know Jax, and they know he'd never betray us. He nearly died to keep me safe." My voice chokes up as I recall Jax breaking a fae promise he made to the dean for my sake. "I trust him as much as I trust any of my mates."

Bennett's scowl softens, and he reluctantly steps aside.

"Thank you," Jax says, bowing his head in respect before turning to give me a gentle kiss. "I'll be out soon."

CHAPTER FOUR

JAX

As I make my way down the long, winding staircase that leads to the dungeon, my heart feels heavy with a mix of anger and disbelief. Kieran, my best friend, the serpent fae I've known since we were children, is locked away down here, and I can't help but wonder what he's gotten himself into this time.

I refuse to believe he'd hurt my mate. Intentionally or otherwise.

As I step into the cold, damp chamber, my eyes immediately find Kieran, slumped against the wall in chains. Even in this desperate situation, he exudes a dangerous energy that sends a chill down my spine. His sharp features and piercing sea-green eyes betray a hint of the serpent fae within him. As I approach him, I can see his black hair falling in unruly waves around his face, and the dim light glints off the metal of his snake bite piercing. The two symmetrical piercings on his bottom lip with a small distance between them make him look even more menacing, like he wears the fangs of a serpent, even when in his fae form. I steel myself for what I know will be a difficult interrogation.

He looks up as I approach, his expression guarded and tense.

"Jax," he says, his voice hoarse. "What are you doing here?"

"I need to know, Kieran," I say, my tone low and intense, as if issuing an unspoken threat. "What's your involvement in all of this? Are you behind the attacks on my mate?"

Kieran's eyes widen in surprise before narrowing with suspicion. "Is that why they dragged me out of my dorm?" he asks, anger lacing his words. "What happened?"

"You're the grandson of the dean," I remind him, my own anger starting to rise. "You have connections to the people who want to hurt Rose. And your disdain for the royal family is no secret. You confronted her in Witches' Woods."

Kieran's expression softens, and I think I see a flicker of guilt in his eyes. "I haven't done anything to hurt Rose," he says, his voice barely above a whisper. "But . . . there's something you need to know. You can't trust her."

"What is it?" I ask, wary of what he's about to say.

"I walked in on Rose and Professor Pyxis fucking," Kieran spits, and I wince as I glance at the security camera in the corner, knowing full-well Rose's parents are hearing all of this right now. "Bent over the desk, right in his gods damned office, where anyone could've seen! I thought you deserved to know that your mate is fucking around behind your back, *again*."

"Kieran," I sigh, crouching so I'm at his level. "He's her soul-bonded mate. I'm fucking lucky she even mated with me, but she did, and Deakan and I both know all about it."

"So, you're fucking him, too?" He shakes his head.

Sitting with my back against the stone wall next to him, I hang my head in my hands. "No, I've only ever slept with Rose."

"But you share her?" he accuses. "With them?"

"Yeah."

"And what about her boyfriend, the witch?" He shifts so he can face me. "Is he in on this, too?"

I nod. "He knows everything, and he's okay with it."

"How are you okay with sharing your mate with other guys? That's your *mate*," he seethes. "Dragons are one of the most territorial orders there are. It just doesn't make sense."

"You mean to tell me that if Rose invited you into her bedroom, you'd tell her no?" I scoff. "You act like you hate her, but I'm not stupid. It's the only reason I'm in here, talking to you, instead of ripping your head off with my teeth."

"What are you talking about?"

"I saw the way you went after those guys outside of practice for catcalling her. And how you screwed up a poisons trial at practice—that you're the only one who has ever won—just because Eli was flirting with her. You're obsessed with her, Kier. You think you can just get rid of all the other guys, then she'll magically fall for you. But it doesn't work like that. Rose loves who she loves, and we all respect that. It's not about possession or territory, it's about love and mutual respect. Can't you see that?"

Kieran stares at me for a long moment, his eyes narrowed in anger as he adjusts his wrists in his binds. "You don't understand, Jax. You can't possibly understand what it's like to be obsessed with the one person you're supposed to hate. She consumes my thoughts, and I'm *losing my fucking mind.*"

I rake my fingers through my hair and exhale. "Why do you have to hate her?"

"Because her parents are the reason mine are dead!" Tears cascade down his face as his entire body shudders with sobs in a rare show of vulnerability. Usually, he's too high to care about anything. His voice quivers as he speaks, his words coming out labored. "They're gone, and she gets to have a house full of parents who love her and dote on her. I have my grandma, who is so broken, she's blinded to the fact that I'm still here, desperate for even the slightest affection."

Someone must take pity on him from the control room, because the manacles around his wrists come undone, and his body collapses under the weight of his grief. Wrapping my arms around him, I do my best to hold him together.

Rose

My hand trembles where I've got it held against the switch on the wall that releases the manacles for Kieran's prison cell, and I watch on the security screen as his legs give out. In a state of shock from Kieran's words, I can feel the world spinning out of control. It's like I'm caught in the eye of a storm, untouched as I witness someone else fall apart.

For a moment, it feels like time has slowed down, like every second is stretching out into an eternity. The sound of metal clanking against stone breaks through my thoughts, but I can't seem to look away from Kieran's raw, unfiltered pain.

How long I hold that button, I don't know. Long enough for me to lose feeling in my arm from holding it over my head. Long enough for my parents to clear out of the control room. All that remain are my mates and Mekhi. Long enough that the tears have stopped flowing, leaving only dried riverbeds in their wake.

"Rose," Mekhi murmurs from beside me. His hand is on my shoulder, but I didn't register it until just now. "Are you okay?"

I turn to him, feeling disjointed and mechanical in my movements as though they're not my own, and offer a weak smile. "I will be," I say, trying to keep my voice steady. "He didn't do it."

That brings me greater relief than I know how to express. Jax and Deakan are Kieran's best friends, and the only thing he's guilty of is a few harsh words and outing me to the entire campus at our Spar Games meet. I know it in the very marrow of my bones.

The only question is, what *does* he know?

In the quiet of my bedroom at Convectus Castle, my mates and I gather while my dads interrogate Kieran. The soft light filtering through the sheer curtains casts a warm glow on the familiar surroundings, offering a semblance of comfort amidst the tumultuous times. The scent of lavender still lingers in the air, a reminder of the beautiful gardens below.

Theo, engrossed in the variety of books on my shelf, runs his fingers lightly along the spines, pausing occasionally to read a title that catches his eye. As a professor, the vast collection of knowledge fascinates him, and I can see his mind absorbing every detail with keen interest.

Deakan, ever the food connoisseur, can't help but investigate the assortment of snacks and treats I have stashed away. His eyes widen with delight each time he discovers a new flavor or delicacy, and his enthusiasm brings a touch of lightheartedness to the room.

Mekhi, familiar with the castle after living with my family for a year, leans against a nearby wall with a relaxed demeanor. His eyes scan the room with familiarity and affection, his presence a calming force amid the uncertainty.

Meanwhile, Jax's attention is drawn to the array of priceless possessions scattered around the room. As a dragon fae with a penchant for hoarding treasure, he studies each item with an expert eye, appreciating the craftsmanship and the history they hold.

With everyone settled, I take a deep breath and broach the subject weighing on my mind. "Should we even go back to university at all? With all the threats and the Dean still at large—is it safe?"

The room falls silent as each of us contemplates the question. It's Theo who breaks the silence, his voice measured and thoughtful. "It's important not to let whoever's behind these threats dictate our lives. You have a right to an education and a future."

Deakan nods in agreement, a half-eaten treat still in hand. "Theo's right. We can't let fear control us. But maybe there's a compromise?"

Mekhi, his brow furrowed, suggests, "What if we live off-campus and take a couple of days off to settle into our new home? It'll give us some distance from the immediate danger while still allowing us to continue our studies."

Jax, still admiring a particularly ornate piece of jewelry, adds, "That sounds like a reasonable plan. We can't stop living our lives, but we also need to ensure your safety."

"Your safety, too." I scowl.

"Well, obviously." He sets down my bronze unicorn, grinning.

As we all consider the proposal, I can't help but feel a sense of relief at the unity and support my mates provide. With their help, I know we can face whatever challenges lie ahead.

Theo, still perusing the books on my shelf, suddenly looks up as if struck by an idea. "Why don't we all move to Sanctuary?" He turns his attention to the others. "It's a place I built just off-campus during my griffin nesting phase. There's a small house there already, and we can easily expand it into the cave's tunnels on the back end of it. It's hidden and secure, perfect for our needs."

The suggestion is met with a murmur of interest, and everyone turns their attention to him. Sanctuary—a haven just outside the university—seems like an ideal compromise.

Jax, his interest piqued, asks, "Will there be enough room?" His gaze finds mine. "Rose keeps picking up strays. What if she collects more?"

I narrow my eyes at him. "Should I put you down?" I fold my arms over my chest.

He feigns outrage, clutching the base of his neck as though he's got a string of pearls there. "You'd never," he breathes.

I saunter over to him and give him a little pat on his cheek. "Nah, I like your dick too much."

Theo grins, a sense of pride evident in his expression. "It's cozy, not going to lie. It's nestled in the jungle. The house itself is made of stone and wood, blending with the palms so you don't even see it until you're right upon it. There's a small pond nearby, a fountain, and the attached cave has tunnels that stretch out for miles, giving us plenty of room to expand and customize as needed."

Mekhi seems to warm up to the idea. "It sounds perfect. A safe haven where we can regroup and plan our next move."

Jax, intrigued by the thought of exploring the tunnels, chimes in, "I like it. It's the best of both worlds—close enough to the university for our studies, but far enough to offer some protection."

As we envision our future in Sanctuary, the atmosphere in the room shifts from one of uncertainty to one of determination. We refuse to let the threats derail our lives, but we'll face them on our own terms and in a place we can call home.

AFTER MY DADS finish interrogating Kieran, I take a nap back at the family house at Rift Pass. By the time I wake, it's near supper time. We worked through lunch today, and I'm starving, but I can't find the will to eat.

I've got Bee on my hip as I sway her through the halls. With a disgruntled sigh, she pats my face with her hands, trying to get me to dance with her. Under most circumstances, I'd oblige, but grief has my heart squeezed, and I can only manage a smile that doesn't reach my eyes as I bounce her.

Once I reach Mom and Dads' room, I pause in the doorway as I watch her use her Luna magic to dry her hair. She's seated on the bed, and it stretches from wall-to-wall, and I'd ask her where she got it if it wouldn't give my dads heart attacks.

I clear my throat, announcing my presence.

Mom's attention catches mine, and she sets down her hairbrush. "Hey, baby," she coos, and Bee does grabby hands, practically jumping out of my arms for Mom's.

I sit next to her at the foot of the bed. "Mom, I think we're going to move off campus."

She turns to me, hope warming her features. "Back home?"

I shake my head. "Theo has a place in the jungle near campus, though I'm worried that'll cause Kieran to spiral even more."

She considers my words for a moment. "Because Deakan will be going with you, and Kieran won't have a roommate anymore?"

"Nor will he have Jax right next door." I sigh. "But until we locate Dean Fallgren, I think it's safer if we're all together. We'd all move in together eventually anyway."

"I hope you're being safe." She side-eyes me. "New mating bonds can be . . . intense."

"Of course, we are." I cover my face as heat flushes my cheeks.

Mom chuckles. "Okay, okay. I trust you. But be careful, alright? I spent my entire life thinking I'd never have kids, and then a couple of years later I'm having the safe sex talk with one of my own. It's a little disorienting."

"I'd rather it be you than any of your mates." I stand, shaking my head. "Glad I'm not Bennett."

"Pretty sure he got that talk last summer when he was spending a lot of time with Teresa."

Teresa is the leader of a pack of wolf shifters who'd been cured of their werewolf affliction during the war. I suppose that's one good thing that came from all of this.

Mom follows me downstairs, where we find everyone gathered in the living room while Theo reads an email out loud.

"What's going on?" I ask, taking a seat between Mekhi and Deakan on the couch.

"The Provost just sent an email to faculty that Dean Fallgren is missing, so he's stepped in as interim dean until they can find a replacement for her." Theo slides his phone back in his pocket.

We exchange looks of concern before my attention falls on Auguste. Out of each of my dads, he's the best tracker there is.

"Already on it," he muses. "We'd gone after her last night, but she'd taken off. She must know we're onto her."

"How are we keeping Kieran safe?" I hug my middle, and Deakan gives my thigh a comforting squeeze. Not that I think his grandma would do anything to hurt him, but who knows what she's thinking?

Kieran has been nothing but awful to me, but that doesn't mean I want to see him caught in the crosshairs of a battle he didn't ask to be part of.

"Might want to ask your man about that." Bennett huffs, leaning back in his chair and crossing his arms.

I turn my attention to my menagerie of men, my brows furrowed in confusion. "Which one?"

Mekhi, sitting on my other side, raises his hands in a gesture of innocence. "Don't look at me." He shrugs. "I was against it."

"What?" I ask, genuinely curious about the decision.

Theo winces, rubbing the back of his neck. "We're all moving to Sanctuary."

"I know, but I was asking what they're going to do with Kieran," I clarify, my gaze flitting between Theo and Jax.

Deakan shifts in his seat, shooting Jax a sidelong glance. "Kieran, too," Theo confirms, his voice laced with a hint of reluctance.

"What?" I sit up straighter, my heart thrashing in my chest. "But he—"

"Has no one," Jax interrupts, his voice barely a whisper as he stares down at the floor. He reaches up and runs a hand through his curls, clearly uneasy about the situation.

I chew on my lip, trying to process the news. The tension in the room is palpable, each of us weighed down by the gravity of the decision. It's clear that our alliance with Kieran is a fragile one, but I can't help but feel a pang of sympathy for him—he's been through so much, and now his grandma is gods-know-where.

"I read his mind the entire time we were interrogating him. He had nothing to do with hurting you, aside from him breaking the news that you're the high princess at the Spar Games tournament."

Finn takes Bee from Novaleigh when she starts to cry. "And he doesn't know where Dean Fallgren is?"

"No, but he made a fae promise to let us know if he hears from her." Casimir's voice rings out from the kitchen, his tone reassuring, though I have reservations about fae promises in general after one almost killed Jax.

In the open floor plan of the house, I can easily see Casimir as he talks, standing by the counter alongside Gideon and Grimm. The trio is working together to prepare homemade pizza, a dish that Gideon— in all his Italian roots—is enthusiastically teaching the two fae how to make properly. Casimir carefully spreads the tomato sauce onto the rolled-out dough, while Gideon instructs Grimm on how to evenly sprinkle the mozzarella cheese and arrange various toppings.

"I guess this is really happening," I whisper. "Where is he now?"

"Packing his things." Deakan puts his arm around me, and I lean into him.

"How will we have enough room?" Mekhi grumbles, but he's not upset with any of us. I think he just doesn't like Kieran. "Especially with Bennett moving in, too? He'll need his own room."

Before, it'd just been Theo living at Sanctuary. And now, there's a whole zoo of us moving in. Mekhi and Bennett are transferring from another school so they can both attend classes with us. It's way more than Theo bargained for, and I'm feeling a little guilty about it.

Deakan, on the other hand, has a huge smile on his face, and a quiet purr sounds from where I'm pressed against his side. As a lion shifter, his primal need to be part of a pride has him feeling deep contentment.

It must've been so hard for him before he'd been adopted.

"There's a cave system on the back end we can open up." Theo pulls up some pictures on his phone and passes them to Bennett. "I've only got the one bathroom, but it shouldn't take me more than a few weeks to build another one."

"Let us know if you need any help," Mom offers.

"Thanks." He smiles at her.

"Can I come visit?" Novaleigh sets her book down, looking up at us with wide eyes. "I want to see your new house."

"Of course." I smile at her. "You can come stay whenever you want."

"And when I attend Bedlam Academy?" She grins back at me.

"Let's cross that bridge when we get to it." I glance nervously at Theo, but in our bond, I only feel pride from him.

Providing for his soul-bonded mate, and those I care about, means a lot to him.

We all continue chatting about the move, discussing logistics and what all we'll need to expand the place while we wait for pizza to be done. Before laying down to take a nap, I'd made a giant pasta salad I think the guys would like as it will go well with the pizza.

Carbs on carbs—our favorite.

Over supper, we put a plan in place, dividing tasks for gathering intel about the dean. Hours pass, the sun dipping below the horizon and casting the world into twilight. The atmosphere inside the house is heavy with concentration and determination, but it's punctuated with moments of lightness—shared smiles, laughter, and whispered words of encouragement.

It's these moments that remind me why we're fighting so hard—for the love that binds us, and the future we want to create.

And hopefully, we can right the mistakes of our past.

As the night deepens, I find myself standing on the edge of the balcony overlooking the waterfall that spills at our feet, staring out at the star-studded sky.

Theo comes up beside me, his warm presence a comforting anchor in the midst of the chaos. "Sorry we didn't consult you first about Kieran," he murmurs, wrapping his arm around my waist. "But after what he said, I figured you'd prefer he be taken care of and loved on, rather than cast aside and forgotten."

I lean into him, grateful for his support. "Thank you, Theo. I don't know what I'd do without you." Everything he says is true.

I'm not one to take any shit, but if Kieran can play nice, I can, too. We owe it to him.

Sighing, I pull my phone out of my back pocket. "I should probably text Lopey." I send my best friend a text, filling her in on our decision to move to off campus and promising to catch up with her once we make it back to campus.

Her reply is quick.

> Everything okay?

I shoot her a message back.

> Not really but will fill you in soon. Xoxo

With Lopey informed and reassured, I feel a weight lift from my shoulders. Turning to Theo, I lean into his side, and he wraps his arm around me, pulling me close.

"I just hope this move will keep us safe," I say softly, staring out into the night.

Theo kisses my forehead and whispers, "We'll do everything in our power to make sure it does."

Together, we stand in the darkness, surrounded by the beauty of the night and the promise of a better tomorrow.

But even as we cling to hope, I can't help but worry about the secrets that still linger in the shadows—where the hell is the dean, and is she really the one behind these threats? Is it all connected?

There are so many unanswered questions, and I can't shake the feeling that the answers will change everything.

CHAPTER FIVE

ROSE

All day Sunday, Theo, Jax, and Deakan teach Bennett and I how to sift. As first year students, we haven't learned that yet, despite our knowing way more magic than even fourth year students.

Bennett and I have a bit of a rebellious streak in us, and our parents had decided sifting was a skill they'd teach only after we showed we could use it safely. Looking back, I don't really blame them. We would've used it to pull pranks on everyone or spend time in places we probably shouldn't, like seedier parts of the realm.

After we've got sifting mastered, Mekhi will have to use a portal stone to get around since witches can't initiate sifting. They can be passengers, and only fae that shift into beasts can start it.

As Luna fae, we don't really have beasts other than we can go feral—our teeth elongate, we focus on more primal needs like fucking or fighting, and our nails sharpen. As the source of all magic, we possess the ability to slip through the cracks of space and time, emerging on the other side in an instant.

The sensation of sifting is like passing through a narrow, twisting tunnel, with only glimpses of flickering light and shadow flashing past you. Sometimes, it's a little disorienting, especially if you're not entirely clear on what the destination looks like. It's like traversing across space, coming across another slit and crawling up through the floor or emerging from the wall. Your body feels stretched and pulled as you squeeze through the narrow gap, but then you suddenly find yourself standing in a new location. The disorientation fades as you ground yourself.

And sometimes, you fuck up.

Sifting requires intense focus and concentration, as you have to imagine the destination clearly in your mind and hold onto that image as you slip through the crack in space. It's like walking a tightrope between two worlds, with only your intention to guide you. If you're distracted, you can end up somewhere you don't want to be. Ponds, the bathroom, the Spar Games pitch, or even the sea.

Despite the mental and physical strain, the rewards of sifting are immeasurable, for you can go almost anywhere, anytime, with nothing but your own power and will.

As the sun sets, we gather around the railing to watch spirit fish spill over the waterfall and then glide through the air. Their wings catch on the last rays of light, flashing brilliant colors of ultramarine and green. We're all silent, lost in the beauty of it. It's like magic made tangible, an experience that never gets old no matter how many times you see it.

A yawn escapes me, and Theo tucks me under his arm as the last of the sun fades behind the mountain, and the balcony is bathed in the soft light of multiple moons, creating an otherworldly serenity.

"Bennett and I have got to finish packing." Mekhi steals me from Theo, a tiny smirk on his face as he threads his fingers through my hair. "Only another hours' worth and then we can sift in before bed. See you in a little bit?"

"Okay." I smile up at him. "Love you."

"Love you, too." He kisses me, and I lean into it, trying to put every emotion I feel for this man into it since he's the only one of my men without a mating bond. Just because one isn't there—yet—doesn't mean I don't feel for him what I do for the others.

We say our goodbyes to my family, and Bennett and Mekhi sift back to their campus, while my mates and I sift back to ours.

While Jax works on his side of the room, Theo assists me with packing my belongings into the trunk at the foot of my bed. He carefully takes the things I hand him—clothes, books, shoes, and a few pieces of wall decor—and arranges them neatly inside the trunk.

When it comes time to empty out the bottom drawer of my nightstand, my cheeks heat, and Jax casts me a knowing grin as I march the contents over to the trunk rather than handing them directly to Theo.

"Here, I can take that for you—"

"No, it's okay," I interrupt. "I've got it."

Jax calls out from where he's seated on his bed, folding a stack of his clothes. "Rose doesn't want you to see her tentacle vibrator, it's pink and purple, and—"

THWAP.

I've launched the silicone appendage across the room, hitting him square in the chest. It falls to his bed in the "on" position, vibrates across the bed, and plunges to the floor, where it buzzes loudly across the wood.

The guys are laughing so hard, not a sound comes out, making the noise of the vibrator all the more traumatizing.

Our door flies open, and Deakan and Kieran stand in the hallway, hands raised, magic gathering in their palms as they prepare to defend us from whoever is attacking us.

They take in the scene in front of them, and their expressions transform from serious to utterly confused. Jax is on the floor howling with laughter, while Theo is attempting to stifle his own laughter with his hand.

As for me, I'm standing there frozen in mortification as my vibrator is buzzing away on the floor.

"Somebody, quick, shut off the killer vibrator," Jax howls, and our newcomers join in.

"All of you are cut off," I warn as I launch myself across the room to wrangle the damn thing into submission. It takes me a few tries at different buttons. First it starts wobbling one way, then another, before I finally figure out the configuration I need to get it to shut off.

"Not getting any, anyway." Kieran props himself with both hands above the door frame while Deakan makes his way inside.

"And never going to." I scowl.

"Not with that attitude you won't," Kieran replies coolly, though the glint of light off his lip piercings belies his smirk. "They've got to be doing something wrong if you have need of those," he murmurs before disappearing back into the hallway.

"You okay in here?" Deakan stalks across the room and pulls me into his arms. "I've just got to pack my hoodies and I'm good to go."

"Don't forget those. I need more to steal." I tilt my head to stare up at him, getting lost in his amber eyes. They're like pools of crystalized honey.

"You can steal everything from me, babe."

"Is that so?" I stand on my tippy toes to give him a kiss. "Bet I can't steal your food."

He sucks in a breath before returning the kiss. "You can steal my food, but I'm going to be really sad about that."

I chuckle, turning around in his arms to face the room. "Go pack your hoodies, and I'm going to finish up here."

He gives me one last lingering kiss on the back of the neck before heading next door.

I stalk over to the bathroom, opening cabinets and pulling out toiletries and placing them into a bag. As I reach into the back of the cabinet, my hand brushes against something cool and metallic. Intrigued, I pull out a small, ornate box. It's about the size of my palm and has intricate designs etched into the metal. I run my fingers over the embossed surface, admiring the craftsmanship.

Curiosity gets the better of me, and I pop open the lid. Inside, nestled in plush velvet, is a delicate silver chain with a small, sparkling diamond caught in the beak of a giant, black bird. A crow, I think. Or is it a raven? I never can tell the difference.

My breath catches in my throat as I reach for the bracelet, lifting it out of the box to admire it in the light.

"What do we have here?" Theo presses behind me, resting his chin on my shoulder. "That's beautiful. Did Mekhi make that for you?"

When Mekhi and his uncle first came to Bedlam from Earth, they made a living selling handcrafted jewelry and weapons—some of the finest in the whole realm.

I shake my head. "I don't know, I've never seen it before."

Slipping it into my pocket, I turn around to face him and prop my butt on the sink. Throwing my arms around his neck, I stare up at him, lost in the gold flecks in his eyes.

A smirk tips his lips. "What other toys you got in that drawer?"

Heat flushes my cheeks, and I groan as I bury my head against his neck. But a thought burrows its way into my brain, and I can't get it out unless I speak it, so I croon, "A couple of butt plugs and a strap-on I've been dying to try on one of my mates."

Theo pulls back and his eyes widen, a slow smile spreading across his face. "Oh really?" he drawls, his voice dropping into a low, seductive tone. "Which mate do you want to try it on?" His fingers trail down my spine, sending shivers down my body. Heat blooms low in my belly.

"Who's going to let me?" I beam at him, tugging my lip between my teeth.

"Deakan seems the most adventurous," he hedges, raising a brow at me. But I meet his thousand-yard stare with one of my own. The Adam's apple at his throat bobs. "But if you insisted, I might be able to be convinced. I can't make any promises I'll like it, though."

I can feel the corners of my eyes crinkle as I beam at him. "Would you share me with one of the others?"

"At the same time?"

I nod.

He sighs. "It'll be a little awkward for a bit. Right now they still kind of feel like interlopers in our bond, despite the fact I can feel theirs inside you, which admittedly, is weird. It's bad enough I can smell their arousal every time yours pops off."

"Oh, come on." I laugh. "I'm only horny like . . . half the time." He raises a brow, and I wince as Jax clears his throat. "Three-quarters?"

Theo's head tilts toward me, and I give him a playful push as I head into the room. "Can you blame me? You guys are fucking hot!"

Jax looks up from his kneeling position, struggling to fit his extensive treasure horde into his trunk. The numerous trinkets and shiny objects seem impossible to fit in the limited space.

"Do you need to put some stuff in my trunk?" I glance back at mine, noting that it's only half-full.

"Are you sure?" he asks, wincing at the thought of encroaching on my space.

Jax carefully examines each piece of his treasure horde before attempting to fit them into his trunk. There are a variety of items, each unique and valuable in its own way.

There are shimmering, multicolored gemstones that seem to emit their own faint light, ranging from deep blues and vibrant greens to fiery reds and warm oranges. He has an assortment of delicate gold and silver jewelry, intricately designed necklaces, bracelets, and rings adorned with precious stones.

He also has a collection of rare coins from different realms, each embossed with the face of a long-lost ruler or mythical creature. Lying among his treasures are enchanted trinkets that emit a faint magical aura, including a small crystal orb that seems to swirl with an ever-changing nebula inside, and a tiny golden music box that plays a haunting melody.

I gesture to the massive amount of stuff piled around his bed. He draws his magic from his treasure, so one can hardly blame him.

"If you're sure." Jax's cheeks flush.

As I scoop up a handful of his possessions, I marvel at the craftsmanship of an ornate dagger with a dragon-wing hilt and an ancient-looking leather-bound book with gilded edges and runes etched onto its cover.

Theo and I carefully transport Jax's eclectic treasures to my half-empty trunk, taking special care to arrange them in a way that ensures their safety. Soon enough, our belongings are neatly packed and ready to go.

Theo turns to me and says, "Let me spell the place so it looks like you are all still living here. Same with next door." With a step back and a whisper under his breath, Theo raises his hands in a gesture of concentration, and a faint shimmer appears in the air around him. As he continues to chant softly, the shimmer grows in intensity, taking on the shape of a complex and intricate pattern. It's like watching a spider weave a web, each thread carefully placed and woven into the overall design. The pattern glows with a soft, warm light, and it seems to pulse with a life of its own.

When done, he pops next door for a few minutes while I inspect under the beds and in the closet in case we forgot anything.

Theo comes back, putting an arm around my waist.

"Guess this is it," I whisper, taking one last look around the now-empty room. It was only ours for a semester, but it holds so many memories—some fond, some not-so-fond—that will stay with me forever.

My soul-bonded mate presses a kiss to my temple. "Let's go home."

I take a deep breath and close my eyes, focusing on Sanctuary, the place that will become our home and refuge. I visualize the thick, magical jungle surrounding it, the ancient trees with their tangled roots, the ivy-covered columns of the hidden temple, and the comforting presence of the house Theo built for us before he knew what he'd been doing it for. The energy of the place seeps into my mind, providing the necessary anchor for sifting.

A gentle tug on my arm, and Theo's heat washes over me, followed by the warmth of Jax and his reassuring presence. We all focus on the image together, ready to be transported to our refuge.

The familiar tingling sensation begins to course through my body as I initiate the process of sifting. As I concentrate, it's as though I'm tearing a hole in the very fabric of the floor beneath me, creating an opening that leads to a rip in the fabric of space on the other side. Climbing through the opening and into the fissure in space, I feel my body gently unraveling and reassembling itself, guided by the connection to the image in my mind. This sensation used to frighten me when I first learned to sift, but now it feels like a warm embrace, as though the magic recognizes me and welcomes me home.

When the tingling subsides, I open my eyes, and I'm standing in front of Sanctuary. The jungle sounds fade into the distance, replaced by the serenity of our secret haven. The sun filters through the thick canopy of leaves, casting dappled shadows on the ancient stone steps. Vibrant, jewel-like colors of the stained-glass windows catch my eye as I take in the beauty of this place. The combination of the old stone structure with the newer addition creates a harmonious blend of the past and the present, a testament to Theo's love of ancient history.

He wraps his arm around my shoulder, and I lean back into the hug. "Great job," he whispers in my ear.

"And we didn't even end up in the swamp!" Jax chuckles as he puts his hands on his hips, marveling at the place.

"That was one time!" I spin on him and send a wave of water at him that he easily dodges. It splatters against the tree behind him, sending a cascade of droplets to the ground.

I turn back around, my white tennis shoes sinking into the mossy earth, cushioning my tread as I pass under the stone archway leading into the flower-filled courtyard. The sound of the trickling fountain fills the air, soothing my soul and washing away any lingering worries. Every element of this place is designed to lighten the burdens of the mind, and each piece is imbued with magic to help it along.

I stroll over to the marble bench, my fingers trailing over the cool surface as I remember the moments Theo and I shared here, each one etched into my heart. Just as his soul called to mine, this home served as a beacon, guiding me to a place of safety and comfort.

With a small smile, I continue toward the house. The white stone columns, the huge wooden doors, and the tiled roof gleam under the canopy of trees, somehow managing to appear both elegant and inviting at the same time. As I approach the entrance, the scent of blooming petals from the flower boxes washes over me, and I can't help but take a deep, calming breath. The flowers have bloomed even more since we last left, a riot of colors adorning their beds.

Exerting a forceful shove, I heave open the weighty door and step into the welcoming interior of the house. The space, though modest in size, feels *right*. Though I grew up in giant homes and castles to accommodate our enormous family, there's something about the close proximity of everything that infuses warmth into my bones.

Theo snaps magic at the fireplace, allowing a crackling fire to dance in the stone hearth, casting flickering shadows on the walls. Thick, plush rugs cover the floor, softening each step and adding to the sense of comfort. The room is a mixture of old and new, with a cathedral-like ceiling supported by ancient stone columns that rise to meet intricately carved wooden beams. Tall, arched windows line the walls, allowing natural light to fill the space, and the floor is made of smooth, polished stone. Furniture in the space comprises an eclectic mix of comfortable, well-worn pieces and handpicked newer additions, all arranged to create an atmosphere that feels both lived-in and inviting.

The main living area is an open space that seamlessly blends together the various aspects of the home. To one side, there's a small but well-equipped kitchen, where we've spent hours preparing elaborate foods I love from Earth. A sturdy wooden table, surrounded by mismatched chairs, takes up the center of the room. It's here that we've shared those meals and heartfelt conversations.

Nestled in the far corner of the living area is a cozy nook, with floor-to-ceiling bookshelves overflowing with tomes both ancient and new, each one containing knowledge and stories that have transported us to countless worlds. A plush, oversized armchair sits nearby, accompanied by a small table holding a few spell ingredients.

I make my way toward the back of the house, where a narrow hallway leads to the more private spaces of the home. To the left, a door reveals a bedroom filled with soft, inviting fabrics and dappled sunlight filtering through the sconces on the wall. The scent of lavender wafts through the air, lulling me into a sense of peace and tranquility. To the right, the bathroom, simple yet elegant, with its walled-in shower and a separate clawfoot bathtub, and a large, ornate mirror.

At the end of the hallway, another door leads to the entrance of the interconnected cave system.

I turn to Theo, my eyes filled with tears of happiness. "I forgot how much this place feels like home."

Theo smiles sheepishly, scratching the back of his neck. "When I built the place, I just did what I thought would be perfect."

Jax walks over and claps him on the shoulder, grinning. "It is perfect, man."

The comforting atmosphere wraps around us like a warm blanket, and it truly feels like we've come home.

After a quick shower, I shoot a text to the others, letting them know I'll wait up for them. I curl up in bed with Theo and Jax, the flickering glow of the fire illuminating the cozy room. The stone walls keep the cool night air at bay, and I'm grateful for the warmth of their bodies pressed against mine. A contented smile graces my lips and I close my eyes, just to rest them for a little bit.

I DID NOT, in fact, wait up for them as I had initially intended. Nestled in the heat of Theo and Jax, I was soon lulled into a deep, dreamless slumber.

As I begin to stir, a slow, luxurious stretch pulls me from my sleep. I awaken to find that the bed is much more crowded than when I'd fallen asleep, filled with the familiar forms of several more men.

"Shh," Theo murmurs, his arm wrapping around me as he pulls me snugly against his side. "Classes are canceled today while they sort out the Dean Fallgren situation. I have a staff meeting at three, but until then, we can sleep in."

Cracking open my eyes, I meet his still-closed ones. "And if I don't want to sleep?" My skin gives off its blue glow, illuminating the room even more.

A slow, wicked grin spreads across his face as he opens his eyes. "Then we can find other ways to occupy our time," he whispers, his voice low and suggestive, sending electricity down my spine.

I arch my back, feeling the heat of desire rise within me. "I like the sound of that."

Theo leans in, his lips brushing against mine in the softest of kisses, his breath warm and tantalizing. "Good, because Mekhi has something to tell you."

I sit up, my eyes adjusting to the dim light, and find Jax, Deakan, and Mekhi all sharing the bed with us. My heart swells with affection for them, and I can't help but grin. "Hey," I say, pressing tender kisses to each of their sleepy faces, feeling a surge of warmth and love for each of them.

My gaze lands on Mekhi, curiosity piqued by his smug expression. "What did you do?"

He runs a hand through his dark, tousled hair and grins sheepishly. "So, you know how we've been researching a spell for birth control? Well, I found one that'll actually work."

"How did I know you would be the first to come through for me?" He and I have never had sex, but it's not for a lack of trying. "Tell us more, babe."

The room is filled with a sense of anticipation as we all rise from the tangled sheets, preparing ourselves for the ritual. Mekhi retrieves a worn, leather-bound book from his bag and begins to explain the process. "It's an ancient spell, so the wording is a bit . . . archaic. But I've translated it as best as I could. We'll need to gather some herbs and ingredients for the incantation."

Theo takes the lead, glancing over Mekhi's shoulder before he retrieves a wooden chest from the corner of the room. The trunk, etched with intricate runes and symbols, looks like it's been in use for centuries. And it might've been—he collects all kinds of cool stuff. As he sets it down, I can feel a subtle thrum of magic radiating from it. He lifts the heavy, creaking lid to reveal an assortment of herbs, vials, and crystals neatly organized within.

My curiosity piqued, I lean in for a closer look at the shimmering vial filled with iridescent liquid. Theo notices my interest and explains, "This is the essence of moonflower. It helps to attune the energies of the ritual to our natural cycles." He then gestures toward a bundle of deep purple leaves that seems to hum with energy. "And these are twilight sage leaves, a potent herb known to strengthen the connection between our intentions and the magic we'll be working with."

Lastly, he points to a small, luminescent crystal that pulses like a heartbeat. "This is an aurora quartz. It's used to amplify the magic and enhance our focus during the ritual." I nod in understanding, impressed by the careful selection of ingredients, each playing a specific role in the spell.

We gather around the chest, our fingers brushing against one another as we pick out the necessary components for the ritual. Mekhi carefully selects a sprig of the twilight sage leaves, crushing them between his fingers and releasing a heady, earthy aroma. Theo retrieves the pulsing aurora quartz, and Deakan uncorks the shimmering vial of moonflower essence, taking a cautious sniff of the contents.

I chuckle. "You know, this means you get to go first, right?"

Mekhi smirks at me. "Oh, I know. It's why I didn't get in until thirty minutes ago. I was hunting down everything we need."

I shake my head. "Not going to be too exhausted?" I raise a brow.

"Are you kidding me?" He sets the stone bowl down on the night-stand and pulls me into his arms. "I've wanted to do this since I first saw you at the Tristique Island's markets."

"But that wasn't even my real face." I laugh. Until recently, Bennett and I always wore glamors in public to protect our identities as royals.

"It didn't matter." He cups my face. "In my heart, I always knew it was going to be you."

Tears prick at the back of my eyes, and I bury myself against his neck. "It's too early to cry, Mekhi."

"Nah, it's late for me, remember?" he murmurs. "It takes forty-eight hours to kick in, so after we do the ritual, I'm going to bed."

"Then let's get it done." I pull back, pressing my lips to his.

The guys exchange amused looks as we begin the preparations. Theo sets up a small altar in the center of the room, carefully arranging the ingredients in a specific order as Mekhi instructs. The magic in the room begins to crackle and intensify, heightening our senses and filling the air with an almost electric anticipation.

With the ingredients assembled, we gather in a circle around the flickering fire, the shadows of the flames casting a warm, golden glow across our faces. Mekhi leads the ritual, his deep voice resonating with power as he begins to chant the ancient words. I can feel the magic building within the room, a tangible energy that crackles through the air.

As the incantation continues, I sense the power swirling around me, seeping into my very being. The connection I share with each of these incredible men deepens and solidifies, the threads of our bond woven tighter by the shared magic. I notice the way the herbs catch fire, releasing a plume of fragrant smoke that curls around us, adding to the mystique of the ritual.

Mekhi's voice rises to a crescendo, and I feel a sudden surge of energy pulsing through my body, as if a protective barrier is being woven into my very essence. I glance around at the guys and say with a hint of sarcasm, "Maybe the man with a breeding kink shouldn't be in charge of birth control spells."

Mekhi grins at me, the firelight dancing in his eyes. "Ah, but you see, then none of us would be in charge."

"All of you!?" I meet each of their eyes, seeing no lies. "Unbelievable," I whisper.

As the incantation comes to an end, the energy in the room begins to dissipate, leaving us all with an odd sensation of having been changed somehow. The fire returns to its normal, comforting flicker, and the smoke from the burned herbs slowly clears.

We remain silent for a moment, each of us processing the experience we just shared. The air in the room is still thick with the remnants of the ritual's magic, leaving a warm and comforting atmosphere in its wake. Jax is the first to break the silence, a playful grin spreading across his face. "So, how do we know it worked?"

Deakan chuckles and pats Jax on the shoulder, his eyes dancing with amusement. "I guess we'll find out soon enough." Fae pregnancies are usually less than a month long, depending on the order.

Theo wraps a strong arm around my waist, his voice warm and

laced with a hint of humor. "And if it doesn't, I guess I'll be teaching you and our kid."

"All of you are cut off until I'm at least two hundred," I declare, backing away and pressing myself against the door. "No one is touching me with any of your baby makers."

Jax shares a knowing glance with Deakan, mischief dancing in their eyes. Something seems to pass between them before they both turn their attention back to me.

"That's fine." Jax slowly unbuttons his shirt, each deliberate movement accentuating the muscles beneath, before hopping onto the bed with an inviting smile.

Deakan follows suit, his fluid motions almost hypnotic. It isn't long before the others catch on, stripping down until they're just in their boxers. The sight of their sculpted bodies, every inch of taut muscle on display, is undeniably alluring.

I grip the doorknob, my breath hitching as I struggle to tear my eyes away from the tantalizing sight before me. "You're evil, the whole lot of you."

My skin glows a bright blue, betraying the desire I'm trying so hard to suppress. With every ounce of willpower given to me by the gods, I manage to pry the door open, swearing colorfully as I slip through it and into the hallway. The sound of their laughter, rich and warm, follows me as I retreat.

As I make my escape, my footsteps lead me straight into the kitchen, where I stumble upon a sight that makes me freeze in my tracks. Kieran, shirtless with a serious case of bedhead, sits at the table casually eating a bowl of cereal. I'm wearing nothing but Theo's crisp white button-down shirt, the kind you'd wear beneath a suit, which barely covers my thighs and leaves quite a bit of skin on display.

Kieran looks up from his breakfast and meets my gaze, a surprised expression crossing his face. His eyes flicker over my appearance for a moment before he clears his throat and averts his gaze back to his cereal.

My cheeks warm, and I attempt to project an air of nonchalance as

I saunter to the cupboard, retrieving a bowl and some cereal for myself.

As I pour milk into my bowl, I'm keenly aware of the heavy silence in the room. The gentle clink of his spoon hitting the edge of the ceramic and the distant pitter patter of rain outside the window seem almost deafening. Each of us sneaks furtive glances at the other, the unspoken words hanging heavily in the air.

I take my seat at the table, deliberately leaving a few empty chairs between us. The space may not do much to alleviate the pressure, but at least it provides a small barrier.

Kieran's knuckles whiten as he grips his spoon a little too tightly, betraying the tension that courses between us.

"Good morning," I squeak.

"Mornin," he drawls, reaching for his glass of orange juice.

The sound of him guzzling the juice draws my attention, and I watch as his throat bobs and the juice leaks down his chin before landing on his chest. With the back of his hand, he wipes it off.

"'Tis rude to stare," he says, a hint of amusement in his voice.

I raise an eyebrow, a biting retort at the ready. "I'd offer you a straw, but I'm not sure that would help."

My comment makes Kieran chuckle, his eyes crinkling at the corners as he tries to suppress a smile. He leans back in his chair, crossing his arms over his chest, the corded muscles, and intricate tattoos on display. His raven hair is tousled, a result of sleep, and his seafoam-green eyes hold an intensity that's difficult to ignore.

"You know, Rose, I'm trying to be on my best behavior here," he admits, his tone softening just a bit. "I'm grateful that you guys let me stay."

I pause, spoon halfway to my mouth, taken aback by his sincerity. "Yeah, well, you may be a jerk, but you're our jerk now." It's a clumsy attempt to ease the tension, and my cheeks probably redden further at my words.

He smirks, looking away from me for a moment before returning his attention to his cereal. "Thanks, I guess."

We continue eating in relative silence, the strain between us simmering, but not quite boiling over. It's a delicate dance of sidelong glances and small, shared smiles that hints at something more beneath the surface.

In the background, muffled sounds of video games and laughter drift from the bedroom, a reminder that my mates are not far away.

As I finish my breakfast, I push my chair back and stand up, gathering my empty bowl and spoon. Kieran watches me intently as I rinse the dishes and place them in the dishwasher.

When I turn back to face him, he clears his throat and rises from his seat. His low-slung sweats emphasize his lean hips and strong legs. "I should, uh, get dressed and give you some space," he mumbles, his gaze flickering between me and the floor.

I nod, trying to ignore the sudden tightness in my chest. "Yeah, sure. I'll see you around, Kieran."

His tongue toys with his snake bite piercing, his eyes lingering on me for a moment longer before he heads toward his makeshift room he's sharing with Bennett somewhere in the cave system.

As I watch him walk away, I can't help but wonder what the future holds for the both of us. What's it going to be like living under the same roof with all this unresolved tension and desire simmering just beneath the surface?

CHAPTER SIX

ROSE

With the rain tapping gently against the windows, I curl up on the couch in our shared living space, a book clutched in my hands and my feet in Deakan's lap. Sitting on my plate balanced on my lap is a slice of homemade bread Bennett and I made today, still warm from the oven. It's slathered in butter and cinnamon and sugar.

As the comforting aroma of the homemade bread fills the room, my mind drifts back to the attraction I'd felt earlier toward Kieran. I can't help but worry about what it might mean, especially considering the animosity his family has for mine. And I'm pretty sure serpent fae can only mate with certain orders on account of their poisonous venom.

Why I even entertain that thought is beyond me. I guess I really am my mother's daughter.

I take a deep breath and try to sort through my feelings. Although the attraction had been intense and unexpected, I decide that it's too inconvenient and risky to allow any romantic feelings to blossom between us.

With a resolute sigh, I resolve to keep my emotions in check, focusing instead on the love and support I receive from my mates and family. The stakes are too high, and I can't afford to let myself be distracted by complicated feelings for someone whose very presence could threaten our safety and unity.

Determined to move past my confusion, I take a bite of the warm, cinnamon-and-sugar-laden bread, letting the flavors and textures ground me in the present moment.

Deakan notices my distraction and gives my leg a comforting squeeze. "Everything alright?" he asks, concern etched across his face.

I offer him a reassuring smile. "Yes, I'm fine. Just lost in thought for a moment."

Soft laughter, Deakan's deep purring, and the rustle of turning pages fill the room, providing the perfect soundtrack for a cozy, lazy afternoon. But despite the peaceful atmosphere, my thoughts soon turn to Theo and his staff meeting.

The front door clicks open, and I glance up just in time to see Theo stepping into the house, his shoulders tense, and a deep furrow creasing his brow. He locks the door behind him, his movements slow and heavy, as if the weight of the world has settled upon him.

"Hey," I murmur, setting my book and plate aside and rising to meet him. My heart aches at the sight of him, so visibly exhausted, the stress of the meeting having clearly taken its toll.

He musters a weak smile as I approach, wrapping his arms around me in a tight embrace. "Hey," he whispers into my hair, his breath warm against my ear.

"What happened at the meeting?" I ask, my voice barely audible, dreading the answer.

He squeezes me gently, and his eyes finally meet mine, a flicker of frustration shining through the weariness. "It was a lot, Rose. Your parents were there, along with the council and the royal guard. They're trying to figure out what happened to Dean Fallgren and investigate the threats against our family. They hired a replacement, too. He's powerful, but I haven't been able to work out what fae order he is. The new dean asked a lot of really good questions, though, and seems like he'll be changing things up from what Dean Fallgren had in place."

I don't miss the way he says *our* family. Despite the heaviness of the conversation, our bond hums between us, giddy with the easy declaration of love.

I furrow my brow, my own frustration bubbling up at the thought of the missing dean and the danger we all face. "Did they have any leads? Anything more we should be worried about? And did anyone mention the missing bracelet?"

Last semester, someone took an artifact from Professor McColt that he'd been keeping safe in a trunk for years, only for someone to snatch it after I'd seen it. It feels deliberate. Like maybe someone wants me to be on edge.

If that's the case; it's worked. The bracelet enables the bearer of it to control any royal.

Theo sighs, rubbing his temples as he shakes his head. "Not really. There's a lot of conjecture, but nothing concrete yet. They're working on it, but progress is slow."

"And our relationship?" I press, my heart heavy with the knowledge that the secrecy surrounding our connection adds to the already complicated situation.

He hesitates for a moment before answering, the tension in his voice palpable. "We still need to be discreet, Rose. The council wasn't told about our bond, and your parents want us to keep it that way for now. They don't want to risk further upheaval or scandal within the academy. It wouldn't be a good look for the court if your parents let you break the rules, and I don't know how the new dean will react to his faculty being involved with a student. The guy is powerful. We've just got to lay low for a little while."

Though I'm not surprised by this answer, it doesn't make it any easier to accept. I lean into Theo, seeking comfort in his embrace as I murmur, "I wouldn't want them to risk anything. We'll get through this. All of us, together."

Theo wraps his arms around me, his breath warm against my hair as he nods. "I know we will. I have faith in us, in our family. For now, though, we should get some sleep. Everyone has to be on campus in the morning for an assembly of announcements—and introduction of the new dean."

Rose

I LEAD Bennett and Mekhi through the lush, vibrant jungle that surrounds Bedlam Academy. The air is thick and damp, the scents of flowers and claggy earth mingling together. They both look around in wonder, taking in the unique beauty of their new surroundings. I'm excited to show them the campus where I've spent so much time.

"We'll start with the cafeteria," I say, pointing toward the building where students can fuel up before and after classes. Nearby is my second favorite place. Large glass windows overlook the pitch, the frosted glass blurring the shock of green turf and stands of bleachers. "That's where the Spar Games take place," I explain, knowing both Bennett and Mekhi are eager to try out for the school's team next year.

Next, I show them the impressive greenhouse, its glass walls covered in condensation and brimming with exotic plants from all over the magical realms. "You'll find some of the rarest and most enchanted plants here. The greenhouse is an essential part of our education in potion-making and herbology," I tell them as they peer inside.

As we continue exploring the campus, I point toward the towering observatory. "Theo's observatory is where students study the stars and celestial magic. It's a great place to stargaze or just find some peace and quiet away from the chaos of school life," I explain, before leaning in to whisper in Mekhi's ear. "Or sneak a quickie with your mate."

"Let's go there." He starts to tug me toward it, and Bennett growls, tugging him back in the direction we were originally headed.

We walk past the ancient bell tower, its weathered stones holding centuries of history and secrets. "Rumor has it that the tower is haunted," I say with a mischievous smile, watching their expressions shift between excitement and feigned apprehension.

Approaching the lighthouse, we pause to take in the breathtaking view. "This is one of my favorite spots on campus," I confess, admiring the way the lighthouse stands sentinel over the sea, its light cutting through the darkness like a beacon of hope. To the north, the sea stretches out, a wild and untamed force that adds to the enchantment of the academy.

"There's so much more to see," I say as we continue our tour, "but I think these are the highlights. I know you'll love it here."

Gesturing to the sky, I point to the crow circling ahead. "Not sure if those are standard issue, or what, but he or she follows me everywhere it seems."

"Do fae have familiars?" Mekhi asks, using his hand to shade his eyes from the sun as he looks up.

I glance at Bennett. "Not that I'm aware of?"

Bennett shakes his head. "The only instance I know of is Rune."

Rune is our grandma's mate, who can manifest a giant jaguar-type cat that's sentient and an extension of himself.

Glancing at the sky every so often, we continue our tour. I spot Lopey walking across the courtyard, her dark brown hair pulled back into a messy bun, and her warm brown eyes light up when she sees us. She's wearing her usual quirky, mismatched clothes.

"Guys, you remember Lopey, right?" I say to Bennett and Mekhi, motioning for Penelope to join us. They might have met her briefly before, but now that they'll be spending more time on campus, I want them to get to know her better. "Lopey, come over here!"

She approaches with a warm smile, and I make the introductions. "Bennett, Mekhi, this is Lopey. She's one of my closest friends here. Lopey, you remember my twin brother, Bennett, and my boyfriend, Mekhi?"

"Of course," Lopey says, extending her hand to each of them in turn. "It's nice to see you both again. I hope you're enjoying your tour of the campus. The food is the best part, though the selection of cereal kind of sucks. You'll want to pick up your own at Shatterlee Market if you can."

Mekhi chuckles. "Will do," he replies, returning her smile. "The food could be crap and I'd still want to be here, at the same school as Rose."

"How do you get all these men to throw themselves at your feet?" Lopey leans in conspiratorially. "We can't all be stunning princesses with giant boobs—"

I give her a playful shove. "They are not giant."

"Yes, they are," Mekhi raises a brow at me as he slides an arm around my waist.

"I'm not listening to this." Bennett covers his ears, walking a few paces ahead.

Lopey chuckles, but her gaze lingers on my brother a little too long, and her cheeks flush. "Seriously though, how does one get a guy, let alone multiple? Help a girl out here."

"Wait a minute. You want more than one?" My mouth drops open, scandalized. My precious little mouse shifter wants multiple men?

"Surprise." She winces.

"I don't know; I just have a big mouth, I guess?" Turning to face her, I study her. "Who are you interested in?"

She tugs her lip between her teeth before managing to squeak out, "I don't know, just save me a few good ones and I'm set."

"Um, gladly, but—"

Bennett takes that as his cue to break formation and saddle up on Lopey's side, making her cheeks flush. "Just how many are we talking?" His gaze lingers on my best friend for a moment, a flirtatious smile tugging at the corner of his lips. "I can learn to share for the right one."

Lopey blushes, but she grins back at Bennett. "When I first started here, I thought one, but the more I hang around your sister, the more I see the merit in several . . . attachments."

"Interesting," he muses.

I trade looks with Mekhi, but keep my mouth shut.

As we continue the tour, Bennett and Lopey exchange playful banter, their chemistry evident. It seems she is quite taken with him, and I can't help but smile at the thought of my brother finding someone as good as my best friend.

CHAPTER SEVEN

JAX

I shift in my seat in the auditorium, slipping my hand into Rose's next to me. On my other side is Deakan. Mekhi, Bennett, and Kieran are here, too, along with the rest of the student body. We're all on edge, awaiting the announcement of the new dean of Bedlam Academy. Ever since Dean Fallgren went missing, the campus has been in a state of uncertainty.

Glancing over at Kieran, I take in the glazed look in his eye, distant from whatever substance he's taken now. Grief wells up inside my chest.

I'm already failing him.

But he doesn't seem to notice my presence. He's lost in his own world, a solitary figure in the room full of people.

His hand trembles slightly, but he tries to steady it by keeping it busy with a guitar pick. He flips it over his knuckles, passing it from one finger to another in a bored, restless manner. It's as if he's trying to distract himself from the turmoil within, but the pick flipping only serves to accentuate the subtle shaking of his hand.

We heard him playing late last night, the sound of his guitar and haunting, melancholic voice carrying through the cave tunnels.

As the lights dim, a spotlight illuminates the stage, which is lined with the faculty members, including Theo. They exude an air of importance, their poised, expectant faces highlighted by the harsh glow. The murmurs of the audience gradually fade as all eyes turn toward the stage in anticipation for what's to come.

The curtain parts, and a man stands confidently at the podium, his presence commanding attention. A fleeting moment of recognition flickers in my mind, but it's like trying to catch a wisp of smoke—elusive and impossible to grasp, leaving my head slightly foggy.

The new dean is a striking figure, his dark hair framing a sun-kissed face, and his intense golden-green eyes seem to pierce into every corner of the room. An undeniable force radiates from him, captivating everyone present. It stains the air, thickening it.

Whoever this guy is, he's powerful. I couldn't even begin to guess his fae order. He gives the same kind of aura as Theo or Rose's dad, Finn, but it's even more intense.

"Good evening, esteemed faculty, students, and staff," the dean begins, his voice deep and resonant. The audience is enraptured, hanging on every word, as though he put the very magic in their bones. "I'm Dean Kairos Corvus, and I'm honored to lead Bedlam Academy into a new era."

He takes a moment to let his words settle, and a hushed silence fills the auditorium. The intensity of his presence is palpable, and it feels as though the very air crackles with power.

"In addition to our regular curriculum and the pursuit of excellence, we will embark on a journey of discovery, exploring the depths of our magical world," Dean Corvus continues, his eyes scanning the audience. "In particular, I would like to draw attention to the myth of the Arcane Scholar. It is said that this legendary figure holds the key to unlocking hidden knowledge and secrets long lost to the fae world."

He pauses for effect. "But the scholar is real and is amongst you now."

Whispers of intrigue flutter through the audience.

"In light of our pursuit for knowledge and mastery, I'm announcing a competition among our most gifted and dedicated students. If interested in applying, there will be a ritual you must complete in four weeks' time. After that, those entering the competition will have to solve a series of challenges, both academic and magical, designed to test the limits of your abilities. The winner of this competition will not only earn the esteemed title of the Arcane Scholar, but they will also play a crucial role in unraveling the mysteries of our magical world, potentially ushering in a new era of understanding. As a reward for their exceptional skills, the Arcane Scholar will have the extraordinary privilege of being personally mentored by me."

Dean Corvus takes a step back from the podium, his fingers curling tightly around the top edge of it. As he does, a screeching echoes through the microphone as the wooden legs of the podium grind against the stage floor. The sudden noise causes many of the fae in the audience to wince and cover their ears, while others who are more adept at magic use their abilities to dampen the sound for themselves and those around them.

Making his way to the center of the stage, Dean Corvus raises his hands up toward the ceiling, his eyes closed in concentration. A pulse of power ripples out from him, suffocating the room and robbing the air from my lungs. For a brief moment, all magic in the auditorium is smothered, as though the dean has taken control of it all. It's a feeling unlike anything I've ever experienced before, and I can feel the fear and awe coursing through my veins.

Just as suddenly as the power appeared, it vanishes, leaving me feeling exposed and vulnerable. But my magic surges back into my body, as though it had never left. In the wake of Dean's display of power, a palpable sense of fear lingers in the air, and I can see it on the faces of my fellow fae.

But to my surprise, Dean Corvus grins at us as though nothing out of the ordinary had happened. It's a cocky grin, the kind that makes me want to roll my eyes and tug Rose closer to my side. But at the same time, I can't deny the fact that I'm in the presence of one of the most powerful fae I've ever encountered. And that's both thrilling and terrifying.

"So, now that you all know what a privilege it would be to be mentored by me, you should know that with the pleasure of being named the Arcane Scholar comes great risk. This competition is not for the faint of heart. It will push you to your limits, both physically and mentally. You will face daunting challenges, the likes of which you've never experienced. Many will enter, but few will progress, and there may even be some who won't make it through unscathed. Yet, for the one who perseveres and succeeds, the rewards are immense. The Arcane Scholar will have the opportunity to procure a spell granting absolute safety for themselves and their families against all threats or attempts of magic suppression. In a world where magic is both a gift and a weapon, this protection is invaluable."

Murmurs reverberate through the audience. Rose leans over to me. "How the hell can he do that? He's got to be from Romarie if he can stop magic suppression."

Fae from Romarie can suppress magic due to the metal they possess in their realm. "You're right—"

The dean continues, "And before I bid you goodbye for the day, I've discussed this with the council and we're doing away with the rule about first years not using magic. It serves no one to not allow you to practice and grow outside of the classroom."

As Dean Corvus wraps up his announcement, the auditorium resonates with enthusiastic applause, the atmosphere brimming with anticipation. Students exchange eager glances, their minds racing with the potential rewards of this unique competition. The title of the Arcane Scholar sparks their imagination, and the chance to win and become a part of something extraordinary is too alluring for many in the room to resist.

He locks eyes with Rose, and I feel her body trembling beside me. A raging blush creeps up her neck and across her cheeks, illuminating her stunning blue aura that begins to radiate hot around us. Mesmerized by the sight, I can barely breathe as her supernatural beauty overwhelms me.

Rose abruptly stands, her eyes wide with embarrassment. "Excuse me," she mumbles, stumbling as she flees from the auditorium.

The guys and I exchange worried glances before rushing after her, confusion and concern pumping through our veins.

We catch up to Rose in the hallway outside the auditorium, her back pressed against the wall as she tries to catch her breath. The blue glow has receded, leaving her flushed and flustered.

"Rose, are you alright?" I ask, my voice laced with worry. "Did he hurt you?"

She shakes her head hesitantly, avoiding eye contact. "No, I just . . . I don't know. That man, the new dean, there's something about him."

Mekhi places a comforting hand on her shoulder. "It's okay, we all felt it too. There's something powerful about him, but it's hard to pinpoint."

Bennett chimes in, "He did give off a really intense vibe, but maybe he's just using one of those amplifiers they make in Romarie?"

Rose bites her lip and manages a nod, but it's clear she's still rattled. There's definitely more to our new dean that meets the eye, but time will tell. For now, all I want to do is support Rose.

Rose

THE GLOW of the fireplace bathes the room in a warm, flickering light, casting dancing shadows on the walls. It pops and it cracks, filling the space with a cozy soundtrack. Our living space is adorned with a mix of modern and vintage furniture, creating a homey atmosphere that invites relaxation and conversation. A large, plush rug spreads across the wooden floor, softening the space and adding a touch of comfort.

A tall bookshelf, filled to the brim with books on magic, history, and various other subjects, covers one wall, while an array of artwork hangs on the opposite wall, reflecting Theo's love of celestial events. The scent of cinnamon and sugar, from the freshly baked bread we made earlier, still lingers in the air.

Theo pulls a large, old book from the shelf, the leather cover worn and embossed with runes. "I found this in the library," he says, opening it to reveal yellowed pages covered in delicate, handwritten text. "It has information on past Arcane Scholars and their discoveries. It might help us understand the competition better."

"I didn't realize there'd ever been a competition before." Bennett stops his pacing. He uses magic to twirl a pencil in the air without touching it. "Does it say who won?"

We gather around the book, leaning in to examine its contents. The ancient text is accompanied by illustrations of various magical artifacts, diagrams of spells, and intricate maps of faraway territories and distant realms.

Mekhi points to a passage, his face a mix of fascination and concern. "It says here that some Arcane Scholars disappeared during their tenure, never to be heard from again."

"I don't like it." Jax leans forward, eyes darting across the page. "I feel like I've met this dean before."

"What do you mean?" I hoist myself onto the table but let out a squeak just as Deakan slides me onto his lap instead. He gives me a wry grin.

Jax runs both hands through his hair. "I get a strong sense of déjà vu when I look at him, but it's almost as if he's glamored himself."

"He probably did," Theo muses, flipping the page. "While I don't sense anything nefarious with him, he's a little intense."

"Are you suggesting we shouldn't enter the competition?" Bennett's phone buzzes, and he pulls it out, smiling as he rapidly types a response.

"Who has you grinning like that?" I tease.

He just raises an eyebrow at me while continuing to type away without looking, a playful smile on his face.

"One has to question the value of being mentored by the dean when you're a royal and have access to powerful fae during family gatherings. I'm not sure the risk is worth the reward." Theo leans back, sliding the worn book away from him.

"But you'd all be safe," I murmur. "If something happened to any of you, *again*, it would destroy me. I can't bear the thought of more heartache."

"That's what feathers are for," Theo says, placing his hand on mine and gently rubbing his thumb along the top. "I'll give each of you one of mine, and when all of your wings come in, we'll be set."

Tears well up in my eyes at his willingness to do that for my other mates. Fae feathers don't grow back, which is why fae rarely reveal their wings to anyone other than their own mates. A single feather is a cherished possession, and one from a strong fae like Theo? Invaluable.

I intertwine my fingers with his before bringing our hands to my lips to tenderly press a kiss to his knuckles. "Why don't we do the feather ritual first, and then the rest of us will have a safeguard in place if something happens during the competition. This way, none of us will stay dead if gods forbid, something happens?"

"I love your big brain." Deakan nuzzles against my neck before placing a nibble against my shoulder.

I swat him away. "I'm serious! If one of us wins, we're all set. It's fine if you guys don't want to do it, but I'm going to. Maybe he can help us figure out where the missing bracelet is."

My parents have dedicated everything to tracking the bracelet that can control my family, but it's as though it's vanished completely.

The guys exchange uncertain glances, their expressions reflecting a mix of reluctance and concern. Theo's apprehension is evident in the way he fidgets with the worn book on his lap, but eventually, he sighs and concedes. "Alright, I suppose we're doing this together."

Kieran, still quiet and withdrawn, pushes his chair back abruptly, the legs screeching against the wooden floor. He stands up and walks away, his footsteps echoing as he traverses the hallway before disappearing into the dimly lit caves. I can't help but worry about him, the heavy atmosphere in the room weighing on my chest.

I slip off Deakan's lap, feeling the warmth of his body as I do so. Leaning in, I press a tender kiss to his lips, lingering for just a moment before pulling back. "I'll be right back," I reassure him, my eyes darting in the direction Kieran had disappeared. My heart swells with a need to support and care for all of them, and I'm determined to ensure we face whatever challenges the competition might hold together, as a united front.

And that means the serpent fae who's retreating to his room.

I follow the path Kieran took, the dim lighting from the hallway spilling into the cave's entrance. The cavern is cool and damp, and the sound of dripping water echoes faintly in the distance. The air grows heavy with a sweet, acrid scent that I recognize as a popular fae drug known as nectarsmoke, commonly smoked to soothe one's mind and dull emotional pain. It's relatively harmless, and its effects last only an hour or so.

As I venture further into the cave, I find Kieran's makeshift bedroom nestled in a corner. The small space is illuminated by an array of delicate lights strung up on the uneven walls, casting a warm and inviting glow over the rough-hewn space. His guitar rests on a stand near a cozy-looking bed, dressed in rumpled sheets that match the earthy tones of the cavern. Various trinkets and personal belongings are scattered about, giving the space a lived-in, intimate feel, despite his just moving in.

Kieran sits on the edge of his bed, taking a drag from a joint of nectarsmoke between his fingers. As he exhales, tendrils of smoke fill the air, swirling and twisting in mesmerizing patterns before dissipating into the dimly lit room. His eyes, heavy-lidded and glazed, find mine as I approach.

"Kieran," I say softly, hesitant to startle him. "Is everything alright?"

He takes another slow drag, his gaze never leaving mine. The tension between us is palpable, our shared history of animosity and burgeoning affection creating an emotional whirlwind that makes my stomach churn. He's in love with me—he admitted as much in the dungeon—but my royal status and his aversion to the aristocracy have made our connection fraught with conflict.

Kieran exhales, releasing a cloud of smoke that lingers between us like a barrier. "Do you think it's fair?" he asks, his voice rough and unsteady. "You all get to enter this competition, be in this together, while my only family is missing? I know it doesn't matter to you because of what my gran tried to do, but she's all I have. It doesn't matter to any of you."

His words sting, and I feel a desperate need to reassure him that he is valued and cared for. I take a tentative step closer, my heart pounding in my chest as I search for the right words to mend the rift between us.

"Can I sit next to you?" I ask hesitantly, my voice a mere puff of breath passed between my lips.

Kieran studies me for a moment, his eyes searching mine for sincerity. Finally, he reclines back on the bed, a sliver of his abs peaking from where his band t-shirt rides up. He lazily extends an arm in invitation, and I carefully lower myself onto the soft sheets next to him.

As we sit in silence, Kieran offers me the joint, an unspoken invitation to share in his reprieve from reality. I hesitate for a moment, unsure if I want to indulge. But the longing in his eyes urges me to try it, if only to feel a little closer to him, to understand him better.

It isn't addictive, so I take the joint from his fingers, my hand brushing against his ever so slightly, and raise it to my lips. As I take a tentative drag, the smoke fills my lungs, and I immediately cough, my chest burning from the unexpected sensation. Kieran chuckles softly, the sound more comforting than condescending, and offers a reassuring smile.

As we continue to pass the joint between us, my coughs lessen, and a soothing warmth begins to spread through my body. The tension in the air gradually dissipates, replaced by an intimate vulnerability that opens the door for honest conversation.

"Kieran," I begin again, my voice filled with sincerity. "I want to help you find your grandma. And I don't want you to feel left out anymore. I want you to have a feather too. If Theo isn't willing to give you one, I'll ask one of my parents for one."

My words hang in the air as Kieran's eyes widen with surprise. The offer is a bold one, and it's evident that he didn't expect me to extend such an olive branch. As we sit there, sharing a joint and baring our souls, I realize that this is a pivotal moment in our relationship, one that could either bring us closer or push us further apart.

The nectarsmoke dances lazily around us, tendrils of blue and violet weaving through the air. The scent of the smoke is both sweet and earthy, the perfect blend of fae magic and nature. I take a deep breath, letting the fragrance fill my senses, and notice how it seems to help calm my racing heart.

Kieran's makeshift bedroom is both cozy and intimate, reflecting his personality and interests. Soft, warm light emanates from tiny lanterns that are scattered around the room, casting dancing shadows on the walls. He's got another guitar propped against the cavern wall, surrounded by a collection of handwritten music sheets, their edges worn and well-loved. A silent witness to countless nights of restless sleep.

As the seconds tick by, Kieran appears to be lost in thought, his eyes tracing the flickering shadows on the wall. His expression is unreadable, a mix of vulnerability and contemplation. His grip on the joint tightens ever so slightly, betraying the tension building inside him.

The cavern seems to shrink around us as the silence stretches on, the weight of my offer bearing down on us. The faint sound of water dripping from the cave's stalactites echoes through the chamber, creating a soothing, rhythmic soundtrack to our shared introspection. The cool air of the cavern presses gently against my skin, a comforting reminder of the realm's embrace.

Finally, Kieran turns his gaze to me, his eyes softened with gratitude and something more—an emotion I can't quite place.

"Thank you," Kieran says, his voice a hoarse rasp. "That means more to me than you'll ever know."

His words dance along my spine, awakening it, and I can't help but wonder if it's the nectarsmoke or the intensity of the moment that's causing my reaction. The smoke seems to take on a life of its own, curling and coiling around us as if to capture the essence of our newfound understanding.

He hands the joint back to me, and I take another drag, trying to emulate the smooth way he inhales. I cough again, but it's less intense this time, my lungs adjusting to the foreign sensation. Kieran chuckles softly, the sound warm and soothing, like a balm for our frayed emotions.

"So, you've really never tried nectarsmoke before?" he asks, a playful glint in his eyes.

I shake my head, the corners of my lips turning up in a sheepish grin. "No, never. I guess I've been a bit sheltered."

He studies me so long that I have to turn to face him to make sure he hasn't fallen asleep on me. His lips part, and he blows a smoke ring, using air magic to send it circling a stalactite a few feet away. It bobs and weaves around it. "Shelter can be a refuge from the storm, but it can also be a cage if you don't venture beyond its walls. In the end, it's the storms we weather that shape who we become." The smoke ring solidifies before pinching off the point, sending it crashing to the ground.

I think that's the most he's ever said to me before. If this is what it takes to get him to open up to me and not be so closed off? I take another drag, holding the smoke in my lungs a little longer this time before exhaling. "That's true. I'd been adventurous until it got my brother killed."

Kieran smiles, his eyes crinkling at the corners. "Let me guess. You blame yourself."

I hum. We continue to pass the joint back and forth, sitting in quiet contemplation. I notice the way Kieran's tense shoulders gradually begin to relax, the lines of worry on his face slowly melting away.

I'm struck by the realization that despite our differences and the animosity we've felt toward each other in the past, Kieran is someone I can relate to on a deeper level. While our experiences have been vastly different, we both know the pain of loss and the burden of carrying on in the face of tragedy.

I can see now that beneath Kieran's tough exterior is a fiercely loyal and protective soul, someone who's had to forge his own path in a world that's been unkind to him. Our shared struggles draw us closer together, allowing us to see past the surface and find understanding in one another's experiences.

CHAPTER EIGHT

ROSE

Over the next few days, Theo teaches us magic to help him construct the caves so they're more of a living space rather than a series of tunnels and caverns. When you're working with wood to build a house or furniture, it's straightforward—wood here, nails there. But working with magic to move literal earth is a whole other beast, and it's overwhelming to say the least.

Part of me wants to just call in someone from the Terra order to just fix it all for us in a few days, but I don't want to put any of us at further risk. It was a big move to bring Kieran—a known associate of our enemy—here, but with a fae promise helping keep him in line, I can't really argue about bringing in my mate's best friend. And after our little heart-to-heart, I'm warming up to him.

Besides, having him here is built-in entertainment. When he plays guitar, it carries through the cave system and reaches the room I share with my men. And when he sings? I'm not sure whether I want to sob at its beauty or find him a recording deal somewhere.

His clear, melancholic singing is like a river of golden honey, a soft and soothing melody that carries through the cave system and wraps around each of us like a warm blanket, that speaks to each one of our sorrows. His voice is buttery and rich, yet tinged with an undercurrent of raspy sadness that leaves me feeling melancholic and heavy with emotion. Every syllable carries a medley of emotions that speak to the soul in ways words cannot.

As we continue our work, I find myself thinking about the unique spaces each of us has claimed as our own. Bennett, for instance, has a little cavern for his room at the far end of the cave after going through several corridors. His reasoning is he wants to be far away from our room, but you can't really blame him for that. I wouldn't want to hear him with his mates, if he had any.

"Why don't you two head back and we'll keep working on this?" Jax suggests, tossing Mekhi and me each a bottle of water. Grateful, I eagerly take a swig, relishing the cold liquid as it quenches my thirst.

Despite the layer of grime coating everyone, I can't help but let my gaze linger on my mates, all of them shirtless and drenched in sweat from their labor. The dim light of the cavern seems to accentuate the contours of their bodies, making them appear even more alluring.

Theo's muscles ripple beneath his tanned skin as he works diligently to reinforce a section of the wall. The sweat glistening on his chest, combined with his focused expression, only adds to his appeal. Jax's normally wavy hair has taken on an unruly, curly texture from the humidity, and his flushed cheeks seem to enhance his already striking features. My eyes begin to wander over to—

"Jesus Christ, get out of here with that!" Bennett shouts, tossing a shirt at my face. "I'm going to shower then grab some food from campus."

Startled, I let the fabric fall away, and it's then I realize my blue glow has flooded the entire cavern, bathing my mates in its ethereal light.

The warmth of embarrassment spreads across my cheeks as I come to terms with the fact that my fae nature has betrayed my emotions. My glow, an involuntary response triggered by pain, healing, or arousal, now exposes my appreciation for my mates' sweat-soaked forms.

My mates exchange amused glances, a mixture of smirks and chuckles filling the air. "We'll be here, working."

"Sorry, guys," I mutter, spinning to face the empty hallway, desperately trying to hide the blush that threatens to overtake my face. As much as I might wish for the ground to swallow me whole, there isn't a whole lot I can do about it.

Mekhi slips an arm around my waist, his touch both protective and comforting. "Let's go," he gently guides me down the hallway, and I can't resist casting a glance back at my mates. Their warm, teasing grins linger in my mind as Mekhi and I leave them behind.

The ache of our muscles and the exhaustion from the day's work seem to slowly dissipate as we make our way back to our room, the excitement of a quiet, romantic evening with Mekhi making my heart race in anticipation. We haven't had the luxury of private time lately, and the thought of simply enjoying each other's company is alluring.

Upon entering our shared bedroom, I can't help but smile as I notice that our mates have made an effort to tidy the space in preparation for our date night. Clothes that were once scattered across the floor have been picked up and folded, and a faint scent of citrus fills the air, undoubtedly the result of a quick cleaning charm.

Mekhi and I take turns in the bathroom, washing away the layers of dirt and sweat that cling to our skin. As I step out, wrapped in a fluffy towel, I find that he's laid out a comfortable outfit for me: a pair of soft leggings and a cozy oversized sweater. I quickly change, grateful for the thoughtful gesture.

As we step into the living room, I'm struck by a scene that appears to have been lifted straight from a romantic film.

"How the hell did you guys find the time to do this?!" I whisper in amazement. "We've been in the caves all day!"

"Every time one of them had to take a bathroom break, they worked on setting this up for us," Mekhi explains with a grin.

"Really?" I gasp, taking in the breathtaking sight.

"Even Bennett and Kieran pitched in."

The room has been transformed into a cozy, intimate sanctuary. Warm candlelight flickers, casting mesmerizing shadows on the walls, while the soothing melodies of our favorite indie songs drift from a discreetly placed speaker in the corner.

In the center of the room, Mekhi has set up a low table, adorned with a clean white tablecloth and a simple but elegant arrangement of wildflowers straight from our courtyard. The mouthwatering aroma of homemade pasta wafts through the air. He's even managed to find a decent bottle of fae wine, a luxury that's hard to come by on Academia on account of all the students. As long as you're mature, you can drink legally, but the council overseeing each of the universities doesn't make it easy to procure it.

We sit down to enjoy our meal, and I can't help but be struck by how effortlessly the guys have crafted this perfect moment for us. If there were any lingering doubts as to how they'd all get along—this annihilated them.

The flickering candles, the mellow glow of the fae lights dancing along the walls, and the taste of the delicious food he's prepared all combine to create an atmosphere that feels truly magical.

As the evening progresses, our talks take the same cadence as so many before; we discuss everything and nothing: our dreams, our fears, and the endless possibilities that our future holds. It'll make what I ask him later so much easier. I find myself losing track of time, drawn in by the warmth of Mekhi's voice and the depth of his eyes. The chaotic sounds of moving rock fades away, leaving just the two of us, cocooned in our shared love and the comfortable, familiar rhythm of our conversation.

The butterflies in my stomach dance wildly as I summon the courage to bring up the subject I've been mulling over for months.

Mekhi and I gather our dishes, rinsing them off before placing them in the dishwasher. Taking his hand, I guide him into the bedroom and sit down beside him. My heart sprints in anticipation, pounding a rapid rhythm against my ribcage.

Drawing in a deep breath, I try to steady my nerves. "Mekhi, there's something I've been wanting to talk to you about," I begin, my voice rich as I try to push as much feeling into it as possible.

He gazes at me with kind, attentive eyes that seem to see straight into my soul. His hand, warm and reassuring, gives mine a gentle squeeze. "What's going on? You know you can talk to me about anything."

I nod, swallowing the lump that has formed in my throat. "I know, it's just . . . this is important, and I want to make sure I say it right."

His smile, soft and tender, warms me from within as he brushes a strand of hair behind my ear. "Take your time. It's just me. I'm here, and I'm listening."

Emboldened by his gentle encouragement, I gather the courage to continue. "Mekhi, we've been through so much together, and I can't imagine my life without you. I . . . I want to ask if you would consider taking the mating bond with me. I know we've joked about it before, but I'm serious when I say I don't want to spend life without you."

Without any of them.

His dark eyes widen, and for a moment, he seems at a loss for words. Mekhi's chiseled features, marked by a scar across his chest visible where he's got his shirt unbuttoned, are softened by the candlelight. His bronzed skin glistens with a fine sheen of sweat, only serving to highlight the sculpted muscles that make him so undeniably attractive.

As he processes my words, I feel my heart thudding wildly in my chest, anxiously awaiting his response.

Mekhi's eyes search mine for a moment, taking in the depth of my sincerity. A crooked smile begins to form on his lips, the warmth in his face intensifying. "It's because of my kinks, isn't it?"

A giggle escapes me as I swat him with a pillow, but then I pause. "Wait a minute. What other kinks do you have?"

Mekhi chuckles, his hand coming up to rub the back of his neck. "Oh, you know, just a few things here and there. Nothing too crazy." He winks at me, and I can't tell if he's teasing me or if he's being serious. One way to find out I guess.

I roll my eyes, but a smile plays at my lips.

He pauses, taking a deep breath as he continues. "In all seriousness, before you, I think you know how terrible things were for me. But then you come along, this beautiful, bright light helping to guide me out of the dark. You're it for me, Rose. It's only ever been you."

As he speaks, the warmth in my chest swells, and I can hardly believe the depth of emotion flowing between us. His magic brushes mine just as he gently lifts my hand, pressing a tender kiss to my knuckles. "Rose, I would be honored to take the mating bond with you."

Relief and joy wash over me, and my heart feels like it might burst from happiness. I throw my arms around him, pulling him into a tight embrace as I breathe in deep, inhaling deep. His skin carries a sweet, spicy aroma with a hint of exotic citrus. It's a comforting smell, one that feels like our home in Australia.

As we pull apart, our foreheads resting against each other, our breaths mingling, I search for the right words to say. "I'm serious about the birth control thing, though. And I can't bear the thought of losing you, so you need to perform the immortality ritual, or we can't go through with the mating."

Mekhi's eyes hold mine, reflecting the weight of my words. "They don't offer the ritual to witches until our fourth year," he explains, his voice soft yet steady. "But with the recent threats against our family, I imagine your parents would be willing to teach me sooner. There's always a feather in the meantime."

"Theo can help if they won't, though I can't see them refusing," I reassure him, my heart swelling with the knowledge that we're working together to navigate this.

"I'll give them a call tomorrow. As for now, I think there's something we've wanted for a while." A small, grateful smile graces his lips. "And don't worry—we've all checked our fertility status."

My curiosity piqued, I lean back slightly to scrutinize his face. "How did you manage that?"

"If you drip a bit of blood onto a Sascord plant, it'll turn purple if you're fertile," he explains, gesturing toward the window.

Still somewhat skeptical, I rise to my feet, the cool floor biting my toes as I approach the window cautiously, my eyes narrowing as I lift the sill and peer down. There, nestled below the window, are four potted plants, their vibrant green leaves basking in the moonlight, not a hint of purple to be found.

Relief seeps into my bones at the sight of the untouched green plants, and I can't help but let out a small, incredulous laugh. "Shocker," I admit, turning back to Mekhi. "I never thought I'd be so happy to see green plants in my life."

Mekhi chuckles, his crooked smile returning as he wraps his arms around my waist, drawing me closer. "I know what you mean," he murmurs, pressing a tender kiss to my forehead. "I just wanted to make sure we could focus on each other tonight, without any worries or distractions."

I nestle into the warmth of his embrace, my heart brimming with love and gratitude for this incredible man who stands by my side through thick and thin. "Thank you, Mekhi," I whisper, looking up into his eyes, which are filled with warmth and devotion. "That means the world to me."

He brushes his thumb gently against my cheek, his dark eyes gazing deeply into mine. "You mean the world to me, Rose."

Our surroundings seem to fade away, the flickering candlelight and the soft melodies of our favorite songs wrapping around us like a warm blanket. In this private sanctuary, the rest of the world disappears, and only our love and commitment remain, filling the air and our hearts as Mekhi's fingers find the button on my jeans.

His lips trail my jaw before resting near my ear. He whispers, "You know I love you, right?"

"Of course," I breathe, goosebumps lining my skin where his breath stirs against my neck.

"Good." He nibbles on my flesh. "Because in a minute, you're going to think I don't."

I let out a soft sigh as he works my zipper down, and I help him pull the jeans over my ass and step out of them. With Mekhi, I always thought it'd be slow and sensual with him, but tonight, his touch is more urgent, his hands moving quickly to strip me of my clothes. His lust and desire are evident in the way his dark eyes roam over my body, drinking in every inch of me with a hunger that sets my blood on fire and lights the room with my glow.

I can feel his hard length pressing against my thigh, and I know what I want first. Palming him through his shorts, I slide them down, thrilled to find him wearing nothing underneath. He sucks in a breath when I drop to my knees, understanding my intention.

"You don't have to do that," he whispers, gaze heavy as he tilts my chin.

My lips curve into a wicked smile just before I take him into my mouth, relishing the groan he releases as I taste him. He fills me completely, fingers tangling in my hair as I suck and swirl my tongue around him, taking him deeper until he's throbbing against the back of my throat.

I can feel his control slipping as I continue, and when I finally pull away, he looks like he's about to lose it. His eyes, wild and fierce, find mine, and I can't help the satisfied smirk that appears on my lips.

"Rose," he breathes, voice hoarse. "You'd better stop before I make a fool out of myself."

A smirk adorns my face as I pop him out of my mouth. "Let me guess, you want to spill your seed in my pussy?"

My words, carefully chosen for his breeding kink, sends a full-body shiver down his spine, and he groans, a deep rumble that vibrates through the air. "Yes." His hand cups my cheek before grabbing my chin. "Will you let me film it?"

"You want to film us?" I raise a brow, studying him.

"The guys and I thought it might be hot." He grins.

He helps me to my feet, and I narrow my eyes. "*Might be?*" He leads me to the bed, but I push him onto his back and crawl on top of him. I give him a slow, passionate kiss, our tongues entwined and exploring before I pull back to whisper in his ear. "If it only *might* be hot, I'm not so sure we should be having sex—"

Mekhi's hand grips the hair at my scalp, holding it firmly while he gets me to look him in the eye. "It'll be the hottest fucking thing they've ever seen. How about we show them what they're missing?"

"You do that, and they're likely to interrupt us."

"Let them." He smirks, flipping me onto my back so fast, all the air leaves my lungs on a yelp. "Show them that just because I'm not fae, doesn't mean I can't make you scream."

He looks so sure of himself; I can't help but giggle. "I don't know, babe . . . it would take a lot for me to scream."

Mekhi grins, lowering himself against me, his hard length pressing into my soft curves. "I know I can, and I'm going to prove it to everyone."

He reaches for the nightstand, where my phone is plugged in. "Video call them." He grins.

My mouth falls open. "You're serious."

"Hell yeah, I'm serious."

I laugh, shaking my head as I dial Deakan's phone because I know he's got it hooked up to the sound system in the cave right now.

Mekhi takes the phone from me, propping it on the window ledge so the guys have a full view of the whole bed before proceeding to lock the door with an enchantment. He crawls over me on the bed, a wicked gleam in his eye.

"Hey." I hear Deakan's voice from my phone.

I don't get a chance to respond before Mekhi's hands travel the length of my torso, lingering at the waistband of my panties. In one swift motion he yanks them off, and I breathe in sharply.

His fingers dance delicately over the lace of my bra. "Such a pretty package to unwrap." He grins down at me.

With a grand wave of his hand, the fabric covering my chest disappears, spilling my breasts into his hands.

"Is that Rose's bra?" I can hear Jax ask through the muffled speaker on the phone. "How the hell did it get in here?"

How did he sift my whole bra into the cave system? I'm not given the chance to ponder his words as Mekhi descends upon me, burying his face between my thighs and unleashing a surge of pleasure at my core.

"Oh, shit," Theo curses next.

Mekhi's tongue flicks around my clit, exploring every inch with a delicious tempo. Before I know it, I'm lost in a sea of pleasure that builds higher and higher until I can hardly contain the mounting sensation. My voice escapes as a piercing keening moan that fills the air like a siren song.

"Are they . . .?"

"Shit, let's go—"

I barely hear the muffled sound of them running through the tunnels, but do hear the pounding on the door and shouts to let them in.

Mekhi chuckles, the vibration of his laugh traveling between my legs, making me moan louder. His fingers join his mouth, and I'm so close to my peak that my eyes roll back in my head.

"Let us in, Rose!" I hear Deakan's voice. "Please!"

Mekhi pulls away, and I glance up to see him smirking. "You don't get to come until I tell you that you can."

I whimper, "They'll let me come all over their cocks." I raise my hand to summon magic to let the guys in, but a hand around my wrist stops me.

"Uh uh," he tsks. "Not until I've had my fill."

"Please," I beg, my voice trembling with anticipation. He lowers his mouth, swirling his tongue against my clit, applying just the right amount of pressure.

My breath comes in pants, and I feel the pleasure coiling tightly in me, but before I can come, he backs off again. He pauses just long enough to drive me insane before continuing, sending jolts of fire through my veins until I'm so close to bliss, I can almost taste it. But each time I come close, he pulls away, keeping me on edge until I scream with unfulfilled desire.

"Mekhi!" I whimper. "You're so nice to me outside the bedroom, why do you have to torture me?"

He chuckles, stopping my hand when it goes between my thighs in an attempt to get myself off. Using magic, he pins them above my head so I can't touch him.

"You love it." He slides two fingers inside me, while using his thumb to rub at my clit in slow, agonizing circles. "And you're going to thank me when I'm done and you're coming all over my face."

I lose myself to his touch, and I'm no longer aware of the pounding on the door or the guys' pleas for me to let them in. All I know is

Mekhi and his magical fingers, luring me ever closer to the edge of an orgasm that seems to always be out of reach.

Bucking my hips, I try to get closer. He pins me down, and I'm completely at his mercy as he edges me just to the brink before backing off.

"Please," I cry, and I think I might have actual tears.

Mekhi crawls fully onto the bed next to me, laying down. "You need to come, baby?"

I nod, sweat slicking my skin.

He grabs me by my hips and hauls me up until I'm hovering over his face, my hands still bound from some invisible forced tied to the ceiling. "You can come now, but you're going to paint my face with it so there's no confusion as to who made you come like this."

Mekhi's hands clamp down on my thighs, forcing me to sit on his face as he drags his tongue along my core, settling against my clit, flicking it over and over. I arch my back, rocking against his mouth as I finally tumble over the edge into an orgasm that shatters me into a million pieces.

He slides me off him when my body goes limp, and I collapse onto the bed, my breathing coming in ragged gasps.

"Holy shit," I breathe.

"Told you." He traces my nipple with his tongue, glancing back at where my phone is still broadcasting us to Deakan's phone.

I pull myself up so I'm on my elbows, no longer restrained, and give him a lazy grin. "Pretty sure you said I was going to scream," I tease.

"Who said I'm done?"

I yelp when he drags me under him. My laughter is cut off when he slams his lips against mine, smothering me in a passionate kiss. I taste myself on him.

His hands move down my body, dragging me closer until I'm flush against him, his body a firm weight against me. My legs wrap around his waist, and I can feel his cock pressing against me.

He breaks away from me, smirking. "Might not be any time soon, but I will put a baby in you someday."

My eyes widen, and I don't have time to respond before he's sliding into me. I gasp, clinging to him as he seats himself to the hilt.

"Fuck, it feels good to be home," he grins down at me. But there's sincerity and all the love I know him to possess for me in his gaze, too. "I love you, Rose."

"I love you, too," I breathe.

He moves slowly, each stroke sending sparks of pleasure through me. The sound of our skin slapping together, his grunts of pleasure, and my moans of bliss fill the room. I've dreamt of this moment a thousand ways, but nothing could've prepared me for this. The way he leisurely rolls his hips at just the right angle has me clinging to him as though I might shatter.

Mekhi increases his pace, his hips pistoning faster and harder as he drags his pelvis against my clit until I'm screaming his name, my nails digging into his back and my teeth clamping down onto his shoulder. He slows his thrusts, groaning as he shoots thick ropes of come into me.

Like a spark to gunpowder, our magic surges toward each other, filling our chests and spreading through our limbs, bathing us in a bright glow. It coils me tight, riding the edge of pleasure and pain until I'm shuddering against him, my body clenching around his as my orgasm rocks me. Our breaths come in staccato gasps, fanned by the heat radiating from our skin. His arm snakes around my waist and his warmth becomes one with mine as our hearts beat a frantic rhythm against each other.

Spreading my thighs, he watches as his semen trickles down my inner thigh. His fingers dip into the puddle, scooping up the evidence of our lovemaking and he thrusts it back inside, a mesmerized look on his face as he does so. He settles back onto the bed so I'm in the crook of his arm.

"We going to talk about that?" I chuckle.

"Let me enjoy this before we allow the cavalry in," he whispers against my shoulder. "I can feel you here." He lays his hand over his heart.

"I can feel you, too." I smile, turning to face him.

"You know, after that time at the lake when we didn't have any condoms, I obsessed over it. For *months*." He chuckles. "Kicking myself for not just being with you then, and that's probably what caused my kink. But I'm glad it happened this way now."

"Made it memorable." I grin.

Loud pounding sounds on the door, and it's then I register the guys have been trying to get our attention through the phone this whole time.

"Please let us in," Deakan whines.

Pressing my lips to Mekhi's, I linger before pulling back. "I think we've tortured them long enough."

He sighs, reaching over to shoot a charm at the doorknob.

The guys stumble in, shirts off, still just as filthy as they were when I left them. They stalk toward me, and I scoot back, hands out like I'm trying to keep a wild animal from attacking.

"You guys are not filthying up our bed," I warn, but they pay no attention.

Jax drags me by my ankle to the edge of the bed, and my laughter fills the room as he buries himself between my thighs.

It's sometime before midnight when the guys and I are in a tangled heap, thoroughly fucked and spent, when I notice my phone still sitting in the corner of the window.

Sitting up on my elbows, I say, "guys?"

"Mm?" Theo hums against my chest.

"Did you ever disconnect the video call to Deakan's phone?"

KIERAN

*L*ast night, the sound of Rose's pleasure echoed through the ancient caverns, reverberating off the walls and floors and filling the air until it was all I could hear. Her moans, louder than thunder and softer than a whisper, seemed to echo through my body as if I was there with her. The way she begged for release still fills my ears even as we dine across from each other before classes begin.

I fucked my fist to the sound of her cries, and I have never come harder in my life.

Rose's cheeks have taken on a fiery red hue that matches her namesake perfectly, radiating an inner beauty that nothing else comes close to matching.

Mekhi and Rose secured their mating bond last night, so I'll likely be subjected to the two of them all over each other for the rest of the month. I grit my teeth, trying to push back the jealousy that rears its ugly head.

Downing my protein shake, I scoot my chair back and rinse the glass before putting it in the dishwasher. Grabbing my bag by my chair, I make my escape like my ass is on fire.

I burst through the front door, feeling the heat of the jungle hit my face as soon as I enter the courtyard of Sanctuary. The scent of damp earth and fog hit my nostrils, which is a welcome reprieve from the cloying, intoxicating scent of Rose's arousal. Jogging to the boundary, I sift out as soon as my feet touch the other side.

Being here—with them—is a terrible idea. I'm in desperate need for a distraction, something to keep my thoughts from spiraling back to her. Instead of heading to the campus, I find myself sifting to Occasus, seeking solace in the chaotic anonymity it offers.

Seems as though if my grandma were in hiding, she'd be here. It's also a great place to hide the bracelet Rose's family is looking for. I offered to help her find it this weekend when we go to look for my grandma, but I'm going to start here, first.

The central foothills of Occasus are home to a sprawling, walled-in metropolis—the city of Espero. It's as massive as it is overwhelming. Since the war, the sentry turrets situated in each corner of the city tower over any building and house armed guards with orders to shoot to kill anyone caught looting. Just about everything else goes on behind its walls, but stealing from him is off-limits. Whoever *he* is. It's something I guarantee Rose's parents know nothing about. I don't even want Rose to know about this place.

She might've indulged in a little nectarsmoke, but the stuff they sell here? She's too pure for it.

The royal guard doesn't step foot here, thanks to a redirect glamor on the city said to be conjured by a powerful dark fae with a cruel appetite. Anyone with pure hearts find themselves with the sudden urge to turn around when approaching the place. I'd discovered it not long after our first Spar Games tournament this year. Burly thugs, cloaked in a mix of fur, hide, and scales roam the streets, splitting from the shadows in a hunt for their next victim.

It's why all its seedy activities go without punishment. It has a flesh market nestled at the eastern edge of its vast timber forest. The air here is thick with putrefaction and danger, teeming with characters you wouldn't want to encounter in a dark alley. The scent of blood and death is carried on the wind along with the stench of the meat stalls that sell nothing but illegal goods. The air makes you itch in a way that nothing else can. It's like a soft itch that you can't scratch, but it's everywhere and all at once.

The streets are chaotic, filled with drunken brawls, shrieking hookers, and the deadly sounds of out-of-control magic battles. The buildings of Espero are made from whatever materials could be scavenged. Stone, wood, and anything in between. The only thing they all have in common is the dingy, greasy feeling they hold to the touch.

The ground is swampy and wet with stagnant water and the remains of frequent downpours. Noxious vines and roots cover side streets and buildings like webs, swaying and crawling in the shadows. Creatures dangle from their webs, their bodies limp and lifeless, their blood dripping down the sides of their faces to pool at the tips of their noses.

I cloak myself in a glamor, blending seamlessly into the crowd as I weave through the bustling throng. My sharpened fangs make their presence known to anyone bold enough to attempt to pickpocket me.

The flesh market is far from where I wish to be, the sight of those for sale—some barely more than children—leaves a bitter taste in my mouth. Two months is hardly enough time for me to put a plan into action to help them. I'll do whatever it takes, though, because for them? I'll do it.

Finding a secluded corner, I wait, my body thrumming with anticipation. Soon, a tall figure emerges from the shadows, meeting my gaze with a knowing smirk. We exchange tense words, my eyes narrowing, my heart heavy with the reason I've come to this wretched place.

Reluctantly, I pass a bag of coins into the toothless witch's waiting hand, and in return, she hands me a small jar. This is a small price to pay for those I need to help. Biting into the gasket atop the container, I cringe as my fangs pierce the rubber, the sensation unnerving. After a few moments, I withdraw, licking the last traces of my venom from my lips.

She seals the jar with a lid, slips it into her pocket, and tips her hat at me before vanishing back into the teeming masses. As I continue through the market, another stall catches my eye, luring me in with its wares but I press on, ready to leave Espero's horrors behind.

As I continue through the market, the alluring scent of an intoxicating substance wafts through the air, so at odds with the reek of this place, drawing me towards a dimly lit stall. The vendor, a mysterious figure draped in shadows, displays an array of vials filled with shimmering powder.

"What is this?" I ask, curiosity piqued by the otherworldly substance.

The vendor's eyes gleam with mischief as they reply, "Aeris Luminis, a rare and potent elixir from the depths of the Romarie. It offers a momentary respite from the burdens of life, a brief escape into a world of wonder. Even for those with serpentine blood."

I hesitate, weighing the consequences of dabbling in such a substance. Serpent fae are impervious to all poison, though some drugs have some effect on us, particularly those from Romarie, who specialize in metal—especially those found in blood. Whatever this is, it's got to be incredibly potent to do anything to a serpent. But my need for a distraction, a way to silence the relentless thoughts of *her*, ultimately overrides my caution.

"How much?" I growl, my voice barely audible over the din of the market.

The vendor leans in, whispering the price into my ear. I grimace, realizing the cost is steep, but ultimately, the allure of the Aeris Luminis proves too strong to resist.

Handing over the coins, I secure a vial of the mystical powder, knowing I'll probably regret this. But that's what my life seems to be, just a series of regrets.

As the transaction concludes, I clutch the vial of Aeris Luminis tightly in my tattooed hand, my heart racing with a mix of anticipation and unease. I steal one last glance at the bustling market, then decide it's time to leave. With a deep breath, I focus on the familiar landscape just outside Sanctuary and activate my sifting ability.

In an instant, the cacophony of the market fades, replaced by the soothing sounds of the jungle surrounding Sanctuary. The stark contrast between the chaotic market and the verdant serenity outside the house is jarring, but I welcome the solace. I make my way through the house and to the cave entrance, where the lingering traces of our work to make the caves inhabitable become more apparent—our efforts to create a safe haven away from the world outside.

Once inside, I find my isolated corner within the cave system, not far from the room where my friends and their mate resides. In the dim light, I carefully uncap the vial of Aeris Luminis, the powder inside shimmering with an ethereal glow.

I just don't want to feel anything anymore.

As I raise the vial to my lips, I pause for a moment, grappling with the potential consequences of my actions. But the thought of my demons haunts me, an unrelenting presence in the depths of my mind. Desperate for an escape, even if it's fleeting, I consume the Aeris Luminis and brace myself for the journey into the mystifying realm it promises.

CHAPTER TEN

ROSE

"So, he's actually living with you guys?" Lopey slurps on her straw across from me, eyes wide, as we sit together in the lively college cafeteria. The sounds of laughter and spirited conversations surround us, mixing with the clatter of trays and silverware.

"Yep, he's joined us off-campus."

"And your brother is there, too?" she asks with forced nonchalance.

I narrow my eyes at her attempt to pretend she isn't more than a little interested in him. "Yes, Bennett is there, too." I study her for a while, trying to place the peculiar expression on her face. The fluorescent lights overhead cast a glow on her delicate features, emphasizing her rosy cheeks and soft brown hair.

Before I can decipher her expression, Eli plops his tray down, sliding in next to her. "Hey, Pen," he drawls. "Hi, Rose."

He's a vampire from Dallas, part of my Aunt Maeve's line. His hazel eyes sparkle with mischief, and his Southern drawl is charmingly disarming.

"Hi, Eli." I greet him with a friendly smile. "How have you been?"

"Can't complain," he says, his accent wrapping around each word like honey. "School's keeping me busy, but that's nothing new."

Lopey chimes in, her voice still soft but more confident than before. "Yeah, it can get pretty hectic. But it's all part of the experience, right?"

Eli grins, leaning his muscled arms on the table. "Speaking of experiences, there's a party happening off-campus Friday. A bunch of us from the team are throwing it. Y'all should come."

The smell of pizza wafts from a nearby table, momentarily distracting me. I glance at Lopey, who hesitates for a moment before looking back at me, seeking my opinion. I nod, offering her encouragement. "Sounds like fun. You could use a break from all the studying, though I'm not sure I can make it. I've got class at night. I can send Bennett to the party in my stead . . . but make sure you guys aren't out too late. We've got our game on Saturday."

I don't mention that the mating bond I secured less than fourteen hours ago is riding me hard right now to find Mekhi and take him in a janitor's closet.

Lopey's eyes light up, and she turns to Eli. "Alright, I'm in."

Eli's grin widens, and he leans back in his seat, looking pleased. "Great, I'll text you the details later. Put your number in my phone." He slides it toward Lopey, whose whole chest and face are red.

As we continue to chat, the cafeteria around us a vibrant tapestry of life, I find myself feeling grateful for the connection that seems to be forming between the two of them.

But even that is a fleeting thought, because my mind is elsewhere, filled with the anticipation of meeting Mekhi again. It's been too long since we've been together—an hour, maybe—and I can feel the heat building up inside of me. I excuse myself from the table, telling Lopey and Eli that I have to go take care of something.

I make my way out of the cafeteria, needing air. Pulling out my phone, I shoot off a text to Bennett, letting him know about the party I need him to go to so he can keep an eye on my bestie for me. Then I shoot off a text to the group chat with my mates.

> My bond is feeling needy. Any takers? I've got twenty before my next class.

A rapid-fire barrage of texts buzzes on my phone, and I can't suppress the grin that spreads across my face as I read them.

> Gonna take more than twenty, pretty girl. Where are you? I'll write you a pass for your next class. – Theo

> Stuck in poisons class. Give me five and I can be there? – Jax

> On my way to the cafeteria. Where are you? I'm going to need that pass, too, Professor. :P – Deakan

> I'm in Potions 201 :(- Mekhi

I hit share on my location, in case any of the others decide they can make it. Palming my new necklace, I prop myself against a tree while I wait for Deakan to show.

Deakan soon arrives, and I can feel the heat emanating from him as he wraps his arms around me. The familiar scent of his sea salt and lemon washes over me, and I breathe it in deep as I nuzzle against his neck.

He hoists me into his arms so my legs wrap around his waist, without a care that we're in public as he presses me against the tree. Lion shifters are a bit exhibitionist, and it probably won't take long before the whole school knows who all my mates are if they didn't already know.

Well, all except Theo.

"Miss me, love?" he murmurs against my skin, his breath hot against my ear. "I missed you."

"Always."

My skin glows under the shade of the tree, as Deakan's lips find mine in a heated kiss. Our tongues tangle together, and I can feel the urgency in his touch as he grips my hips tighter. His lion is restless, and I can feel the predator inside him wanting to take over.

But we're interrupted by the sound of someone clearing their throat.

"My office, please, Miss Drake."

I turn around to find Theo standing there, his tattoos glamored and a business suit on. He wears glasses, which I've learned he does to help muffle his griffin eyesight, rather than add to it.

"Have we been naughty, Professor?" I pout as I slide down Deakan's body, landing on my feet.

The only thing betraying him is the slight dimple at the corner of his mouth where he's working to keep the grin off his face. Instead, he raises a brow, and inclines his head toward the bell tower.

Deakan slips his hand in mine, and we follow behind Theo. We pass students milling about, some with food in various stages of being eaten in their hand, and others carry book bags or ingredients for classes. A pair of unicorn shifters take flight from the courtyard, and I can't help but follow the sight.

My attention catches on the crow circling above, and I'm so busy watching it I don't hear the others trying to get my attention.

"Rose." Deakan nudges me. "Are you going to go in?" He gestures to the door.

I hadn't realized we were already at the Bell Tower. Blinking, I shake my head, and slip through the door Theo has held open for us. We climb the stairs to his empty classroom and circle the top row until we reach his large, glass-encased office. He's got the large dome above his classroom open, giving us an unobstructed view of the daytime sky. There's a hint of lilac and lavender, with sweetness that clings to the edge of the slight breeze drifting through the open window of the Bell Tower. Puffy, white clouds float lazily across the sky, and I can feel the warmth of the sun on my skin, even in the glass enclosure.

Deakan finds the plush couch and lounges on it, while I perch myself atop Theo's desk as he shuts the door.

"You here to punish me, Professor?" I tease, and he shakes his head with a grin, loosening his tie. "Or are you here to teach me a lesson?"

"You probably should do *something*; you should've heard the depraved thoughts running through her head." Deakan grins from his spot on the couch.

"You can't read my mind." I laugh, stretching out on Theo's tidy desk, bearing my neck.

All royals have the ability to read minds, eventually. Maybe I will once my wings come in. Though I'm not sure I want that ability, because it seems like it could cause more heartache than anything.

"Nah, but I can *feel* all the obscene thoughts in the bond. Just look at her skin." Deakan's hand grips the erection evident in his jeans.

"Is that what you need?" Theo stalks toward me, pausing once he's settled between my thighs. His hand grips my chin, pulling it forward to meet him.

Our breaths mingle, and before he can kiss me, I run the flat of my tongue along the side of his face, tasting his salty skin. Theo's body rumbles with a chuckle, his eyes closing briefly before opening to stare me down. His pupils are blown wide with desire, and I can feel his arousal pressing against my center.

"Rose," he growls, his grip on my chin tightening. "You're playing with fire."

I smirk up at him. "Maybe I like the heat," I whisper, and Theo's grip on my chin doesn't lessen, but his expression does soften.

Arousal surges through my veins as his lips crash to mine, and I'm lost in the sensation of his tongue wrestling with my own. His hands snake around my body, one gripping my hip and the other threading through my hair. The couch squeaks, and I realize Deakan has moved closer.

But the sound of chatter from the stairwell reaches our ears. Theo tears himself off me, stepping back and adjusting his suit while I slide off the desk and move to the couch, all my libido gone.

"Oh, good, you're here," a voice calls from the entrance to the classroom.

My breath catches in my throat as a powerful presence enters the room, thickening the air and sending shivers down my spine. It's unmistakable. Dean Corvus, the man whose mere existence commands attention. The new dean's striking features and intense golden-green eyes seem to pierce into every corner of the room, captivating everyone present.

Beside him, a sandy-haired man with piercing blue eyes enters, dressed in a suit. Dean Corvus introduces him as the lead detective from the Royal Guard, Detective O'Brien.

"Rose, Deakan." The dean tips his head at us.

I wasn't aware he knew our names. It's not a big campus, but this is the first I've ever spoken to him.

"Hi," I murmur.

"Hey." Deakan puts a possessive hand around my thigh, and it doesn't escape the dean's notice.

"I do hope to see you try out for the Arcane Scholar competition." The dean grins. "The ritual is coming up fast." His gaze is pointed directly at me.

I shift in my seat. "We'll be there."

"Dean Corvus, to what do I owe this pleasure?" Theo, also known as Professor Pyxis, extends a hand for the man to shake, drawing his attention away from me.

They exchange pleasantries, and then Dean Corvus addresses the reason for their visit. "Well, Professor Pyxis, as we discussed in our faculty meeting, we've brought in the Royal Guard to investigate Dean Fallgren's disappearance. It's time for your interview."

Detective O'Brien nods solemnly. "We'll need to interview all faculty members who had close contact with Dean Fallgren, and as you two had a few heated disagreements, we thought it best to start with you, Professor Pyxis."

Theo's face remains impassive, but I can feel the tension radiating off him. "Of course. I understand the need for a thorough investigation, and I'm more than willing to cooperate."

I can't help but steal glances at Dean Corvus as they converse, feeling a pull of attraction despite my loyalty to my mates. The undeniable force that radiates from him is both thrilling and terrifying, a testament to the power he holds.

He glances at Deakan and me. "Excuse us, please. We need to have a private conversation. I recommend you continue your studies else-where for the time being."

Deakan and I exchange a glance, and then we get up and exit the room, leaving the three men to their conversation.

Once we're out of the room, I can't help but feel anxious.

"I didn't know Theo and Dean Fallgren had any arguments. What do you think they were about?" Deakan spoke in hushed tones.

I let out a long breath as a memory hit me. "I didn't know they had either, but I'm pretty sure I know what it would have been about. He was really pissed when he'd heard about Dean Fallgren putting a magic suppressant necklace on a student—even more so when he found out it was *me*."

Deakan puts his arm around my shoulder. "Well, the dean made her bed. She wasn't exactly well-liked."

Remembering our upcoming classes that demand our attendance, we reluctantly part ways, our lips meeting in a tender, lingering kiss that promises more. As we separate, a soft agreement to reunite later escapes our lips, sealing our shared anticipation for the time when we can continue our stolen moments. The encounter with the new dean and the detective remains in my mind, making it hard to focus on my studies. As I walk to my next class, I can't help but worry about the situation. All I can do is hope that Theo's connection with Dean Fall-gren won't cause any more problems for him.

Or for us.

CHAPTER ELEVEN

DEAKAN

Stepping into the Herbology 101 classroom, the familiar damp air and earthy scent surrounds me. The lush green plants fill the greenhouse, their leaves shimmering in the stippled sunlight filtering through the glass ceiling. I take my seat next to Rose, and Kieran slides into a chair on the other side of her, his demeanor lax and a glazed look in his eye indicating that he's probably high. As much as Kieran's feelings for Rose trouble him, I can tell he's making an effort to hide it around us.

Professor Blush enters the room, a flurry of butterflies and flower petals accompanying her. "Students, students, students!" she sing-songs. "Just wait until you see what I've got for you today."

As the professor begins her lecture, I steal glances at Rose, captivated by the way her eyes light up with interest as she absorbs the new information. She catches me staring once or twice, offering me a sly grin before returning her attention to the lesson. I can't help but feel my chest swell with pride and affection, seeing her so engrossed in her studies.

On the other side of Rose, Kieran is less focused on the lesson, a mischievous smirk playing on his lips as he doodles something in his notebook. He seems to be struggling to keep his eyes on the plants and away from Rose. The tension between them is palpable, and I can sense his inner turmoil. As much as I want Kieran to be part of this, I know it won't be an easy road, and I haven't had the courage to bring it up with Rose. He needs her as much as we do, but no one seems ready to admit that, yet.

Professor Blush calls our attention to a plant with vibrant, glowing leaves. "This is the Luminous Laceleaf" She holds it in the air. "Its magical properties allow it to emit a soothing, ethereal light when the sun goes down. With proper care and the right incantations, it can even help guide lost travelers in the dark."

I glance at Rose, imagining how the soft, glowing light would reflect off her skin and enhance the glow hers gives off when she's horny. She meets my gaze, raising a brow, no doubt clued into exactly what's going through my head.

The lesson continues, with Professor Blush showing us several other magical plants and their properties. Eventually, we're paired off to practice our newly acquired knowledge. Rose and I end up together, while Kieran partners with another student.

As Rose and I work with the Luminous Laceleaf, she playfully nudges me with her elbow. "Maybe you could use one of these to guide you to where my clit is," she teases, her eyes sparkling with mischief.

I chuckle and respond with a cheeky grin. "You and I both know I have no problem finding that."

Kieran, leaning back in his chair, swivels toward me and says, "Happy to point you in the right direction."

I cock an eyebrow Rose's way, and her cheeks turn bright red.

Kieran chuckles, turning back to his assignment.

With the lights off and shutters over the greenhouse glass, the plant's leaves emit a soft, ethereal glow, bathing our workspace in a warm, soothing light. I can't help but admire the way the gentle light dances on Rose's face, highlighting her features and making her eyes sparkle.

"Alright," Professor Blush instructs the class, "I want each pair to attempt channeling their magic into the Laceleaf. The goal is to strengthen the plant's natural light and guide it to a specific direction. This will require focus and a strong connection between you and the plant."

I watch as Rose reaches out to touch the Laceleaf gently, her slender fingers hovering just above its leaves. She closes her eyes and takes a deep breath, focusing her energy on the plant. I follow suit, feeling the pulse of my magic flow from my fingertips, connecting with Rose's energy as it weaves around the Laceleaf.

Since we've bonded, our magic works beautifully together, with very little trouble coordinating efforts.

The Laceleaf's glow intensifies, becoming brighter and more vibrant under our combined efforts. Gradually, the light begins to move in a specific direction, pointing towards the far corner of the greenhouse. Rose opens her eyes, watching our progress with a mixture of awe and excitement.

The rest of the class continues working, but I can't help but glance over at Kieran. He's struggling to direct the light of his Laceleaf, the glow wavering and flickering erratically. His partner, a scorpion fae with a temper, appears increasingly frustrated with his lack of focus, but Kieran's gaze keeps drifting toward Rose and me, an odd mixture of yearning and fascination in his eyes.

I can't help but feel a pang of sympathy for Kieran, understanding the complexity of his emotions. I make a mental note to talk with him soon, to discuss our situation openly and figure out the best way to navigate our relationships with Rose.

Eventually, Professor Blush calls for the class's attention. "Well done, everyone! I'm impressed with your progress today. Remember, practice makes perfect, so I encourage you to continue working with the Luminous Laceleaf outside of class."

As the class comes to an end and students start to pack up, Rose turns to me, her eyes gleaming with accomplishment. "I'm glad I bit you. We make a great team," she says with a grin, her cheeks still flushed. "You're trapped with me forever."

"Best thing that ever happened to me." I slide my arm around her shoulders. "Wouldn't change a thing."

As we gather our things and prepare to leave the greenhouse, I notice Kieran's physical state has deteriorated. His posture is hunched, and dark shadows underline his glassy eyes, which seem unfocused and distant. His skin has taken on a pallid hue, and a thin sheen of sweat glistens on his forehead. His movements are jittery, uncoordinated, and he appears to be fighting to keep his balance.

Rose seems to notice his alarming condition as well, shooting him a deeply concerned glance before addressing him.

"Hey, Kieran, you okay?" She pauses at his table.

"I'm fine," he grumbles, clutching the potted plant in his hand. "Just not feeling well."

"I noticed you were having some trouble with the Laceleaf. Maybe we can all practice together later? I think we could learn a lot from each other." She props herself against a desk opposite him.

Kieran's gaze snaps up to meet Rose's, his eyes searching her face for any signs of mockery or insincerity. To his relief, and mine, he finds none. Instead, there's only the genuine offer of friendship and support.

"Yeah," Kieran replies after a moment's hesitation, a small but genuine smile forming on his lips. "That sounds good. Thanks, Rose."

As we continue our conversation with Kieran, I glance around the room and notice Jax standing near the exit. His eyes are narrowed, and he seems to be observing something—or someone—with great interest. Following his gaze, I see Bella standing off to the side, her silver eyes locked onto Rose.

Her shock-white hair and alabaster skin seem even more pronounced in the greenhouse, surrounded by lush greenery. The same formidable aura we'd sensed in her during our previous encounters is still present, and it's clear she's a force to be reckoned with. Yet, her gaze on Rose is peculiar, a mixture of curiosity and intensity.

As the class finishes clearing out, Bella approaches Rose with an eager smile. "Hey, Rose. That was really impressive today. I've been working on Luminous Laceleaf manipulation for ages and never quite got the hang of it like you just did." She hesitates for a moment before continuing, "Would you like to grab coffee sometime? Maybe you could give me some tips."

The sudden keen interest from Bella catches Rose off-guard, and she exchanges a quick glance with me before responding, "Uh, sure. That sounds nice, Bella. Maybe later this week?"

"Great! Just let me know when you're free," Bella says, her enthusiasm seemingly genuine, though I can't help but notice Jax's raised eyebrow and the way his protective instincts kick in. There's something about Bella's interest that seems a bit too intense.

Back at Sanctuary, we head back to the caves, where it's pitch black so we can continue to practice with the Luminous Laceleaf. As we work together, sharing tips and techniques, I can see Kieran becoming more comfortable around Rose and more confident in his abilities.

Operation: bring Kieran into the fold continues.

CHAPTER TWELVE

ROSE

The day's classes are over, and the sun has already dipped below the horizon, leaving a sky streaked with purples and pinks. My heart races with anticipation as I walk toward the designated meeting spot where Kieran and I planned to start our search for Dean Fallgren. Alongside our mission, we'll also search for the missing bracelet—she's the one most likely to have taken it.

As I approach the spot, I find Kieran leaning against a stone wall, his brow furrowed with worry. When he sees me, a small smile brightens his face, and he pushes off the wall to greet me.

"Ready to go?" he asks, his voice tight with emotion.

I nod, my heart going out to him. "As ready as I'll ever be. Let's go."

Kieran offers me his hand, and I take it, my stomach fluttering with a mix of nerves and the unspoken attraction between us. Despite our complicated history and all the reasons why we can't and shouldn't be together, it's hard to ignore the spark that passes between us with each touch.

Closing our eyes, we focus on our destination, and a sensation of weightlessness envelops us as we sift, teleporting to Luporia. When we open our eyes, we find ourselves in a charming, snowy village nestled in the mountains. The air is crisp and clean, and the soft blanket of snow that covers the ground sparkles under the moonlight.

"This is where my grandma lives during the summer, and where I used to spend my weekends as a kid," Kieran explains, his breath visible in the cold air. "Let's get you inside."

I glance around, taking in the small, cozy-looking houses that line the cobblestone streets. It's hard to imagine Kieran's past here, surrounded by family and laughter, knowing the pain he carries with him now. I want to offer comfort, but I know that my presence is a reminder of his loss.

We make our way through the village and up a winding path toward a slightly larger house nestled against the mountainside. The wooden structure looks old but well-loved, and I can't help but wonder what stories the walls hold. As we approach the door, Kieran hesitates, his hand shaking as it hovers over the doorknob.

"You okay?" I ask, my voice gentle.

He nods, swallowing hard. "Yeah, just . . . it's been a while since I've been here. Not since my parents died."

"I understand," I assure him, giving his hand a reassuring squeeze. "But we're in this together. We'll find her, and we'll find the artifact."

Kieran takes a deep breath and pushes open the door. Stepping inside, we're greeted by a dimly lit interior, filled with memories and the echoes of a happier time. It's clear that no one has been here in a while, and the air is heavy with an unsettling silence.

As we move through the house, searching for any clues that could lead us to Dean Fallgren and the artifact, our hands brush against each other, and we share furtive, longing glances. Each touch and shared look adds fuel to the fire of our attraction, and I feel torn between the powerful feelings growing between us and the weight of our past.

Our search leads us to a small study, where the walls are lined with ancient books and trinkets. Kieran's fingers graze over the spines of the books, a distant look in his eyes as memories of his family flicker behind them.

We carefully comb through the study, examining each book and artifact in the hopes of finding any clues about the missing artifact or

Kieran's grandmother. Our search is slow and methodical, as we're mindful not to overlook even the smallest detail. I can see the stress etched on Kieran's face, his desperation growing as the minutes tick by without any significant discovery. Raven hair falls into his face, and my fingers itch to brush it back, so I can see his eyes.

But I don't do that.

After an hour of fruitless searching, Kieran pulls out a dusty photo album from a hidden compartment in one of the bookshelves. With a hesitant, almost reverent touch, he opens the album to reveal pictures from his childhood. In the photographs, he's laughing and playing with his parents, the warmth and love in the images palpable even through the printed pages.

"They were so beautiful," he murmurs, his voice cracking. "My parents. They loved each other, and they loved me."

I find myself drawn to Kieran's side, captivated by the glimpse into his past. As I look at the photographs, I can see the resemblance between him and his parents—the same eyes that reflect both strength and vulnerability, the same smile that could light up a room. It's odd seeing him so small, with no tattoos, no piercings.

"We were happy, once," Kieran continues, his voice hoarse. "Before the war. Before everything changed."

Feeling the weight of the history between our families, I want to offer him solace, but I'm not sure how to do so without making things worse. Instead, I place my hand gently on his shoulder, hoping the gesture will offer him some comfort.

In some of the pictures, I recognize Mr. and Mrs. Cavë, little Jax, Deakan, and who I presume are his mouse shifter parents. I snap a picture of it with my phone, so I can show the guys later.

After a while, we reluctantly return to our search, moving from the study to explore the rest of the house. We make our way to Kieran's childhood bedroom, a small but cozy space filled with memories of a simpler time. The walls are adorned with posters of his favorite bands and sports heroes, and the bookshelves overflow with well-worn novels and comics. In the corner is a dusty drum set, and pegs on the wall where I presume he kept his guitar.

"It feels like a lifetime ago," Kieran confesses, running his hand over the old wooden bed frame. "Sometimes I can barely remember what it was like to be that carefree kid."

As we continue our exploration of the house, we find more clues to Kieran's past—drawings and letters from his grandmother, tokens from his travels with his family, and mementos from his youth. But even as we uncover these precious memories, we're no closer to finding any hints about the whereabouts of Dean Fallgren or the missing artifact.

Despite the lack of progress, our time spent together in this house is bringing us closer, the undeniable connection between us growing stronger with each passing moment. In the quiet spaces between our search, we share stories and laughter, forging a bond that transcends our tumultuous history.

However, I'm also acutely aware that each intimate exchange only adds to the complexity of our relationship. The barriers between us— our loyalties, our families, and the weight of our past—make it impossible for us to ignore the potential consequences of our deepening feelings.

As we stand in the hallway, our focus on a framed picture of his parents at the end of the hall, I know that we must soon return to our search. But for now, in the midst of the snow and the memories of his family, we steal a few more precious moments together, allowing ourselves to be vulnerable in each other's company.

We decide to move our search outside, hoping that maybe we missed something in the surrounding landscape. But before we step out into the snow-covered grounds, Kieran notices me shivering in my jungle-appropriate attire. I've only got on a pair of tennis shoes, shorts, and a long-sleeved shirt.

"Here, you should wear this," he says, disappearing into a nearby room and returning with a cozy-looking hoodie and a pair of sweat-pants. "These are from when I was a teenager, so they might fit you."

I gratefully accept the clothes, slipping them on over my own. They're soft and warm, immediately providing some relief from the chill. They smell like him: the musk of cologne, and the warmth of summer sun. It's comforting, familiar, and brings a feeling of safety like curling up in a safe place where nothing can touch you.

"I really like you in my clothes." Kieran takes a step closer, his tattooed fingers toying with the drawstring on the hoodie I've got on. "Keep these."

"Are you sure?"

"Yeah, I'm sure." He grins down at me, so much emotion behind his serpentine stare.

I pull the hood up when a gust of wind rattles the windows. "How'd a serpent fae end up here?" This village is snowy year-round.

"Well," Kieran muses as we step outside, the cold air biting at our cheeks. "My grandmother is actually an ice fae who adopted my mom after her own family was lost. So, this place has always been her home, and she wanted to share it with her adopted family."

Interesting that she'd teach at Bedlam Academy if she likes the snow, and not at Moonfire Academy, where it's cold year-round.

The once-pristine snow is now marred by our footprints, leading to and from the house. The air is crisp and cool, contrasting sharply with the sweltering heat of Academia.

"We used to build snow forts and have snowball fights out here," Kieran recalls fondly, his breath visible in the chilly air. "It was a lot of fun, just being a kid without any worries."

I can't help but smile, imagining a young Kieran laughing and playing in the snow, his cheeks flushed from the cold and exertion. The image is bittersweet, a reminder of the innocence that was taken from both of us by forces beyond our control.

We trudge through the snow, exploring the property and searching for any signs that might point us in the right direction. As we investigate a small shed, Kieran discovers an old, worn map tucked away in a corner, partially hidden behind a pile of firewood.

"Hey, look at this," he says, carefully unfolding the fragile paper. "It's a map of the village and the surrounding mountains. There are some markings on it—maybe they're places my grandmother visited or planned to visit?"

We study the map together, trying to decipher the cryptic symbols and markings. While some are familiar landmarks, others remain a mystery. We carefully note the unknown locations, deciding to investigate each one as part of our search.

As the sun begins to set, casting a warm, golden light over the snow-covered village, we realize that we've been at this for hours without any breakthroughs. We're both tired and disheartened, but the thought of giving up isn't an option.

"Let's go back inside," I suggest, squeezing Kieran's hand reassuringly. "We can regroup and plan our next move. We'll find her, Kieran. I promise." The zing of magic snaps in the air at my vow.

It's the least I owe him after what he's been through on account of my family's war. He paid an unfathomable price, and I hope that with this vow—one that'll kill me if broken—he'll understand my willingness to right the wrongs of our past mistakes. There's no question I'll find her, because family is everything to me. If she's a threat to them, and it'll help ease Kieran's heartache, I'll spend the rest of my life trying to find her.

"Don't make promises, Rose," he whispers, pain etched into his features. "Not for me."

"Why not you?" I take his hand, tugging him toward the house.

As we walk back to the house, our fingers intertwined, the cold air gets left behind and replaced with a soothing warmth, we prepare to continue our search from the safety and comfort of the cozy living room. Kieran lights a fire in the hearth, the flames licking the logs, creating a cozy ambiance.

With the flickering light from the fire illuminating the room, we spread the old map across the coffee table, poring over the symbols and landmarks we've discovered so far. It feels like a puzzle, each piece hinting at something bigger.

As we study the map, I notice a small wooden box on a shelf, slightly ajar. Curiosity piqued, I reach for it and find that it's filled with old photographs. I hold one up and look at Kieran. "You were so young in this one. You all looked so happy."

He walks over and takes a look, a smile spreading across his face. "Yeah, those were some of the best times. My parents always tried to make every moment special." He picks up a photograph of himself as a young boy holding a giant guitar on his lap, flanked by two stunning adults, his mother and father. Their love for their son is evident in their warm expressions.

As we flip through the pictures, we come across images of Kieran and his parents in happier times—at the beach, in the snow, practicing musical instruments. Despite the underlying sadness of what we know happened to them, there's also a sense of beauty in seeing these precious, frozen moments.

But the night is growing late, and our search can't be put on hold any longer. We set the photographs aside and turn our focus back to the map, identifying several locations that seem worth exploring. Despite our fatigue, we agree to check them out in the coming weeks, hoping that one of them will hold the answers we seek.

As the night wears on and our investigation reaches a natural pause, we decide it's time to head back to Sanctuary. We gather our belongings, put away the artifacts and photographs, and prepare to leave the warm, cozy home that once belonged to Kieran's family. Despite the somber nature of our task, I can't help but feel grateful for the connection it's given us, for the chance to understand Kieran better, and for the deepening bond that has formed between us.

We stand in the snow outside the house, bundled in the borrowed clothes, ready to sift back to Sanctuary. Kieran wraps his arm around me, pulling me close to him, and I can feel his heartbeat against my chest. It's a bittersweet moment—we're closer than ever, yet we're keenly aware of the obstacles between us.

Kieran looks into my eyes, his own filled with a mix of emotions: gratitude, resolve, and something deeper, an unspoken longing that etches itself into my soul. He gives me a meaningful look, the weight of the moment evident in his gaze.

Slowly and without a word, we both focus our energy and sift back to Sanctuary, arriving near the entrance of the cave system. The contrast between the snowy village and the lush warmth of Sanctuary is startling, but we adjust quickly.

Kieran gives me one last lingering look, his eyes soft and intense at the same time. "Thank you, Rose," he says quietly, his voice carrying the weight of everything that has happened, and everything we've yet to face.

I nod, unable to speak, my heart swelling with the intensity of the moment. And then, with a small, reassuring smile, Kieran turns and disappears into the cave system, leaving me standing there, filled with a mix of hope and the undeniable feeling that we're on the brink of something extraordinary.

CHAPTER THIRTEEN

ROSE

The cool island breeze weaves its way through my hair as I stand on the shores of the lush island, its vibrant foliage a dazzling sight to behold. My heart beats with anticipation, fueled by an intoxicating mix of nerves and excitement.

As I glance around, I see my friends and fellow competitors preparing for the contest that lies ahead. Kieran's jaw is set with fierce focus, his eyes scanning the island with intensity. Deakan and Jax exchange a tense look and offer each other a reassuring nod. Bennett, Lopey, Eli, Bella, and some of my Spar Games teammates are psyching themselves up for the upcoming trial.

Dean Corvus, tall and commanding, stands at the head of the group, his charismatic presence capturing our attention. "Welcome, everyone, to the Arcane Scholar competition!" he booms, his voice echoing with undeniable energy. "The first challenge you'll face is a magical obstacle course. This course is designed to test your agility, creativity, and magical prowess. You will encounter various challenges and obstacles, requiring you to utilize your magic to succeed. Only twenty participants to complete the course will advance to the next round."

My pulse quickens as I take in the enormity of the task before us.

Jax and Deakan each place a reassuring hand on me, as I told them this morning to give their all to win, not letting the fact that we're competing against each other hold them back.

A shiver of nervous energy races through me as I survey the island. Dean Corvus, with a grand sweep of his arms, reveals a path through the dense jungle, where a myriad of magical obstacles awaits. Some seem deceptively simple, like floating platforms suspended in mid-air. Others, such as enigmatic portals shimmering like liquid silver or swirling vortexes hinting at unknown danger, spark my curiosity and trepidation.

I take a deep breath and steady myself, my magic pulsing beneath my skin. "Remember," Dean Corvus calls out, his voice heavy with significance, "the key to this challenge is to think creatively and adapt your magic to the obstacles before you. Good luck, and may the best fae win!"

The magical signal is both audible and visual. A deep, resounding boom echoes through the air, shaking the very ground beneath our feet. At the same time, a brilliant burst of purple light explodes overhead, signaling the start of the race. We surge forward as one, our collective determination propelling us into the heart of the magical obstacle course. As I move through the course, I push myself to the limit, my magic answering my every call as I navigate the ever-changing landscape.

I come across the first obstacle, a series of floating platforms, each suspended at varying heights above the ground. I focus my magic on maintaining my balance as I leap from one platform to the next, my breaths coming in shallow pants. As I reach the last platform, I realize it's much farther away than it appeared.

Breathing deeply, I channel my magic into my legs and leap into the air, targeting the distant platform. As I soar through the air, I sense a change in the atmosphere; the air around me feels thicker, as if it's pushing against me. I stretch out my fingers to grasp the edge of the platform, but suddenly, I feel a cold, dark energy slithering around my ankles like ethereal tendrils, yanking me downward.

As my descent accelerates, panic surges through my veins. I glance around, trying to find the source of this dark energy. My eyes meet Bella's, her sinister grin confirming her involvement in this sabotage. I grit my teeth in frustration, refusing to let her thwart my progress. Drawing from the core of my magic, I focus on the warmth within me, on the essence of my power. I picture it as a brilliant light, driving away the darkness coiled around my legs.

I sense the dark energy retreat, and as it dissipates, I find myself mere inches away from the platform. With a surge of adrenaline and determination, I channel the last remnants of my strength into one final push, clawing my way onto the platform. Panting and exhausted, I allow myself a moment to catch my breath. I spare one last wary look at Bella before moving on, mentally preparing myself for whatever the course has in store for me next.

Having overcome Bella's sabotage attempt, I move on to the second obstacle: a series of shifting, floating platforms suspended above a murky, fog-covered abyss. The platforms move unpredictably, requiring both quick reflexes and perfect timing. As I glance at my mates, best friend, and brother, I see the fierce determination in their eyes as they, too, prepare to tackle this challenge.

Mekhi makes the first leap, his air magic propelling him through the air with ease. The platform tilts dangerously beneath his feet as he lands, but he quickly regains his balance, his arms outstretched for stability. Seeing Mekhi's success, Kieran and Jax exchange a determined glance before springing onto their respective platforms, their magical energy surging with each precise movement.

Kieran's fire magic wraps around him, providing extra propulsion as he leaps from one platform to the next. Jax, on the other hand, relies on earth magic, using it to momentarily stabilize the platforms beneath him as he jumps. Lopey and Bennett also demonstrate their unique abilities. Lopey's water magic allows her to glide gracefully between platforms, while Bennett uses earth magic to create small footholds, enabling him to traverse the unstable terrain more securely.

As we leap from one platform to the next, Mekhi calls out to us, "Remember, guys, it doesn't matter which one of us wins, just that one of us does!" We all nod in agreement, our determination to succeed for the sake of our group strengthening our resolve.

Inspired by their performance, I take a deep breath, concentrating on my magic, and I make the first jump. The platform wobbles beneath my feet, causing me to lose my footing. Panic surges through me as I begin to slip, but Mekhi's strong hand wraps around my wrist, pulling me back up onto the platform. Our eyes meet briefly, and he gives me a reassuring nod before continuing the challenge.

As we leap from one platform to the next, the fog below grows thicker, the swirling mist obscuring any hint of the ground below. It adds an eerie ambiance to the obstacle, and the tension in the air is palpable. I watch as Lopey's foot slips on one, but she manages to recover, using her water magic to guide her safely to the next. Bennett, who hasn't taken his eyes off her since the trial started, calls out to her, "You okay, Lope? Hang in there!"

Despite the constant fear of falling, we gradually make our way across the precarious platforms. Our breaths come out in short, shallow gasps, adrenaline coursing through our veins as we focus on the challenge at hand. Though we're all competing against each other, it's impossible not to feel the camaraderie that binds us together. We cheer one another on, offering assistance and encouragement when needed, proving that we're not just competitors—we're a family.

The last few jumps are particularly nerve-wracking, as the plat-forms become even more unstable and unpredictable. I can't help but notice how my mates, Lopey, and Bennett have all adapted to the treacherous terrain, showcasing not only their individual skills but also their unwavering resolve.

Finally, we all reach the end of the second obstacle, our hearts pounding and our limbs shaking from the effort. Despite the intensity of the challenge, we take a moment to catch our breath and exchange supportive glances, knowing that there are still more obstacles to come. "Great job, everyone," Jax says, his voice filled with pride.

The third obstacle catches me off guard as we find ourselves entering dense jungle so dark, it's difficult to see, as though the light bends differently here. The sunlight barely penetrates the canopy, casting everything in shadows. I push forward, watching my mates do the same, unease gnawing at the pit of my stomach.

As we continue through the trees, I notice the air is becoming heavy and stifling. I begin to feel disoriented, struggling to remember what the obstacle course is supposed to be. In my confusion, I catch a glimpse of my mates ahead, seemingly moving further away from me.

"Hey, guys. Wait for me!" I sprint through the darkness, desperate to close in on my comrades' fading voices. The forest is a looming wall of black, and I can feel something oppressively evil seeping into my veins with every step.

As I emerge from the trees, a chaotic scene unfolds before me: clashing swords, roaring cries of anguish, and thick plumes of smoke that choke out most of the light. Blood spills over an emerald landscape littered with shattered bones and leaves. There's no time to be scared—I'm in this fight now, and I must find my mates.

I didn't think I'd have to fight anyone in this competition. Frantically, I search the battlefield, the panic rising in my chest. "Deakan! Mekhi! Jax!" I shout, desperately hoping they'll answer. "Kieran?" My voice is swallowed by the chaos, and I fear they can't hear me.

My world shatters as I find Kieran, lying still and unmoving on the ground. My knees hit the ground hard. I crawl, barely able to make out his limp forms only yards from me. "No, gods, no," I beg. I can hear every haunting strum from the last thing I'd heard him play on his guitar. I can see the intense look in his eyes whenever he grants me one of those rare smiles. This can't be the end. It can't be his end. I'm not ready. I'll never be ready, I realize.

Tears stream down my face as I shake him gently, desperation coursing through my veins. "Kieran, no," I beg in a soft whimper, my hands trembling as they hover over his body.

The sight of him lying there, lifeless and broken, is like a sledgehammer to my heart. The reality that he could be gone forever overwhelms me, robbing me of breath and leaving me numb. Desperate for any sign of life, my hands shake as I reach out to touch him, blindly hoping against hope that some kind of connection could bring him back.

Tears blur my vision as I scream for help, for anyone to hear me. But no one comes to my aid; they just keep fighting. I press my hands to his bloody wounds, pouring my magic into him, my blue glow illuminating the jungle.

Still cold. So cold, as if he's been like that for hours.

I scream again, cursing Dean Corvus, begging for my mates to hear me and come help. If they knew he was hurt, they'd come. I cradle his body, picturing my parent's house so I can try to sift out with him.

Fuck the competition.

But nothing happens.

My eyes dart around wildly as I clutch his body to mine. A wail escapes my throat when my eyes land on my mates.

Mekhi's body is mangled against the tree, his blood staining its bark like a gruesome painting. His lips are cracked and pale, the top layer of skin missing, revealing a deep gash in his chest. Deakan's head lays in Jax's lap, the rest of his body several feet away, their hands clasped together even in death. My vision swims with tears as I climb to my feet and stumble toward them, my heart shattering with each step.

I drop to my knees with a thud and scramble to Mekhi's side. My hands shake as I place them on his chest, pushing more and more of my magic into him, willing his body to heal, to be alive again.

But no matter how hard I try, no matter what I do, there is still only an unsettling silence beneath my touch. His stillness haunts me, taunting me with the powerlessness of it all.

His chest doesn't rise.

My precious, beloved magic has abandoned me in my time of need. I grip the edges of desperation and scream out a prayer to the heavens before viciously tearing open my wrists, the hot river of ruby flowing freely from the gashes. Sobbing, I press my dripping wrists to the still lips of Mekhi, Deakan, then Jax, sending forth a silent plea that my lifeblood will course through them and bring them back to life.

"Please, please don't leave me," I choke out, my voice barely audible as it's wracked with sobs. "I can't do this without you. I need you." But their lifeless bodies remain unresponsive to my desperate pleas, my blood staining their faces a deep crimson. "HELP!" I scream. "BENNETT! PENELOPE!"

I cradle their heads in my lap, my tears falling like rain upon them. My grief and despair know no bounds, and I cling to them, as if my touch could anchor their souls to this world. I can't comprehend how this could be part of the competition, how Dean Corvus can allow students to die for a stupid *game*. I'll kill him. Consequences be damned. And when he resurrects, no doubt he's got plenty of feathers, I'll kill him again.

In this moment, I feel the crushing weight of my loss, a void that threatens to swallow me whole, leaving me empty and broken. Time loses meaning as I huddle there with my mates, their bodies cold and still, the pain inside me so raw and unbearable that it feels as though I might simply cease to exist.

As I cling to the lifeless bodies of my mates, my sobs echoing through the once peaceful air, a new sound catches my attention. It's faint at first, barely audible over my own anguished cries, but it grows louder—the unmistakable noise of battle, of magic being unleashed in a fierce and relentless storm.

Through my tear-blurred vision, I see movement in the distance, a figure that seems both familiar and utterly out of place. My heart lurches as I realize who it is—Theo. He's a professor.

He's not supposed to be here.

He fights with a ferocity I've never seen before, his magic a swirling vortex of power, his body a blur of motion as he takes down one opponent after another. His eyes are wild, filled with a primal rage and something else, something darker and more terrifying.

The sight of him, so fierce and deadly, sends a shiver of unease through me. I'm torn between wanting to run to him for comfort, for some semblance of safety, and the instinctual knowledge that there's something very wrong about his presence here.

The sight of Theo, surrounded by opponents in this seemingly hopeless situation, triggers something deep inside me. My chest tightens as my heart races, my breath coming in short, shallow gasps. But it's not only fear gripping me; it's a painful mixture of disbelief and confusion, fighting for control of my thoughts.

As I watch him fight, I can see the graceful, almost balletic way his body moves, each step calculated and precise, even as his face is contorted with an unfamiliar ferocity. He effortlessly dodges attacks, countering with his own powerful spells, the air crackling with magical energy around him.

And then, as he locks eyes with me, I see the raw emotion that lies beneath the surface of his fury. There's a desperation there, a sense of helplessness that doesn't belong in his normally composed demeanor. It's then, staring into his eyes, that a sliver of doubt begins to worm its way into my mind.

"This isn't real," I whisper to myself, the words feeling foreign and uncertain on my lips. "It can't be."

The moment those words leave my mouth, reality seems to waver, the scene before me shifting and dissolving. The screams and sounds of battle fade, replaced by the cries and sobs of my fellow competitors. All around me, students are struggling with their own worst fears, each person trapped in their own private nightmare. Some cower in terror, swatting at invisible beasts and critters, while others relive painful memories, their faces etched with sorrow.

One by one, my mates, friends, and brother emerge from their own personal hells, their faces pale and haunted. Mekhi, Kieran, Jax, Lopey, and Bennett all look shell-shocked, as if they've just returned from the front lines of a brutal battle. We glance at each other; our eyes reflecting the pain and fear we've just endured. No words are needed.

As we approach the finish line, we walk side by side, our once excited and eager spirits now heavy with the weight of our trials. We cross the finish line, our victory muted by the lingering echoes of our nightmares. There's no jubilation, no triumphant cheers. We've won the first challenge, but it feels hollow, as if we've paid a heavy price for this success.

The illusions were so vivid, so real, that they've left scars on our souls. We cling to each other, finding solace in our shared experience, but the darkness of what we faced lingers.

We're victorious, yes, but we carry the burden of this victory with us. Our triumph is bittersweet, tainted by the ordeal we've been through. We'll move forward, knowing that we're stronger for having faced our greatest fears, but the shadows of those nightmarish illusions will stay with us, a constant reminder of the true cost of this competition.

And this is only day one.

CHAPTER FOURTEEN

THEO

I pace the floor of our home, my anxiety growing with each passing moment. The weight of anticipation is almost suffocating, and I can't help but feel a mixture of fear and helplessness as I await the return of Rose and our friends. This competition, the trials they've been facing—I can't shake the feeling that it's something more sinister than it seems.

The door creaks open, and my heart leaps into my throat as they finally arrive. But the moment I see their faces, my relief is immediately replaced by a cold dread. They look . . . haunted, as if they've just emerged from the darkest corners of their own nightmares. Their eyes are hollow, their once vibrant expressions now etched with pain and fear.

Rose doesn't say a word, her gaze meeting mine with an intensity that steals my breath. I can see the turmoil behind her eyes, and the need for solace, for the warmth of our embrace. I close the distance between us, enfolding her in my arms as she clings to me, her body trembling with unspoken emotion.

Mekhi, Kieran, and Jax gather around us, their gazes reflecting the shared ordeal they've just endured. Each of them seems lost, adrift in a sea of torment, and it breaks my heart to see them like this. We stand together, a collective anchor in the storm, trying to support one another against the crushing weight of our shared pain.

I want to ask what happened, to understand the source of their anguish, but I can't bring myself to break the silence. The weight of their unspeakable experiences seems too heavy, too fragile to be disturbed by my probing questions. Instead, I simply provide a comforting presence, an unwavering foundation for them to lean on, as we navigate the shadows of the unknown darkness that has consumed them all.

Carefully, I release my hold on Rose and glance over at Bennett and Kieran, who are leaning against each other for support. Their exhaustion is palpable, and I can see the weight of their experiences written all over their faces. I nod to them, acknowledging the bond we share as family, as friends, and offer my help.

With slow, deliberate movements, I guide Bennett and Kieran through the house towards the caves where their bedrooms are nestled. They lean on me, and I provide a steady shoulder for them to rest on as we navigate the dimly lit halls. There's a sense of unity in our silence, the unspoken understanding that we are here for one another, no matter how dark or heavy the burden may be.

Once we reach the caves, I help Bennett and Kieran into their respective rooms, making sure they're comfortable and safe before leaving them to rest. I feel a deep sense of responsibility for their well-being, knowing that they, like Rose and our other mates, have been through something that has shaken them to their very core.

With Bennett and Kieran safely settled, I make my way back to Rose, Deakan, and Jax. They are still huddled together in the main living area, seeking comfort in their closeness. I can see the weariness in their eyes, the need for rest and the sanctuary of our shared bed.

Gently, I lead them to the bedroom that we all share, the space filled with the familiar scents and memories of our love and bond as mates. Together, we slowly undress and slip into the soft, comforting embrace of our bed, our bodies instinctively seeking the warmth and solace of each other's touch.

As we lie there, entwined and silent, the weight of the day's events seems to slowly lift. We find solace in our closeness, the connection that transcends words, the healing balm of our unconditional love. Though the shadows of their experiences still linger, I know that we will face them together, as one, and that no darkness can ever truly break the bond we share.

CHAPTER FIFTEEN

JAX

The sun's rays glint off the blades of the training weapons, creating a dazzling spectacle as I arrive for Spar Games practice. The air smells of freshly cut grass and warm earth baking in the heat, despite it being late winter. Most of the team is here already, including Rose, Lopey, Eli, and Kieran. It's been a week since our dance with our own personal hell, and it's only now that I understand why Dean Corvus has each competition day months apart. We're just now getting back into our routines after having spent days in bed, near comatose over the horrors we faced.

The one thing I keep clinging to is Rose—she's here, and she's safe. There is no mortal wound across her throat, she's not bleeding out, and I didn't actually watch her die in my arms. My mate is safe.

A warm smile crawls across my face as I witness Rose do warm up stretches. "Rose!" I call out, our bond swelling at the sight of her. As she turns toward me, she jogs over and I sweep her off her feet, spinning her around. She giggles and wraps her arms around my neck, her eyes bright with affection.

If anything, the first round of the Arcane Scholar competition has only brought each of us closer. Though Kieran has definitely been using drugs a little more heavily since that day.

"Hey," Rose murmurs, pressing a soft kiss to my lips before we reluctantly part, knowing Coach will give us a hard time if we're not bringing our best. Especially since most of us haven't been at practice all week. Almost every one of my teammates tried out.

Coach Thorn, with his athletic build and distinctive features that resemble a budget version of Tom Holland, strides purposefully toward us.

"Is this a thing now?" Coach Thorn gestures between us, scowling.

I tuck Rose under my arm. "Has been for a while, sir. Rose is my mate."

"Oh." He clears his throat, shifting on his feet as he crosses his arms and tucks his hands under his biceps. "Just don't let it interfere with the team."

"Wouldn't dream of it." Rose smirks.

Despite the camaraderie, we all understand the pressure to excel in the upcoming tournament, and the weight of expectation hangs heavy in the air. Draconor Academy is a hard team to beat.

"Alright, team." He uses magic to amplify his voice, clapping his hands together. "Let's get started. We're sparring today."

We pair off for one-on-one practice sessions, with Rose and Lopey squaring up against each other.

I face Eli, our confident vampire teammate hailing from the earth realm. He's cocky, but for good reason—he's fast, even for a vampire. Before he was turned, I guess he played high school sports they call football and track.

We exchange a brief nod of mutual respect, the unspoken agreement to give our all in this sparring match. As we circle each other, our muscles tense, ready to spring into action. Eli makes the first move, his fist flying toward my face with remarkable speed. I lean back just in time, feeling the air displace as his strike narrowly misses.

Our dance begins, our movements fluid and synchronized. Each time Eli lunges forward, I counter with a swift sidestep or block, quickly following up with a strike of my own. I can sense his calculating mind, constantly searching for an opening in my defenses, while I do the same.

As we trade blows, I notice the tiny details of our match—the way Eli's muscles tense just before he attacks, the subtle sound of our feet shuffling on the grass and dirt. Our movements create a rhythm, our bodies responding intuitively to each other's actions.

Our teammates watch from the sidelines, their eyes never leaving the sparring match. They lean in, studying our techniques and analyzing our strengths and weaknesses. Occasionally, a shout of encouragement or a helpful observation punctuates the air, driving us to push ourselves further.

Though I have the natural advantage as a fae, Eli's talent and determination make him a worthy opponent. The match ends with us standing close, sweat glistening on my forehead. Vampires barely sweat at all, and they have the advantage of staying relatively cool even with intense exercise or heat. With a shared nod, we acknowledge our progress and the lesson learned in this practice. We extend our arms, bumping fists as a symbol of the teamwork that has been forged in the training ring.

As we step away from the ring and I work to catch my breath, our attention shifts to the next pair of sparring partners. Rose and Lopey square off, both eager to show their skills.

Rose's Luna fae abilities give her an ethereal quality as she moves, an azure glow surrounding her when she's hurt or healing. Lopey, though smaller in stature, is a whirlwind of energy and determination. Their friendship only serves to enhance the intensity of their match, pushing each other to perform at their best.

I stand next to Eli, both of us watching the fight with keen interest. "They're impressive," he remarks, an undeniable note of admiration in his voice.

I nod in agreement, my gaze fixed on Rose, my heart swelling with pride. "They've both come a long way since our first practice."

Our bouts continue, each member of the team engaged in rounds of unarmed combat, testing their limits and refining their techniques.

Throughout the session, however, I can't help but notice that something's off with Kieran. He's always been a fierce fighter, but today, he seems unsteady on his feet, his movements lacking the precision and grace he typically displays. His eyes seem slightly glazed, and he seems to be blinking more frequently than usual.

Concerned, I quietly pull him aside during a break. "Kieran, are you alright?" I study him closely. "Coach will understand if you can't compete right now." We've already got three teammates still sitting out after the competition.

He flashes me a weak smile, trying to appear nonchalant. "Yeah, just a little under the weather."

I'm not convinced, but I decide to give him the benefit of the doubt for now. We'll need him at his best for the game Saturday, and I hope that when he's ready to talk, he will.

Coach Thorn observes Kieran's lackluster performance, his expression clearly dissatisfied. "Kieran, what's happening with you today? This isn't the standard we've come to expect from you."

Kieran grits his teeth, struggling for a response. "I'm sorry, Coach. I'll do better."

We switch partners, giving each of us the chance to spar against different fighting styles. With every rotation, Kieran's struggle continues, while the rest of us focus on refining our skills.

During a water break, I pull Kieran aside, concern for my best friend overcoming any hesitation. "Seriously, man, just let coach know you want to sit this one out. You're not going to get a medal for being a martyr."

Kieran sighs, his eyes downcast. "I don't know, Jax. I just . . . I can't seem to focus."

Losing his parents was the worst thing to happen to him. I imagine that's what he saw last week. Having to relive it again, after he's made so much progress to get through it? I place a reassuring hand on his shoulder. "We're here for you."

By the end of practice, Kieran still hasn't recovered his usual form, but the determination in his eyes tells me he won't give up easily. Even Rose keeps shooting him looks of concern.

As Coach Thorn blows the whistle, signaling the end of practice, we gather around him, muscles aching and bodies slick with sweat.

"Alright," he says, eyeing each of us intently. "Today wasn't perfect, but it was a step in the right direction. We need to keep pushing ourselves, refining our skills, and working together. Remember, the tournament is about more than individual prowess. It's about teamwork and strategy. If any of you need to tap out for the Draconor game, let me know now."

A couple of the third-year students raise their hands, and coach dismisses them. His eyes land on each one of us, but I keep my jaw locked, eyes forward. Gods know we all need the distraction.

Coach Thorn claps his hands, dismissing us for the day. "Get some rest and be ready to give it your all at the next practice."

As we collect our gear and make our way toward the exit, I pull Kieran aside, concern for my friend gnawing at me. "Hey, I know today was rough for you, but don't let it get to you. We all have off days. Just keep pushing forward."

Kieran offers a weak smile, his eyes glazed over and his frustration evident. "Thanks, Jax. I'll do my best."

We take quick showers, and when I emerge, I join Rose, who's chatting quietly with Lopey outside the locker rooms. Slipping my arm around her waist, I place a kiss against her temple.

"Are we all heading to the dining hall?" Lopey asks, her eyes sparkling with energy. "I could eat a horse after that practice."

We laugh, Rose giving Lopey a playful shove. "I don't think they serve horse, but let's go refuel."

"I'm just going to head home," Kieran runs a hand through his hair.

I cautiously eye Rose as she stands before Kieran, her mouth agape in visible concern. "Are you alright? We can make you something to eat or bring you something from the cafeteria," she offers, resting a hand on his forearm.

Kieran responds with a grunt and shakes his head. I can feel the anxiety radiating off of Rose as she watches him sift home.

"He's still having a really tough time, isn't he?" Lopey asks, holding the cafeteria door open. "What did you all see in your fears? There was an assembly in mine, and suddenly everyone was stampeding towards the exit. I was squashed—completely flattened in my mouse form after someone stepped on me. It was awful."

"Oh," Rose whispers gravely as her eyes fill with tears. "He seemed like he was doing better before the competition, but after everything he's endured? He's already lived his worst nightmare. He probably just relived it."

Rose

SITTING in the living room at Sanctuary, we're all trying to recover from the haunting memories of the competition, even weeks later. It's in the quiet evenings when our thoughts get loud and the memories seep in, the very ones we try to contain during the day. Our worst nightmares made real.

I find solace nestled between my mates, with Kieran and Bennett nearby, the warmth of their bodies providing some comfort amidst the shadows of fear and worry that linger in the air.

The moment shatters when my phone rings, the abrupt sound jolting us back to reality. My heart skips a beat as I see the caller ID— my mom. I hesitate for just a moment before answering, the silence in the room heavy as everyone waits for the news I'm about to receive.

"Hey, Mom," I say, my voice tense but steady. "What's going on?"

As I listen to my mom's words, I feel my expression grow increasingly grave. The atmosphere in the room shifts, filling with a familiar sense of unease. My mates, Kieran, and Bennett exchange worried glances, recognizing that something is terribly wrong.

My hand trembles as I clutch the phone. "Another threat?" I murmur, my voice barely above a whisper. "And you think it's from Dean Fallgren?"

The mention of Dean Fallgren—Kieran's missing grandmother and the person believed to be behind the threats to my family—sends a ripple of tension through the room. It's been a while since we'd heard anything from her, and we'd all been hoping that maybe, just maybe, the threats were behind us.

As I listen to my mom explain the details of the new threat—how a severed arm was delivered to their door at our family residence. A chill creeps down my spine and a growing sense of fear and resolve builds within me. Once the call ends, I take a deep, shaky breath and look around at my mates, my brother, and Kieran, my voice trembling as I speak.

"My mom said they received another threat, and it strongly points toward Dean Fallgren," I say, my eyes darting to Kieran. "We need to up our search efforts."

Kieran's face is a mask of conflict. The thought of his grandmother causing harm to my family is clearly filling him with anger, but at the same time, he probably can't help but feel a sense of relief that if she's sending threats, it means she's still alive.

"I won't let her keep terrorizing your family." Kieran's voice is strained with emotion. "I want to find her just as much as you do. I love her, and I hate what she's doing to your family. But at least we know she's alive. If we can find her, we can get her the help she needs."

The room is heavy with tension, our earlier sense of comfort and solace shattered by the reality of the ongoing threats. I look around at my mates, my brother, and Kieran, my brows furrowed. Becoming the Arcane Scholar is my only hope to secure ultimate safety for my entire family, and this new threat only serves to remind me of what'll happen if I don't.

CHAPTER SIXTEEN

ROSE

Golden sunlight streams through the tall windows of the student commons, illuminating the vast room and creating a warm and inviting atmosphere. It's the morning before our biggest game of the season, and our team has gathered around an elegantly set long table, eager to share a massive feast together. The room is filled with the enticing aroma of fluffy scrambled eggs, crispy bacon, golden-brown toast, and a variety of other breakfast dishes artfully arranged on platters and bowls.

The air is charged with excitement and camaraderie, as the teammates engage in animated conversations, punctuated by bursts of laughter and playful banter. Dust particles dance through the sunbeams, creating an almost magical aura as they catch the light.

Every member of the team is present, their faces a mixture of anticipation and determination. Even those who've chosen to sit out this game are here, eager to have some semblance of normal again as they offer their support. They dig into their plates with gusto, savoring each bite and fueling their bodies for the big game later today. Each player seems to understand the importance of this shared meal, not only for the energy it provides but also for the bonds it strengthens among them. The sense of unity is palpable, a powerful force that will undoubtedly carry us through the challenges of the game to come.

Draconor Academy is undefeated for the last six years. We're not likely to win today, but that won't change our motivation. We'll continue to play our hearts out.

Jax slides a large tray brimming with food in my direction, its contents meticulously arranged. The assortment includes a colorful array of fresh fruits, a generously stuffed omelet, golden French toast drizzled with maple syrup, and a plump cranberry muffin that promises a burst of tangy flavor with every bite. His attention to detail and thoughtfulness in selecting my favorites brings a warm smile to my face, though I'm not sure where this is all going to go. I might be able to eat a few bites of everything.

Too bad Deakan isn't on the team. He'd have no problem helping me finish my food.

Lopey sits on the other side of me, nervously picking at her breakfast. I can sense the hesitation radiating off of her and gently nudge her elbow. "Hey, what's going on? You nervous for the game?" It's been a long time since I've seen her disappear from nerves, but I want to check just in case.

Before Lopey can respond, Eli slides into the seat on her other side, a conspiratorial smile on his face. He pulls a box of cereal from a bag, her favorite kind, and places it in front of her. "Morning, Lopey. Brought this for you."

She beams at him, genuinely shocked, but touched. "Wow, Eli, thank you! I can't believe you remembered my favorite."

He winks at her, causing Lopey to flush bright pink. I eye the interaction with cautious optimism before Eli turns around to engage with the rest of the team.

Lopey leans in closer to me, her voice barely audible. "Remember the party Eli invited us to?"

I nod. "How was it?" I know Bennett had gotten in late.

Lopey bites her lip and hesitates, using a silencing bubble around just the two of us as her eyes dart toward Eli before settling on me. "Well, I . . . I made out with Eli at the party."

A grin crosses my face, but before I can say anything, she blurts out, "And your brother, too."

Her cheeks flush a delicate crimson as she braces for my reaction. I chuckle softly and whisper, despite the silencing shroud, "Are you okay with that? How do you feel about it?" Bennett is a good man, and Lopey is my favorite person in the whole world outside of my family . . . so naturally, the fact those two found themselves in each other's orbit thrills me.

She grins, her nervousness replaced with giddiness. "I don't know, it just . . . happened. I mean, they're both so hot, but I wasn't planning on getting involved with *anyone* like that, you know? What if your parents think I'm just trying to weasel my way into being the future queen?"

A giggle bursts out of me. "Jesus, Lopey. I guarantee that's not what they'd think. They love you." I place a comforting hand on her arm, offering her an understanding smile. "Don't let that be the reason not to pursue things with my brother. Just take it one step at a time and figure out what you want."

As our conversation ends and we return to the lively chatter and laughter around the table, I lean into Jax, smiling contently when he slides an arm around my waist.

"Love you." He presses a kiss to my head.

"Love you, too."

Jax

INHALING DEEPLY, I can feel the air charged with anticipation as it enters my lungs. The arena around me vibrates with a contagious, electrifying energy, the crowd restless with excitement. Despite the surrounding commotion, I remain focused on the formidable task before me. My heart pounds in my chest, a steady rhythm of determination, as I scrutinize my opponent from Draconor Academy.

The finals of the Spar Games are not only a showcase of our physical prowess, but also a testament to our cunning, strategy, and the bonds forged among teammates. This climactic event will push us to our limits, demanding every ounce of our dedication and training. With eyes locked on my rival, I mentally prepare myself for the challenge ahead, knowing that victory is not guaranteed, but earned through hard work and perseverance.

"Remember, Jax," Rose whispers, her hand on my shoulder. "Keep a clear head, and you'll outthink him."

I nod, appreciating her faith in me. If I can survive the first round of the Arcane Scholar competition without losing it completely, I can keep a cool head today. So far, we've won two out of three bouts, with Kieran triumphing—just barely, on account of him actually being sober today—in unarmed combat and Rose dominating the non-lethal magic competition. As a champion, I must participate in all three types of matches, and now it's time for the strategy round.

My opponent's face forms a sharp triangle, with a narrow forehead and broad cheeks that give way to a prominent, letter-shaped nose. His square, stubbled jaw anchors the triangle, while deep wrinkles etch around his eyes, echoing the arrow-like slant of his black, wolfish eyebrows. His thick mane of rust-colored hair shoots out in every direction like a punky crescent moon. Although his shoulders are not particularly broad, they are sturdy, much like the jaw that anchors his face. The rippling muscles beneath his arms cause his biceps to bulge like firm, taut spheres, but the patch of freckles that adorns his upper body lends him an air of refinement, rather than roughness.

He moves with a confident, almost arrogant gait, his muscular frame rippling with every step. His pace slows as he approaches, his feet hitting the dirt in a rhythmic cadence like a marching band. He looks like a member of the berserker fae, known for their brute strength, unhinged anger, and unyielding determination. He reeks of perspiration, his sweat-soaked shirt caked with dirt and mud. I can't help but feel a sense of unease in his presence, as if I'm facing something primal and dangerous.

The sun bounces off the stubble on his face, and his eyes squint as he sizes me up. "You ready to lose, Bedlam boy?" he taunts, smirking confidently.

I shake my head, undeterred. "We'll see who's laughing at the end." I grin, my voice steady.

The referee's voice bellows in the arena as he calls for the start of the bout. Instantly, a shimmering game board materializes between us and each of us is handed out cards that represent our weapons and strategies. My heart thunders as I stare at my options, acutely aware that I must think ahead and anticipate my opponent's every move if I want to claim a near impossible victory.

The berserker fae sneers as he rallies his virtual army, sending a horde of digital soldiers rampaging toward my stronghold before I can think about my first move. Panic rises within me like floodwaters, but I quickly suppress it, masking my fear with a confident facade. I manage a counterattack that is swift and calculated only moments later. I erect an impenetrable fortress around my base and launch a covert squad around his flank, with specific instructions to unearth any weaknesses in his defenses. As they disappear into the night, I hear the faintest whisper of his laughter echoing behind them.

The atmosphere around us crackles with energy, each breath of mine halting as the match intensifies. I steal glimpses of Rose and my teammates, their faces taut with anticipation as they silently urge me on.

My opponent's sneer cuts through the air like a scythe. "You really think that'll work?" he mocks. "Thought you elite school pansies would've had brains to go with all that money. Guess not."

My blood boils within me as I unleash my strategy, determined to prove him wrong.

I grit my teeth, refusing to be baited. The Draconor asshole unleashes a relentless attack and I struggle to defend my weakened forces. He presses his advantage, and I can feel the tide turning sharply against me.

As I start to feel overwhelmed, I take a deep breath and refocus, scanning the board for any possibility to regain control. My eyes narrow as I sense an opening in his formation. It's small, but it could be enough to reverse the momentum of the battle. Without missing a beat, I quickly position my soldiers, taking advantage of the opportune strike. I keep my expression neutral, knowing that any hint of my plans will give away my strategy. My veins throb with adrenaline as I stay still, careful not to give away my discovery.

The fae's smug expression starts to fade as I put my plan into action. My forces push through the gap in his defenses, and his eyes widen in surprise.

They flicker between the game board and me, disbelief and panic setting in. "No way," he mutters, realizing he's underestimated me.

"Way," I reply, deadpan, keeping my attention on the board. I exploit the weakness further, dividing his forces and taking control of key resources. The Draconor dick desperately tries to regain the upper hand, but his moves are hasty and sloppy.

He glares at me, clenching his jaw. "Lucky break, Bedlam," he snaps, trying to regain his confidence. "Guess I'll just have to steal your girl when we're through here. She's going to look so pretty as I come down her throat."

"No such thing as luck," I say, focusing on maintaining my advantage. "Just skill and strategy. And if you think I'm tough to beat, go ahead and try taking her. Though I wouldn't, if you care about keeping your precious cargo intact."

"Precious cargo?" he sneers.

"Didn't you hear? She's high princess of the fae. Their family loves collecting crown jewels."

He scoffs. "The only thing she'll be doing is worshipping them on her knees."

"Zero chance of that." I laugh.

As the game progresses, my teammates edge closer to the action, their anticipation and hope tangible. They exchange excited whispers, but I block them out, unwilling to get distracted. Every decision counts, and I'm determined to beat this asshole.

There is a tense silence in the arena as I make my final move, each of us knowing that this could determine the outcome of the match. With a deep breath, I surround the enemy's headquarters, cornering my opponent. His face reddens as he realizes the inevitable outcome.

With a triumphant grin, I play my final card, striking the decisive blow. The holographic soldiers march into his base, and for a moment, time seems to stand still. The anticipation in the air is almost palpable.

The referee raises his hand, and the arena erupts in deafening cheers. "Bedlam Academy wins!" he announces, and my heart swells with pride and exhilaration. My teammates rush over, their faces alight with victory, as they clasp my shoulders and lift me into the air. We've done it—we've beaten the impossible team, and the feeling is more than satisfying.

The team sets me down, and I make eye contact the with berserker, a smirk playing on my lips as my mate tackles me.

Rose croons, "You did it, Jaxy Baby!"

My heart swells with pride and gratitude. If Draconor's team hadn't been so disgustingly sure of themselves, I'm not certain I would've beaten them.

After climbing to my feet, I cast a glance at the Draconor man, who still stares at the game board with a mix of disbelief and bitterness. "Good game," I say, extending a hand in sportsmanship.

He hesitates for a moment, then accepts the handshake. "Yeah, good game," he mutters, nodding grudgingly.

"Now, how about I worship your cock while you pet my hair and tell me I'm pretty?" Rose whispers within earshot of my opponent, but not loud enough for anyone else to hear.

I bark a laugh, picking her up to carry her over my shoulder as I run off the field toward Coach Thorn.

As the arena buzzes with congratulations and excitement, I know that this moment will be etched in our memories forever. They said Draconor couldn't be beat.

I was happy to prove 'em wrong.

CHAPTER SEVENTEEN

THEO

I enter the classroom, and a soft murmur of conversations fills the air. I make my way to the front, setting down my leather satchel and arranging my teaching materials.

The moment my gaze falls on Rose, a jolt of electricity shoots through me. It's something I can't help but feel every time I lay eyes on her, especially now that we're soul-bonded. She's sitting in the back row, leaning against the wall with her legs crossed. A smirk plays on her lips, and I can't help but raise an eyebrow at her expression.

The classroom gradually quiets down, and I clear my throat. "Good evening," I begin, launching into tonight's lesson on the constellations and their significance in the magical world.

As I'm discussing the characteristics of a specific constellation, I notice Rose's hand shoot up. "Yes, Rose?" I ask, trying to keep my voice steady.

She looks at me with an innocent smile and asks a question, betraying none of her affection for me. She knows not to draw attention to our relationship. "Is that the constellation rumored to be responsible for the rise and fall of magical energy levels on Earth during specific celestial alignments?"

I try to maintain my composure, focusing on the academic aspect of her question rather than the fire blazing in her eyes as she stares me down. "Yes, that's correct, Rose," I answer. "During certain celestial alignments, it's believed that this particular constellation, the Astrum Nexus, has a direct influence on the fluctuation of magical energy levels on Earth. When the stars align in specific patterns, the resulting surge or depletion of magical energy can impact the potency of spells, rituals, and even the innate abilities of magical beings."

Throughout the lecture, Rose continues to ask really smart questions, each time with the same unaffected tone, though glee dances in her eyes each time I call on her.

As the class proceeds, I delve into the mythology and magic associated with the stars. The students listen attentively, some jotting down notes while others lean forward in their seats, captivated by the tales.

Kieran, knowing about Rose and me, wears an amused grin as he watches Rose's antics unfold. Though jealousy lurks beneath the surface, he's entertained by her attempts to ruffle my composure. I can tell that he wishes he could be the one receiving her flirtatious attention.

Rose pushes the boundaries a little further, biting her lower lip and running her fingers through her hair. It takes every ounce of my self-control not to react to her subtle teasing. It's too subtle to draw attention from anyone else not privy to our situation.

At one point, I turn to the blackboard to write down some key terms, and I feel a small gust of wind hit the back of my neck, almost like a kiss. Suppressing a sigh, I turn around to see Kieran smirking, a conspiratorial glance passing between him and Rose, though no one else in the room has a clue.

The remainder of the class goes by in a blur. As I wrap up the lesson, I remind the students of their upcoming assignments and dismiss them for the evening.

Students begin to pack up their belongings and file out of the classroom, the sound of their chatter and footsteps echoing in the hall. Kieran lingers, watching me with a raised eyebrow as he gathers his things.

Once the room has mostly emptied, Rose saunters over to my

desk. She leans against it, crossing her arms and raising an eyebrow. "So, Professor Pyxis," she purrs, "how will you punish me today?"

I shake my head with a wry smile. "You're asking for it."

Kieran chuckles as he makes his way to the door. "Let me know if you need any assistance," he says with a grin, the tinge of jealousy still evident in his voice.

As the door closes behind him, I allow myself to let down my guard. I lean in to whisper in Rose's ear, "Just wait until we get home. I'm sure we can find a way to make up for all that teasing." Rose's eyes widen, and a mischievous smile spreads across her face as anticipation for what's to come fills the air.

As Rose and I walk side by side through the dimly lit hallways of Sanctuary, the enchanted sconces cast a magical atmosphere over the ancient stones, and Rose admits to me that she needs my attention in more than one way. "Yes, I want your body," she grins, "but I could also use some help with my studies."

Once we're back in our shared living space, we settle down at the table, preparing for a study session. I intend to help Rose with her studies, and as we flip through her textbooks, I notice a peculiar flower tucked into one of the pages, its petals a deep purple hue and its center adorned with gold flecks.

"What's this?" I ask, curiosity piqued.

"Oh, that?" Rose responds, her eyes darting to the flower. "I found it in the courtyard today, right before Bella showed up."

I examine the flower more closely, my brow furrowing as I recognize its significance. "Rose, this is a God's Breath flower. It's extremely rare and only blooms in the presence of someone who has been marked by a god."

She looks at me in surprise, her eyes widening. "Really? But why would it bloom for me?"

I recall the silver flecks that now dance in her deep blue eyes and remember the reason why my beast has been uncontrollable. She's been chosen, marked by a god, and my griffin senses have been aware of it all along. I never mentioned this to her before, but now seems like the right time.

Kieran, who has been quietly observing our conversation, smirks from the corner of the room. "So, our little Rose has divine attention, huh? No wonder you can't keep your hands off her, Professor."

"She's my soul-bond." I shoot him a warning glare, but he just laughs, clearly entertained by the situation.

Rose looks between Kieran and me, a mixture of confusion and concern on her face. "So, what does this all mean? What do I do now?"

I place a reassuring hand on her shoulder, trying to comfort her. "We'll figure it out together, Rose. For now, let's focus on your studies and keeping you safe."

Jax saunters into the room, his expression narrowing on the books in front of us. "Can't you just give her an A so we can spend less time studying and more time making her scream?"

Rose tosses a pencil eraser at him, earning her a laugh. "I am not a screamer."

"Wanna bet?" I recline in my seat, loosening my tie.

Her throat bobs as she swallows. "Is it time for my punishment yet?"

"Don't sound so eager." I chuckle.

"What are we punishing her for?" Deakan turns his attention away from his video game to see what the commotion is about.

She pushes back from her chair, pure mischief written on her face. "I was naughty," she sing-songs. "Gave him fuck-me eyes the entire class."

Deakan tosses the controller onto the couch. "Let's take this into the bedroom before Bennett gets home and has a coronary."

Rose spins on her heel and takes off like she's on fire, giggles peeling from her throat as she rounds the corner, nearly sends Kieran flying into the wall, before disappearing down the hallway. The guys follow suit, leaving me alone with Kieran. He's leaning against the counter, a smirk playing at the corners of his lips.

"You're not going after her?" he asks, raising an eyebrow.

"Of course I am," I reply, crossing my arms over my chest. "The anticipation of her consequences will only make it better for her."

After a few minutes, I rise from my seat, my tie in my hand as I work to make handcuffs from it as I stalk down the hallway toward our bedroom.

Deakan

A WEEK after the Spar Game, we gather in the living room of Sanctuary, the air thick with tension and anticipation as we prepare for the important ritual that awaits us. It's not just about us as competitors but as a family bonded by love and friendship.

Theo stands before us, his dark hair styled, and his gilded eyes unobstructed by the glasses he usually wears while on campus. In his hands, he cradles a set of his radiant golden feathers. The room is dimly lit, yet the feathers cast an ethereal glow, bathing the space in an otherworldly light.

Kieran, who has been mostly detached from the events, starts to step away from the group to head down the hall toward the caves. Theo notices his retreat and calls out to him, "Kieran, wait. I've got one for you, too."

Surprise flickers across Kieran's face, and he hesitates before rejoining us. Theo's kindness and inclusion have always been essential to our bond with Rose, and Kieran is no exception to this. He might not be a mate, or a boyfriend or Rose's, but he's family all the same.

Bennett stands off to the side, his strong arms crossed over his chest. He watches the proceedings with a mix of curiosity and concern, protective of his sister even though he knows this is something people do all the time.

As we take our positions for the ritual, I sit on the floor with my back against the sofa, feeling the comforting support of the cushions behind me. Rose sits beside me, her chocolate-brown waves cascading over her shoulders, and her large doe eyes filled with a mixture of trepidation and resolve. She takes my hand, and I feel a surge of courage from her touch.

Theo kneels down in front of me, holding one of his glowing

feathers. "This is going to hurt, but I'll be right here, healing you as it happens. Trust me, the protection it offers is worth the pain."

Nodding, I mentally prepare for what's to come. "I'm ready."

Theo starts to chant in an ancient fae language, pressing the feather against my ribcage. At first, my skin tingles, and then the pain arrives, intense and searing. My jaw clenches as I try to hold back gasps of pain, but a few escape, despite my efforts.

Rose's grip on my hand tightens, her voice soothing as she whispers words of encouragement. I focus on her, trying to distract myself from the sensation of the feather burrowing into my skin.

The pain reaches a crescendo, and I can't help but let out a strangled cry, my fingers digging into Rose's hand. Theo's golden eyes meet mine, his face etched with concern as he continues the chant, the feather sinking deeper into my flesh.

Finally, Theo's voice softens, signaling the end of the ritual. The pain begins to ebb away, replaced by a soothing warmth that radiates from the feather now embedded in my ribcage. My breathing slows, and I lean back against the sofa, a sense of relief washing over me.

Rose releases my hand, her eyes shining with pride and relief as she wraps her arms around me, pulling me into a tight embrace. I bury my face in her soft hair, inhaling her familiar scent, and it anchors me to the present, away from the residual pain.

Theo moves on to perform the ritual on Rose's other mates and brother, his hands steady and his gaze focused as he works his magic. The room fills with a symphony of gasps and cries, each of us experiencing the same pain and, ultimately, the same protection.

I take a deep breath as Theo moves on to perform the ritual on Rose. Despite having witnessed the process multiple times now, I can't help but feel a pang of worry for her. But Rose, ever the pillar of strength, doesn't let her apprehension show.

Propped against the back of the couch in just a sports bra and sweatpants, she beams at him, nodding to Theo to begin. Theo repeats the process, placing a golden feather on Rose's ribcage and starting the chant in an ancient fae language.

The room grows quiet, all of us watching with bated breath as

Rose braces herself for the pain to come. As Theo's chant grows more intense, I can see her body tense, her knuckles white as she grips the couch cushion beneath her.

Her eyes squeeze shut, and a pained whimper escapes her lips. We surround her, each wearing expressions of concern and empathy, understanding the pain she's going through.

Theo's voice rises in a crescendo as the ritual nears its end. Rose's breathing grows ragged, her face a picture of agony. Finally, the chant concludes, and the feather disappears beneath her skin, becoming one with her body.

With a soft, reassuring touch, Theo sends a wave of healing magic into Rose's body. The pain recedes, and her breathing gradually returns to normal. She lets out a shaky sigh, her eyes fluttering open to meet Theo's gaze.

We share relieved smiles, knowing that each of us now carries a lifeline, a protection against the unknown dangers that the competition might bring. Even with the weight of our previous experiences hanging heavy in the air, we find solace in the knowledge that we're better prepared as a family to face the challenges ahead.

Rose

THE EVENING LIGHT filters through the windows of Sanctuary, splashing warm hues across the room. My mates, brother, and I gather, having just finished our meal. The atmosphere is heavy with anticipation and anxiety, as tomorrow marks the beginning of the second phase of the Arcane Scholar competition. The memory of the first phase and the horrors we faced during it lingers in our minds, causing a sense of unease to permeate the air.

Deakan toys with his fork, his gaze distant, while Mekhi quietly clears the table, the tension evident in his movements. Kieran leans back in his chair, drumming his fingers against the armrest, and Jax sits hunched over, elbows on the table, his fingers massaging his temples. Bennett attempts a small smile in my direction, but it doesn't quite reach his eyes.

I clear my throat, hoping to alleviate the tension. "We should talk about our strategy for tomorrow. We need to be prepared for anything, considering what we faced last time."

My mates and brother nod in agreement, and we begin discussing various possibilities for the upcoming challenges, trying to anticipate what the competition organizers might throw at us. Our conversation is punctuated by the occasional sigh or furrowed brow, but beneath it all, there's a determination to face whatever comes our way.

Together, we're better.

"We should practice some of our defensive spells and shielding techniques tonight, just in case," Mekhi suggests, his voice steady but lined with concern.

Jax nods, adding, "We should also go over some potential offensive strategies, in case we need to take the initiative. It might help to have a few surprise moves up our sleeves."

As Theo steps forward with an encouraging grin, he claps a hand on Jax's shoulder. "Hey, I may not be competing, but I've got your backs. Let me teach you a trick or two that could help give you an edge in the competition."

Everyone's faces light up with relief, and we all gather in the spacious living area of Sanctuary, making room for us to practice our spells and maneuvers. Theo stands in the middle of the group, the ease and familiarity between us evident in the casual way he carries himself. He's come a long way from being the soul-bonded mate who didn't quite understand what I have with the others.

He gets it now.

"Alright, let's start with some defensive spells," he suggests, demonstrating the proper hand movements and incantations for casting various protective charms. We follow along, teasing each other and sharing laughs as we try to mimic his actions and practice the spells until we get the hang of them.

As the evening wears on, Theo transitions to offensive strategies, encouraging us to think outside the box when it comes to casting spells and manipulating our magic. Time flies by as we learn and grow more confident in our abilities, and the camaraderie within the group deepens.

During a quick break, Theo gives each of us a playful nudge or a supportive squeeze on the shoulder. "Remember, guys, teamwork is crucial in this competition. Lean on each other, trust your instincts, and don't hesitate to ask for help from each other when you need it."

His words only strengthen the bond between us. My mates, brother, and I exchange nods of understanding, prepared to face the trials ahead as a united front. With Theo's guidance, we feel readier than ever.

The next morning, we rise early and gather in the kitchen for a hearty breakfast. The air is charged with a mix of excitement and nervous energy, but the comforting presence of my family help steady my nerves.

As we eat, we discuss various strategies and tactics, bouncing ideas off each other and sharing words of encouragement. Theo takes the lead in the conversation, his years of experience and wisdom invaluable to our preparations.

After finishing our breakfast, we begin to gather our gear and belongings for the upcoming competition. Each of us dons the appropriate attire and checks our magical items, ensuring everything is in proper working order. We don't know what we're walking into today, but if there's a chance we'll be allowed to bring in assistive devices, we're doing it.

Before we leave, Theo gathers us in a tight circle and addresses the group. "Remember, you've trained for this. You've grown stronger and more skilled with each passing day. Trust in yourselves and in each other. I have no doubt that you're more than capable of overcoming whatever challenges await you in the second phase of the competition. If you all pass today, I'll treat you to one of the meals from that cookbook," he points to the red book on the counter. We'd found it after a day trip to Sundahlia a few weeks ago. "Earth food." He grins.

His words resonate within us, bolstering our spirits and injecting us with a sense of confidence. Theo presses a linger kiss to my lips as he cups the back of my neck.

"Be safe. I love you," he whispers against my ear.

"I love you, too."

With a final glance at Theo, who offers us a proud and supportive smile, we take a deep breath and step out of Sanctuary, ready to embark on the second stage of our journey as Arcane Scholar competitors.

CHAPTER EIGHTEEN

ROSE

*D*ean Corvus stands before us, his sun-kissed skin and wind-tousled dark hair giving him a regal air. Despite his intimidating presence, I can't help but feel drawn to him, his immense power almost overwhelming. He explains the second challenge in a smooth voice, his words leaving me feeling breathless. "Now that you've proven your ability to navigate your deepest fears, it's time to test your problem-solving skills," he says, his eyes locking onto mine. "You'll each find a locked chest on this island with your name on it. The chest contains a powerful and dangerous magical artifact, but the lock can only be opened with the correct combination of magical spells. You must decipher the clues scattered around the island to unlock your chest."

The heat rises in my cheeks as I realize I've been staring at him, and I quickly avert my gaze. Despite the intensity of the challenge, I can't help but feel a sense of exhilaration, knowing that if I win, I'll have the chance to work alongside someone as powerful as Dean Corvus.

I lean into Jax and Deakan, whispering, "When y'all lose, I'll let you play with mine."

Jax chuckles and winks at me. "So, what you're saying is, we'll win either way?"

I blow them both a kiss as the competitors scatter, each embarking on their quest to find the hidden clues. The little island is filled with lush vegetation, towering palm trees, and hidden alcoves, providing numerous spots where the clues might be concealed.

The first hint of danger presents itself in the form of an enchanted, serpentine vine that I nearly stumble upon. The vine, seemingly alive, slithers across the forest floor, guided by an unseen force. Its barbed thorns glisten with venom, and I realize that even the slightest scratch could result in a painful, possibly fatal wound. I cast a spell of protection around myself, watching as the vine lunges, its thorns bouncing harmlessly off my magical barrier.

The vine retreats to the base of a colossal tree, and as it does, I notice a rune inscribed on the trunk, hidden beneath the twisting tendrils. Gathering my courage, I maintain the protection spell while studying the rune. It takes several minutes to fully comprehend the pattern, and I only manage to memorize it as the vine grows more agitated, my spell starting to weaken under the constant assault.

Breaking free from the thorny adversary, I venture deeper into the island, my senses on high alert. My path leads me to a treacherous cliff overlooking the ocean, the waves crashing violently against jagged rocks below. It's here that I spot the next clue, carved into the stone face of the cliff, accessible only by traversing a narrow ledge.

I take a deep breath and step onto the ledge, my heart pounding in my chest. A gust of wind threatens to throw me off balance, and I cling to the rock face for dear life. As I inch my way along the ledge, I notice the details of the rune become more visible with each step. The danger intensifies, however, as winged creatures with razor-sharp talons begin to circle overhead, screeching and diving at me. I dodge their attacks while attempting to keep my footing on the precarious ledge.

Barely managing to evade the creatures' relentless assault, I make a mental note of the rune's design and carefully retrace my steps back to safety. My legs tremble from the effort and fear, but I know I have more challenges to face.

I continue my search, following a hidden path shrouded in darkness beneath a canopy of ancient trees. The air is thick with a palpable sense of malevolence. It's within this eerie atmosphere that I come across a rune encased in an orb of dark energy, suspended above a pit filled with wickedly sharp spikes.

Reaching the rune requires a combination of agility and precise spell casting. I use my magic to conjure stepping stones across the pit, balancing precariously on each one

As I navigate the deadly obstacle, with every step, the dark energy surrounding the rune pulses, attempting to disrupt my focus and send me plummeting to a grisly fate below.

Halfway across the pit, I spot Bennett struggling with his own challenge nearby. A swarm of enchanted insects surrounds him, their stingers dripping with lethal poison. I call out to him, offering help.

"Try the parsenny spell Theo taught us!" I shout.

He glances in my direction, sweat beading on his brow, but determination shining in his eyes. "Thanks!"

I don't have time to stick around to make sure he gets out of there because I have no doubt he will, so I grit my teeth and maintain my concentration. At last, I reach the dark orb and dispel the sinister energy with a burst of light magic. The rune inside is revealed, and I take a moment to memorize it before carefully making my way back to solid ground.

Breathing a sigh of relief, I venture on to find the next clue. The dense foliage of the island gradually gives way to a clearing where a pool of water shimmers beneath the light of a single sunbeam. The water, clear as glass, reveals another rune lying at the bottom. As I lean in for a closer look, a hand grips my shoulder, startling me.

I turn to see Lopey, wearing a wide grin. "Found something interesting, Rose?"

"Yeah, but this isn't going to be as simple as it looks," I reply, eyeing the tranquil pool with suspicion. "I think that asshole gets off on watching us hurt."

Together, we approach the water's edge, prepared for the unexpected. As I reach in to retrieve the rune, the water suddenly springs to life, forming tendrils that whip and lash at us. We both dodge and weave, narrowly avoiding the watery onslaught.

But it isn't just water. Drops land on my skin, burning immediately. "It's acid!" I shriek.

"Rose, I'll distract them! Get the rune!" Lopey yells as she begins to cast a series of defensive spells, drawing the attention of the water tendrils.

I nod and quickly cast a spell to part the water, creating an opening to reach the submerged rune without having to touch the water. I stretch out my hand, straining to grasp the rune as the water fights against my spell, attempting to reclaim its territory. With one final effort, I snatch the rune from the pool's depths and rise to my feet, triumphant.

Lopey and I share a breathless laugh, acknowledging our shared victory. "Thanks for the help," I say, flashing her a grateful smile.

"Always." She beams.

Emboldened by our success, we head further into the island, ready to get this over with.

As Lopey and I venture deeper into the island, we hear a shout of frustration from behind a thicket of twisted vines. We exchange a glance and cautiously approach the source of the noise, finding Eli engaged in a heated battle with a swirling vortex of wind. I'm surprised he's made it this far, on account of the fact he's a vampire, and they don't have magic.

"Eli, do you need any help?" I ask, concern lacing my voice.

He grunts, straining against the relentless gusts. "Yeah, I can't seem to get close enough to the eye of this windstorm, and I'm pretty sure the last rune I need is in there."

Lopey shifts on her feet, anxious. "Alright, I'll stay here and help Eli. You should keep going, Rose. We'll catch up with you."

"Are you sure?" I ask, hesitating for a moment.

"Yes, go on. Find the last rune. We'll handle this," Lopey assures me with a confident smile.

I nod, reluctantly leaving them to face the challenge together. As I make my way through the dense underbrush, I can't shake the nagging worry for my mates, wherever they are. I push forward, knowing that I need to focus on my own task.

The search for the final rune takes me to a seemingly impassable chasm. On the other side, I spot the last rune, its glow a beacon of hope amidst the shadows. To reach it, I'll have to use my magic to construct a bridge across the abyss.

With a deep breath, I weave an intricate spell, summoning a series of ethereal stepping stones that hover just above the gaping void. Carefully, I step onto the first stone, testing its stability. It holds firm, allowing me to progress from one to the next, each step a heart-stopping leap of faith.

As I reach the other side, my heart thunders in my chest. The last rune rests on a stone pedestal, its surface etched with a complex pattern. I commit the symbol to memory before retracing my steps across the chasm, my legs shaking from the adrenaline coursing through my veins.

With all the runes now in my possession, I head back toward the starting point, my chest still locked and waiting for me to release its secrets.

Rose

I FIND my mates back near the starting point, all their runes committed to memory. When I open my mouth to speak, nothing comes out. The guys shake their heads, having already figured out that their ability to speak to each other has been taken. We mime to each other, trying to convey safety and love without words as we part to find our own individual chests.

We split up once more, each heading in a different direction, guided by an instinctual sense of where our chests might be hidden. The sun is beginning to dip lower in the sky, splashing long shadows across the jungle floor and lending a sense of urgency to our search.

As I venture deeper into the jungle, I notice subtle changes in the environment. The air feels heavier, and the foliage around me becomes darker and more twisted. I can't help but feel a sense of foreboding, as though the island itself is testing my resolve.

Suddenly, I come across a clearing filled with eerily luminescent mushrooms, casting an otherworldly glow upon the ground. My heart leaps in my chest as I spot my chest, half-hidden beneath the gnarled roots of a massive tree at the edge of the clearing.

The sight of the chest sends a thrill of anticipation through me, but I also sense the presence of unseen danger. I pause at the edge of the clearing, studying the area for any hidden threats or traps. A flock of vividly colored birds takes flight above me, their cries adding to the unsettling atmosphere.

My eyes catch a subtle glint of light in the shadows beneath the tree, a shimmering thread that seems to be part of a magical barrier surrounding my chest. The island has thrown one more challenge in my path—a protective spell that must be unraveled before I can claim my prize.

Gathering my wits, I begin to analyze the barrier, looking for any weakness or pattern that might hint at the key to breaking the spell. The magic is intricate, a web of interwoven strands that pulse with power. I carefully reach out with my own magic, probing the barrier, testing the strength of the enchantment.

As I delve deeper into the spell, I become aware of a faint rhythm hidden within the chaos of the magical threads—a pulsing beat that seems to guide the flow of power. Focusing my efforts on this rhythm, I begin to weave my own magic in sync with the barrier's pulse, slowly unraveling the enchantment.

The process is delicate and time-consuming, but I can feel my progress as the barrier begins to weaken. Sweat beads on my forehead as I concentrate, my muscles tense from the effort of maintaining the delicate balance between my magic and the spell.

With a final surge of effort, I release a powerful counter spell, targeting the very heart of the barrier. The magical threads shudder and snap, dissolving into wisps of light before disappearing entirely. The path to my chest is now clear, and I can't help but feel a swell of triumph at the accomplishment.

I'd take stuff like this over what we endured our first challenge any day.

Exhausted but resolute, I approach my chest, my fingers brushing over the engraved runes on its surface. As the sun sinks lower in the sky and the shadows lengthen around me, I stand before my chest, preparing to unlock its secrets with the runes I have so painstakingly collected. The moment of truth is at hand, and the air is charged with anticipation.

Slowly, I trace each rune in the air, casting the spells in the precise order suggested by the clues I found during my search. With each incantation, a faint glow surrounds the chest, the magical energy resonating with the spells I cast.

The final rune is uttered, and I hold my breath, waiting for the lock to click open. For a moment, there's only silence, and then, with a soft sigh, the chest springs open. I peer inside, curious, and apprehensive about what I might find.

My breath catches in my throat as I recognize the object nestled within the velvet-lined interior. The artifact that had been stolen, the bracelet I thought had been taken by Dean Fallgren, now rests within my chest. It glimmers, its intricate design and gemstones evoking a sense of both dread and euphoria.

A myriad of questions flood my mind. How did it end up here? Could it be that Dean Corvus took it? Or is Dean Fallgren stalking me, waiting for the perfect moment to strike? Paranoia sets in as I glance around the jungle, my heart pounding in my chest.

With trembling hands, I reach into the chest and retrieve the bracelet, feeling its weight in my palm. The implications of its presence here are both confusing and terrifying. I quickly slip the piece into my pocket, hoping to keep it hidden from prying eyes.

As I continue to search the shadows of the jungle, my mind races with possibilities and fears. The discovery of the bracelet has thrown everything into question, and I can't shake the feeling that I'm being watched. My instincts scream at me to stay alert, to be ready for whatever threat may be lurking just beyond my line of sight.

Yet, despite the danger and uncertainty, every muscle in my body sags with relief to have this in my possession. It's no longer lost, which means no one else can use it against my family.

Gripping the stolen bracelet tightly in my pocket, I retrace my steps through the jungle, searching for any sign of Dean Corvus or Dean Fallgren. As I make my way back to the gathering point, the moons illuminate the sky, spilling a veil of shadows across the island. I can't help but feel that time is running out, and the race for the truth has just begun.

CHAPTER NINETEEN

ROSE

aking my way back to the gathering point, I spot my mates, Lopey, and the other competitors slowly emerging from the jungle, each carrying their own chest with a mixture of triumph and exhaustion. I say goodbye to my friends, and my mates, Kieran, and my brother gather our belongings and prepare to shift back to Sanctuary, eager to leave the dangers of the island behind us.

Once we've arrived, I waste no time in seeking out a quiet corner where I can call my mom. The bracelet's presence weighs heavily on my mind, and I know she'll want to hear about this shocking discovery.

"Mom, you won't believe what I found during the Arcane Scholar competition," I blurt out as soon as she answers the call.

"What'd you find?" Her voice is filled with concern, clearly sensing the urgency in my tone.

"It's the bracelet that was stolen . . . the one we thought Dean Fallgren took," I say, my voice shaking slightly.

"What?" There's a beat of silence. "How can that be? Do you think Dean Corvus was the one who took it?" she asks, her voice tense with worry.

"I don't know, Mom. But someone put it in my chest, and I need you or one of dads to come and pick it up. I don't want to risk keeping it with me any longer than necessary," I explain, my grip on the bracelet tightening.

"Of course, I'll be there as soon as I can," she replies before whispering to one of them.

I end the call and gather everyone in the common area, eager to discuss the implications of the bracelet's presence in my chest. As we settle into our seats, I can feel the tension in the room, the air thick with apprehension and curiosity.

"What do you think it means?" Jax asks, his brow furrowed in concern.

"I don't know, but it's clear that someone is trying to send us a message." My fingers nervously play with the bracelet hidden in my pocket.

"Maybe Dean Corvus is trying to set Dean Fallgren up," Deakan suggests, his eyes dark with worry.

"Or maybe it's the other way around, and Dean Fallgren is trying to pin the theft on Dean Corvus," Mekhi adds, his expression thoughtful.

"What did you guys get in your chests?" I tuck into Theo's side as he slips an arm around my shoulder.

"Lopey got a box of cereal." Bennett chuckles before his cheeks flush. "I got a lock of Lopey's hair."

"I got a diamond ring," Mekhi whispers, glancing my way.

"Really?" I cock my head at him. "Do you think you got it because you're great with jewelry and weapons and stuff?"

He shrugs, looking sheepish.

"Mine was this picture frame with a couple I've never seen before in it." Deakan leans over to rummage through his backpack. He pulls out a silver frame, passing it around.

When it reaches me, my heart stills and a gasp escapes me. "Deakan," I breathe. His eyes rise to meet mine, and I jump to my feet, heart thundering as close the distance between us and hold the frame up beside his face. The man and woman both have long, flowing locks of blond hair. The woman has deep-set dimples and amber eyes, while the man is tanned with a spattering of freckles across the bridge of his nose and curls. "They look just like you."

"What?" he takes it from me, studying it as his breathing stills. "Do you think . . . do you think this could be my parents?"

Tears fill his eyes as he looks up at me, and my chin wobbles as I nod my head. "They look identical to you."

"The chest contains what your heart desires," Theo whispers.

I spin around, looking to Jax. "What'd you get?"

He takes a small object from his pocket, holding it up. "Just this little gemstone."

He passes it to me. It emits an ethereal, golden glow and pulsates with an energy that feels incredibly familiar, like it's something my soul yearns for. It's the size of a large marble, and while beautiful, I can't even begin to understand what it signifies.

"Am I that shallow that I'd crave more gemstones above all else?" His eyes are downcast, shoulders hunched.

Kieran frowns. "I got sand."

"Sand?" I face him. "Why would you get *sand*?"

Maybe because he's a serpent? I have no idea.

We discuss the possibilities well into the night, our voices low and hushed as we weigh the evidence and speculate on the motives behind the bracelet's reappearance. As each theory is presented and dissected, one thing becomes abundantly clear: we're being drawn into a dangerous game, and we must tread carefully if we hope to uncover the truth and protect ourselves from those who would use the stolen bracelet as a weapon against us.

CHAPTER TWENTY

DEAKAN

It's been a month since our last Arcane Scholar competition. Class is outside today. I step into the North Woods with Rose, breathing in the scent of damp earth and the fresh dew on the leaves. This place calls to the wildness within me, the lion shifter that's always lurking just beneath my skin. The cool, crisp air kisses my face as I glance over at Rose, her blue eyes shining with curiosity.

The rustling of leaves beneath our feet is the only sound to interrupt the serenity of the forest. Rose moves closer to me, her arm brushing against mine. The heat of her touch sparks a fire within me, but I manage to rein it in. She's so naturally beautiful, with her long, wavy brown hair cascading down her back and her high cheekbones flushed with anticipation for the class.

As we walk side by side, I flash her a cheeky grin. "I bet I'll master my element faster than you."

Rose raises an eyebrow, her eyes twinkling with mischief. "Oh, really? Care to make a wager on that, Deakan?"

I chuckle, the challenge sparking my competitive spirit. "Alright, if I win, you'll have to give me a back massage later."

She smirks and nods, clearly accepting the challenge. "And if I win, you'll do my laundry for a week."

That only involves digging a hole for the ground gnomes to do their job, and I toss in a few coins. Easy.

"Deal," I agree, shaking her hand with a grin.

We make our way to a small clearing where Professor Rowan awaits us. He's a tall, broad-shouldered fae with the typical grace and elegance of his kind. A subtle smirk plays on his lips as he observes our arrival. I'm pretty sure he credits himself with Rose and I taking the mating bond. It was during his class last semester that Rose and I found ourselves naked in class thanks to a spell gone wrong, and it wasn't longer after before everyone knew we were mated.

The rest of the class begins to gather around, their voices a murmur of excited chatter.

"Gather round," Professor Rowan announces, his voice commanding the attention of the entire group. "How about we have a little fun today?"

He begins with a demonstration, summoning fire, water, earth, and air with practiced ease. I can't help but watch Rose as she takes in the spectacle, her eyes wide with wonder. I know that she's far more powerful than any of the fae at the school, the granddaughter of the Luna Goddess herself. But despite her innate power, she's here to learn to control and refine it.

The professor then guides us through several exercises, encouraging us to find our affinity for a specific element. I reach out with my senses, feeling the tug of the earth beneath me and the powerful winds that whisper through the trees. As a lion shifter, I find myself drawn to the fire that lies dormant in the core of the earth, the same fire that fuels my beast.

As we begin to experiment with the elements, I lean over to Rose and whisper teasingly, "Don't forget about our bet, love."

She flashes me a wicked grin, her eyes sparkling with amusement. "Oh, don't you worry. I've got this in the bag."

And so, the friendly competition between us begins, our bond only growing stronger as we explore the depths of our magical abilities.

As the class progresses, I try to summon a small flame in my palm, the fire flickering briefly before sputtering out. I can't help but feel a hint of frustration, my lion side urging me to master this element. I look over at Rose, who's manipulating water with incredible grace and precision. The droplets dance and twirl through the air around her, as if they're responding to her every command.

"You're making it look easy," I say with a teasing smile, though I can't help but feel a twinge of admiration.

She glances at me, her blue eyes shimmering with a playful glint. "Well, you know what they say, practice makes perfect."

I chuckle, my dimples making a rare appearance. "You've got that right."

The sun, perched high above the trees, bathes Rose's skin in a warm, tropical glow. The light plays across her freckles and caresses the tops of her cheeks and forehead. She leans into it with an impish grin on her face, as if she is welcoming someone in.

Rose looks ethereal, like a goddess of the forest. Her perfume drifts to me as I move closer, my amber eyes locked on hers. I can't help but be wildly obsessed with her, my entire being devoted to her happiness and well-being.

"So," I say, raking my fingers through my shaggy blond hair, "how about a little wager within a wager? If I can get this flame to last for more than a few seconds, you have to give me a kiss right here in front of everyone."

The beast in me wants there to be no question as to whom his fire burns for.

Rose laughs, her eyes twinkling with mischief. "You're on, surfer boy. But if you can't, you owe me a foot massage."

With a nod and a confident smirk, I focus on the task at hand. Taking a deep breath, I extend my arm, trying to summon the fire within me once more. The mystical energy of the fae realm, the source of all elemental power here, calls to my lion side, urging me to tame the flames.

The fire flickers to life again, this time stronger and more vibrant. I hold my breath, willing it to stay alight. The seconds tick by, and the flame continues to dance in my palm, radiating a soft glow that bathes my face in warm light.

I glance over at Rose, who looks genuinely impressed. "Well, I believe a certain someone owes me a kiss."

She shakes her head with an amused smile, stepping closer. "A deal's a deal, Deakan."

Our classmates steal curious glances as Rose leans in, pressing a soft, sweet kiss to my lips. The heat of our connection courses through me, reminding me once more just how lucky I am to have her as my mate. As we break apart, I catch the envious stares of our classmates and can't help but feel a surge of pride.

This beautiful creature is mine.

With our friendly competition continuing, we dive deeper into our studies of the elements, the bond between us growing stronger by the minute. Our banter and flirtation only add to the excitement of mastering our magic, making the class one of the most enjoyable and memorable experiences at the academy.

As we continue to practice our elemental magic in the heart of the jungle, the sounds of exotic birds and rustling leaves fill the air. I can't help but feel that the vibrant energy of our surroundings is influencing our progress, our elemental control growing stronger with each passing moment.

After another successful combination of elements, I flash a smile at Rose. "You're getting really good at this, you know. Maybe after class, we could switch gears and I could teach you something else?"

Her blue eyes light up with curiosity. "Oh? What do you have in mind?"

I can't help but grin as the thought of our last surfing adventure comes to mind. Well, before it all went to hell after I dropped her off, anyway. "How about a surfing lesson? We had so much fun last time, and there's still so much I can teach you."

Rose's face breaks into a wide smile, her excitement palpable. "I'd love that."

The anticipation of spending more time together outside of class, sharing in the thrill of surfing, fills me with a sense of happiness that I can't quite put into words. As we continue to work on our elemental magic, my thoughts drift to the waves we'll ride together, the salt spray on our skin, and the feeling of freedom as we conquer the ocean side by side.

The class draws to a close, and we pack up our things. Rose looks giddy with excitement. Her cheeks are flushed, making her look even more stunning than usual.

After we agree on meeting at the beach, Rose heads to the student center to rent a drysuit, while I gather our surfboards and other necessary gear. As I make my way to the shoreline, a familiar rush of excitement courses through me at the thought of spending the day on the water with Rose. It was on this very beach that we had our first "date," and I taught her to surf, and not long after, we became mates. The memory of that day still brings a smile to my lips—the way she looked at me with admiration and trust, the sound of her laughter as we caught our first wave together, the feel of her body pressed close to mine as we rode the surf. Today, I'm eager to relive that experience with her, to recapture that sense of closeness and adventure that brought us together in the first place.

I set up our surfboards on the sand, and the sun casts a gentle light on the surroundings. The cool ocean breeze rustles through my loose blond hair as I take in the beautiful view. The beach, while colder in the winter months, is still a stunning sight, and I can't wait to share this moment with Rose.

She soon approaches, wearing her rented drysuit and a bright smile on her face. Without a beast inside, she doesn't run as warm as I do. She looks stunning and ready to take on the waves. "Well, well, well," she says, a playful gleam in her eye as she approaches. "Looks like the big bad kitty cat is eager to get me wet again." She holds out her arms to show off her attire. "What do you think? I bet I'll be showing you up in no time."

"Fucking hot, but it'd be better off."

She laughs and shakes her head. "Later, babe."

I grin, giving her a wink. "I won't forget that."

Her cheeks flush at my words, but she doesn't shy away. Instead, she steps closer, her eyes full of determination. "Good. Because I'm ready to learn everything you have to teach me."

Our eyes lock, and the air between us crackles with anticipation. Reluctantly, I tear my gaze away and focus on what I want to teach her. "Alright, let's go over the basics again. We'll practice our stance and balance on the sand before hitting the waves."

As we work through the basics, our bodies brush against each other more than necessary, our teasing banter escalating. The flirtatious atmosphere only adds to the thrill of the lesson, and I can't help but hope that this will be the first of many surfing sessions we share together.

After practicing our stance and balancing on the sand for a while, Rose's confidence seems to grow. Her excitement is contagious, and I can't help but feel even more eager to get into the water.

"Alright, Rose, I think you're ready to hit the waves." I park my board in the sand.

She grins and nods, her eyes sparkling. "Let's do this!"

We grab our surfboards and make our way to the water's edge, the cool waves lapping at our feet. Rose takes a deep breath, her chest rising and falling beneath her drysuit. The ocean may be chilly, but I can tell that she's determined to master yet another thing. It's what I love about her—the pride she takes in a job well done, and she won't stop until she's perfected things.

As we wade into the water, I stay close to Rose, offering her guidance and support. We paddle out together, the icy waves crashing around us. Her eyes stay focused on the horizon, waiting for the perfect wave to ride.

When we reach a good spot, I give her a few last-minute tips. "Remember, it's all about timing and balance. When you see the right wave coming, paddle as hard as you can, and then pop up onto your feet. I'll be right here if you need help."

She nods, swallowing hard. "Got it."

As we wait for the right wave, our fingers occasionally brush against each other, sending a jolt of electricity through me each time. I can't help but be impressed by her determination and her willingness to take on new challenges.

Finally, a promising wave starts to form in the distance, and I can see Rose's eyes light up. "Here it comes," I say, squeezing her hand briefly. "You've got this."

Her shoulders square up, her gaze fixed on the approaching wave. As it nears, she starts to paddle, her arms cutting through the water with impressive speed. I watch her, my heart pounding in my chest as she prepares to stand.

With grace and power, she pops up onto her feet, her body finding its balance as the wave carries her forward. My excitement bubbles up inside me, and I can't hold back a whoop as I watch her ride the wave. Her hair streams behind her like a banner, and for a moment, she looks like a goddess of the sea.

As the wave dies down, she jumps off her board and into the water, laughing and splashing. "I did it! I actually did it!"

I paddle over to her, a huge grin on my face. "You did amazing, Rose. I knew you could do it."

As we tread water, our bodies close together, our eyes meet, and the chemistry between us ignites. It's a perfect moment.

CHAPTER TWENTY-ONE

ROSE

For weeks, Deakan and I have spent as much time as possible in the water. The other guys have joined us a few times, though Theo doesn't, because we have to maintain appearances. I can't wait for summer, where we can spend all our free time together. But first, I have to pass my classes.

As I sit in the Sanctuary courtyard, buried in my books, I try to focus on my studies. The sounds of the guys working out around me blend into the background, and for a moment, I'm lost in the pages. That's when I catch a faint, yet distinct, odor that makes my nose wrinkle. The smell of drugs. But not one I've smelled before.

Concerned, I stand up and follow the scent through the house. Pausing at the door to the entrance to the caves, I lean my hand on it, steadying my breathing before pushing it open. The air grows cooler and damper as I venture farther in toward Kieran's room.

He's sprawled out on the ground next to his bed, staring blankly at the ceiling, a thin haze of smoke curling around him. It's clear that he's high, and my heart sinks at the sight of him in such a vulnerable state.

I crouch down beside him, not quite sure what to say. "Kieran," I begin, but my voice trails off.

He looks at me with unfocused eyes, a faint smile playing on his lips. "Hey, Rose. Have you come to love me?" His words end on a chuckle before he continues. "Come lay with me, look at the stars." He gestures to the stalactites on the ceiling. "I made them for you."

Fighting back tears, I try again. "I'm really worried about you. This," I gesture to the drug paraphernalia and the haze surrounding us, "it's not healthy, and it's not helping you."

He's quiet for so long, eyes closed, his smile fading. When he opens his mouth to speak, his words are hoarse, broken. "I don't know how else to make it stop."

I lay down next to him, allowing him to pull me into his embrace on the cold cave floor. Resting my head on his chest, my tears spill onto his shirt. "I want to help you, Kieran. I really do. But I can't do it alone. Please, come home with me. I'll ask my parents for help with the spell they used to find my mom during the war. It might help us find your gran, and you can at least know where she is. It might take some time, but we'll figure it out together."

"You want to take me home to meet your parents?" he whispers.

"You've met them before." I shake my head.

"Oh yeah." He sighs. "Just me and you?"

"I've got to ask the guys if it's okay, otherwise, yeah."

As we sit together in the dark, damp cave, I can't help but feel both relief and trepidation. We have a long journey ahead of us, but I know that together, we can find a way to heal him, whether or not we find his grandma.

I know I need to talk to my mates about my plan to take Kieran to my parents' house. Their support means everything to me, and I can't make this decision without them. I find them still in the courtyard, taking a break from their workout, sweat glistening on their toned bodies.

"Hey, guys," I say, trying to sound casual even though my heart is pounding in my chest. "I have something I need to discuss with you."

Their faces show concern, and they immediately gather around me. I take a deep breath and start to explain the situation with Kieran, how I found him in the caves, and my desire to take him home to seek my parents' help with the spell.

I tell them that it might take a couple of days, especially since it's the weekend and there's no game scheduled. They exchange glances, clearly uneasy about the idea, but they know how much it means to me.

Finally, Deakan speaks up. "I don't like the idea of you going alone, but if you think it's best for Kieran, then we trust you."

Jax nods, adding, "We're always here for you, Rose, and if you need us, we'll be there in a heartbeat."

I feel my heart swell with gratitude, and I give them a small, appreciative smile. "Thank you, guys. I know it's not easy, but I really think Kieran needs some time away from everything. And maybe, just maybe, we can help him find some peace."

My mates offer to go with me, but I gently decline. "I appreciate the offer, but I think Kieran might need some time away from everyone. Just for a little while. I promise I'll keep you updated."

They reluctantly agree, and as I walk away, I feel the weight of their concern and love on my shoulders. I know I'm making the right choice, even if it's a difficult one. For Kieran, and for us all.

With a deep breath, I take Kieran's hand, and together we sift back to my family's home. It's late evening when we arrive, and the house is quiet. A quick glance at the time tells me that my parents have already retired to bed. Instead of leading Kieran to the guest room, I decide it's best if we stick together, so I take him to my room.

My room is a familiar haven, filled with soft colors and mementos from my childhood on Earth. Kieran looks around, taking it all in, his shoulders beginning to relax. As we sit down on the edge of my bed, Kieran hesitates for a moment, looking at me with a mischievous glint in his eyes. "So," he drawls, "you brought me to your bedroom. Trying to seduce me, Rose?" His lips curve into a playful grin.

I can't help but laugh, shaking my head in amusement. "You better be on your best behavior." I raise an eyebrow, feigning seriousness.

He chuckles, and I can see the tension in his shoulders begin to ease. Our banter flows naturally, the room filling with our laughter. I can see Kieran's walls crumbling, bit by bit, as we reminisce about our shared experiences.

"You remember that time," I start, my voice filled with amusement, "when you thought you could beat me in one-on-one combat?"

Kieran's eyes light up, and he grins widely. "Only because you literally recharge if you're hurt. I don't have that luxury."

Our laughter echoes throughout the room, lifting the weight of our troubles, if only for a moment. Time blurs as we share stories, thoughts, and fears. Gradually, Kieran begins to open up.

"I know I shouldn't be using." He props himself again my headboard, head tilted to the ceiling. His Adam's apple bobs as he swallows, and his eyes shutter as though admitting it out loud has robbed the wind from his sails. "I don't know how else to make the pain stop."

I take his hand in mine, twining our fingers as I pull his hand to my lap, wanting him to know he's not alone. That I'm here for him. "The drugs may make you numb to the pain, but they also make you deaf to the music that could have played."

He hums, offering me one of his rare smiles. We find solace in our shared experiences, and our conversation shifts to happier memories we've made together.

As the night deepens, we lie down on the bed, facing each other. Our voices grow softer as sleep creeps in, and we continue painting vivid pictures of our past adventures and dreams for the future with our words.

Gradually, our conversation trails off, and our eyes flutter closed. The covers remain undisturbed as we drift off to sleep on top of them.

CHAPTER TWENTY-TWO

KIERAN

I wake up gradually, the first rays of morning light filtering through the curtains and casting a warm, golden glow across the room. The scent of jasmine fills my senses, and I smile as I realize it's coming from the woman nestled against my chest. Her soft, brown hair is splayed across the pillow, a few strands tickling my nose as I breathe in her calming presence.

My heart swells with love and admiration for Rose, the most incredible woman I've ever known. In the quiet moments like these, I can't help but wonder if she feels the same for me. The way she cares for me, the lingering touches, and stolen glances, I can't shake the feeling that there might be something more between us.

But loyalty binds her, and her heart is torn between her love for her mates and the deep connection we share. I know it's not easy for her, and I'm struggling to find my place among them, all the while knowing they are my best friends.

As Rose shifts in her sleep, her arm draping across my chest, I'm mesmerized by her peaceful expression. Her long eyelashes cast delicate shadows on her cheeks, and her lips are slightly parted, tempting me to lean in for a tender kiss, to feel her soft mouth against mine.

But I hold back, not wanting to cross any lines or cause her more turmoil. Instead, I simply watch her sleep, committing every detail of her beautiful face to memory. This memory, of being in her bed, waking up together as though we'd spent all night making love. The curve of her cheekbone, the slight freckles dusting her nose, the way her hair frames her face like a halo.

My fingers itch to trace the outline of her features, to feel the softness of her skin, but I resist, content to simply admire her from a close distance. As much as I want her to be mine, I can't have her, and it's slowly killing me.

My thoughts are interrupted as Rose stirs beside me, her eyes fluttering open with a sleepy sigh. For a moment, she looks disoriented, but then her gaze falls on me, and her eyes widen in surprise. It's clear that she hadn't expected us to migrate so close during the night, our limbs entwined, her leg hitched over mine as she uses me like a body pillow.

She catches her breath, startled, but I notice that she makes no move to pull away from me. Instead, she seems to revel in our closeness, her eyes searching mine with an intensity that leaves me feeling exposed, vulnerable, and yet inexplicably alive.

"Morning," I manage to murmur, my voice hoarse from sleep and the emotions that tighten in my chest.

"Morning," she whispers back, her voice equally soft and hesitant, as if she's afraid to break the fragile spell that binds us in this moment.

We lay there for a while, neither of us making any effort to separate or to address the emotions simmering beneath the surface. I can't quite read her expression—a mixture of surprise, warmth, and perhaps a hint of fear. But there's something else there, too, something that makes my heart race with hope.

That if I'd have loved her first, things could've been different. If I hadn't hated her and everything she represents, she could've been mine, rather than my having to listen to the sound of her making love to her mates each night.

That maybe, in time, I could be one, too.

It's there, in the faint blue glow of her skin she hasn't apologized for or made excuses for.

The sound of a knock on the bedroom door shatters our quiet moment, like a stone breaking the surface of a serene lake. Rose's eyes flick towards the door, then back to me, as if silently asking for permission to answer it. Reluctantly, I give her a small nod, understanding that we can't keep the world at bay forever.

With a soft sigh, Rose carefully extracts herself from our entwined limbs, stealing away the warmth her body offered. I can't help but feel a sudden chill in her absence, as she pads over to the door. Opening it just a crack, she peeks out, her posture tense and guarded.

"Rose," I hear her mother, High Queen Lana, say from the other side of the door. "I hope I didn't wake you."

Rose hesitates for a moment, her eyes darting back to me, then shakes her head. "No, not at all, Mom. What's up?"

"Pierce managed to track down most of the ingredients from the last time your dads did the locator spell," Lana explains, her voice carrying a hint of excitement. "We've put together a list of what else you'll need, which you can probably find on Academia."

Rose nods, reaching out to accept the list from her mom's hand. She casts a glance back at me, her eyes filled with resolve and a sense of urgency, as if she knows that the faster we can find these ingredients, the faster we can help me get some closure.

"Thank you, Mom," Rose says, her voice filled with gratitude. "We'll start gathering these as soon as possible."

"Take your time," Lana replies gently. "Remember, this spell is time-consuming and complex. It's important that you all work together. And, of course, if you need any help or guidance, your dads and I are here for you."

The sincerity and warmth in Lana's voice is palpable, and I can't help but feel grateful for her support, even if I still harbor some heartache over how their family caused me to lose mine.

As Rose thanks her mom again, she carefully closes the door, keeping her from seeing inside the room. She turns back to me, the list clutched in her hand, her eyes alight with purpose. The quiet moment we shared has been replaced by a renewed sense of focus, and as she rejoins me on the bed. We'll soon be heading back to Sanctuary to find everything else we need.

Jax

WHILE WE MIGHT'VE all come across victorious in our second competition, thus winning Theo's earth meal he promised, I can't really let my competitive side go. Kieran and Deakan have the same drive to compete, so the four of us gather in the kitchen, ready to see who's got the best cooking skills by making Rose the meal. It also serves as a way to spend time together before we embark on the third stage of the competition. We've decided on tacos and chocolate chip cookies, two dishes we know everyone will love, but especially Rose.

We send Rose, Bennett, and Mekhi to seek a couple of ingredients for the locator spell in the courtyard of Sanctuary while we get to work, gearing up for some friendly competition.

Okay, maybe not so friendly. Theo keeps bragging about his mad cooking skills, and Rose can't stop talking about how good his food is. So, I'm pumped to beat him at his own game and show that I can throw down in the kitchen too.

Deakan grabs the cookbook we found in Sundahlia and flips through the pages, his fingers skimming the worn paper until he locates the taco recipe. "Divide and conquer," he says, glancing at each of us with a smirk. "I'll handle the taco meat." He points to Jax, "You take care of chopping the veggies." Then, turning to Kieran, he adds, "Get the toppings ready." Finally, he looks at Theo, "And you, my friend, are on cookie duty."

He really thrives in this family unit, taking on role of the provider and leader. It's as if he's finally found the family pride he's been searching for his whole life, and he cherishes every moment of it.

As he sets to work on the taco meat, his muscles ripple beneath his shirt, his lion nature making him a natural hunter and protector. But he's not just fulfilling his own needs—he's also looking out for his family, making sure they're well-fed and happy. And as we work together in the kitchen, joking and laughing and enjoying each other's company, it seems he knows that he's finally found the place where he truly belongs.

As we gather our ingredients, the kitchen quickly turns into a battleground. Deakan stands proudly over the sizzling beef, throwing in various spices with confident flicks of his wrist, the smell of cumin and garlic filling the air. Although, on closer inspection, he has about half the meat left than what he started with, and he hums with his mouth full of ground meat.

Kieran sets to work on the toppings, dicing tomatoes, shredding lettuce, and grating cheese with a speed that speaks to his viper-quick fae order.

"You're doing it all wrong," Kieran scoffs, looking over Deakan's shoulder. "That's way too much cumin for the amount of meat you've got. It's going to overpower everything." He'd know—serpents can taste it on the air

Deakan rolls his eyes. "Oh, please. I think I know what I'm doing. It's called flavor, Kieran. Look it up."

Meanwhile, Theo is immersed in the art of cookie making, carefully measuring ingredients and lecturing us on the proper technique for creaming butter and sugar.

I chop onions, bell peppers, and tomatoes, trying not to tear up from the pungent aroma of the onions.

"Why are you crying?" Kieran raises a brow at me.

I'm holding the knife, gesturing to the cutting board. "Why the fuck do you think? These assholes."

Theo cackles before leaning over to inspect the bowl of toppings I'm working on.

"Jax, those tomatoes aren't diced evenly at all," he scolds me. "How do you expect the flavors to meld properly if you don't take the time to do it right?"

I growl and toss a rogue tomato chunk at him. "Relax, professor. It's just dinner, we're not being graded, old man." Though when he turns back around, I go back and cut a new tomato with more precision. I can't have the flavors off if I want Rose to like it.

As we work, we continue to bicker and argue over the best methods for each task. Kieran and Deakan engage in a heated debate about the appropriate cheese-to-lettuce ratio for the perfect taco, while Theo insists that his precise method for measuring flour will make all the difference in the cookies' texture.

The chaos reaches its peak when Deakan accidentally knocks a jar of chili powder into the pan of taco meat, creating a small mushroom cloud of spicy red dust. We all cough and fan the air, trying to save our burning nostrils while laughing at the mishap.

"See? That's what happens when you don't pay attention to detail!" Theo gestures wildly, coughing between laughs.

Kieran shakes his head, a smile playing on his lips. "We're really fucking this up, aren't we?"

As if on cue, the smoke alarm begins to wail, and we scramble to open the windows and waft the smoke outside.

Rose pokes her head through one of the open windows, a look of concern etched on her face. "Everything okay in here?"

Deakan grins sheepishly, his eyes watering from the chili powder. "Just a minor setback. Nothing we can't handle. Go enjoy the sunset, we'll have dinner ready soon."

Rose laughs and shakes her head before retreating to the courtyard, leaving us to continue our chaotic cooking adventure. Determined to salvage the meal and prove ourselves to one another, we press on, the kitchen alive with laughter, competition, and plenty of culinary mishaps.

In the midst of the mayhem, Theo somehow manages to burn a batch of cookies, setting off the smoke alarm again. We can't help but laugh at the absurdity of our situation, the smell of charred cookies mixing with the spicy aroma of sizzling taco meat.

"I knew I should've kept an eye on the oven," Theo grumbles, tossing the burned cookies into the trash and starting on a new batch.

"Maybe we should just use magic," Kieran grumbles, placing a scoop of guacamole into a bowl. "At least that's something we can get right. Mostly."

As we near the end of our culinary journey, we start to assemble the tacos, each trying to outdo the others with our presentation skills. Deakan carefully layers the meat, vegetables, and toppings on each tortilla, while Kieran meticulously arranges the plates, ensuring each taco looks like a work of art with a squeeze bottle of hot sauce and sour cream.

I laugh as I watch my friends bicker over whose plate looks best. "Guys, it's just dinner. We don't need to impress anyone."

I'm lying, because I need to impress Rose. But maybe if I can convince the guys they don't, I'll outshine them.

Deakan and Kieran exchange a look before simultaneously saying, "Speak for yourself."

Finally, with our efforts combined, we present a table laden with chaotically plated tacos, an array of toppings, and a fresh batch of golden-brown chocolate chip cookies. Despite the disasters and arguments along the way, we're all proud of our work and excited to share the meal with everyone else.

We call Rose, Bennett, and Mekhi in from the courtyard, and their expressions of cautious optimism make all the chaos worth it. They dive into the tacos, and a choked squeal escapes Rose.

"Oh my gods." She fans her mouth. "How much chili powder did you put in this?" She scoots back from her seat and rushes to the fridge, guzzling milk straight from the container.

Mekhi hums, his mouth full of food. "You guys managed to pull this off without burning the place down, at least."

"Hey now," Kieran says, feigning offense. "We're more talented than you give us credit for."

Despite the bickering, the mishaps, and the smoke alarms, we've created a meal that brings joy to our house—and that, in the end, is what really matters.

CHAPTER TWENTY-THREE

ROSE

I lay in bed, relishing the last moments of sleep as the dawn light filters through the curtains. The soft rustle of leaves and distant birdsong outside my window make it difficult to open my eyes. But soon, the ache of my worn-out muscles nudges me awake. Yesterday was a long day, and I stayed up late, poring over my textbooks before the guys thoroughly wore me out. I'd hoped to catch up on some sleep this morning, but now I'm too anxious to lie still.

I throw off the covers and stand up, stretching out my stiff muscles. As I step onto the cold floor, I realize that my mates have already left for their morning workout, and I'm alone in the house. Sundays are days I like to sleep in late, but it's almost ten by the time I roll out of bed on account of my exhaustion from the competition. The quiet is both unnerving and calming. I wrap a towel around myself and grab my shower supplies, heading toward the bathroom.

As I approach, I notice the door is slightly ajar, and a faint sound of running water reaches my ears. A sweet, fresh scent of soap and shampoo permeates the air, mixed in with the warm, damp smell of steam billowing from the ajar bathroom door.

Guess at least one of them is back already. I lean against the wall, waiting, my heart rate picking up in anticipation.

A minute passes, then another, and the door still hasn't opened. I start to feel impatient and curious. Pushing the door open just a crack, I peek inside, trying to figure out what's taking so long. The unmistakable sound of flesh smacking against flesh as one of them pleasures themselves fills the air, driving me wild with anticipation.

A wicked grin spreads across my face as I slowly set my towel aside, the fabric barely making a sound as it brushes against the floor. I don't want to alert anyone to my presence—I need to be quiet and sneaky if I want to pull this off.

The steam envelops me as soon as I step into the bathroom, blinding me with its opaque shroud. I reach out blindly to grab onto the handle of the shower door and pull it open without a sound, the vapors filling my lungs like smoke. Without warning, a guttural moan fills the air, reverberating off the walls, and that's when I realize what lies beyond the frosted glass. But it's too late—I'm already standing inside, paralyzed with fear at what lurks in the fog.

A strangled squeak escapes me when I notice the span of tattoos adorning his arms and neck. This causes him to spin around so fast I can't make my escape before he's got me pinned to the tiled wall, his pierced erection pressed between us and shooting hot jets of his release across my stomach.

He clamps his arm like an iron vice around my neck, cutting off any supply of air. His eyes narrow to narrow serpentine slits and his sharp fangs glint in the light as he stares me down. My throat is burning, and I can feel my breath coming in short gasps. His knee wedges between my thighs, searing my heated skin.

"Are you trying to kill me?" he hisses, his face inches from mine. His eyes track me, more beast than man right now.

Not daring to move, I shake my head the tiniest fraction, answering his harsh question with a raspy "no."

He's got to be high from the way his pupils dilate, and the faint sweet scent on his breath isn't one I recognize as his.

"Then what the fuck are you doing in here?" He growls, and I struggle wildly against his grasp, fingernails tearing into his arm to try and free myself. "It's bad enough I have to hear you come every night, but now you've got to tempt me in here, too? Either fuck me or don't, Rose, but you can't keep toying with me. You know how I feel about you, but in case you've hit your head. Here's four words: I fucking love you."

Even if I were able to breathe, in this second, I don't think I could. His words spin around my head and my heart at full pelt. When I'm finally allowed a sliver of air, I gasp out a raspy reply, "Thought you were one of my mates." I'm coughing and sputtering as I stumble out of the shower.

"How the fuck did you think I was one of yours?" He opens the shower door, standing there with his gaze locked with mine. I'm acutely aware we're both stark naked, only a few feet separating us.

Instead of covering himself, Kieran deliberately steps out of the shower without a towel, his muscular body on full display, water droplets cascading down his chest and thighs. He injects an air of casualness into his voice, but I can still hear the quiver in it. "It's a big deal to have a serpent fae as your mate. Will the poison kill you, or will it embrace you, allowing you to know the exquisite rush of its high as I part your thighs and fuck you until you forget everyone else's claim but mine?"

The smirk playing at the corners of his lips tells me he's enjoying making me squirm, and I can't help but feel embarrassed by my obvious fuckup. "Enjoying the view?" he teases, running a hand through his damp hair, his eyes never leaving mine. "I'm right here, Rose." He spreads his hands wide. "Ready to burn the fucking world for you. What'll it be? Huh? Don't care for my particular brand of poison?"

I grit my teeth, trying to regain some control over the situation. "You're high," I snap back, forcing my eyes away from him and onto the tiled floor as I scramble to find a towel to wipe his spunk off of me.

He chuckles, his laughter low and warm, like honey and fae wine, but the teasing doesn't stop. "You're welcome to join me if you'd like," he says, gesturing toward the still-running shower. "I can help you wash that off." He gestures to my stomach, where his come now drips between my thighs.

My face grows hotter, and I'm torn between anger and a sense of vulnerability. "You're hurting," I manage to retort, doing my best to keep the ache out of my voice. "You're not in your right mind."

His expression falters, a flash of hurt flickering in his aquamarine eyes. But as quickly as it appeared, it vanishes, replaced by a steely resolve. "That's fair," he admits quietly, his voice barely audible over the sound of the shower. "Because in my dreams, I get to fuck that big mouth of yours, and you finally manage to shut the fuck up and let me have some fucking peace."

He stalks toward me with such purpose, I remain frozen as he leans over me, bracketing me against the wall.

My breath comes in quick, shallow bursts as I combust inside. Small puffs of air stir the hair at my neck as his warmth envelopes me. He's so close, I can hear his heartbeat racing wildly in his chest. Fear of the past and the uncertainty of the future keep me rooted to the spot.

But he's not trying to kiss me or hurt me. It's when he leans back do I realize he's grabbed a towel from a hook on the wall next to my head. He tenderly wipes away his mess off my stomach, but my instincts take over and I snatch the towel when he moves towards the cradle between my thighs.

I take a deep breath, forcing my voice to stay steady. "Finish your shower, Kieran. Sorry about ruining your nut."

Without waiting for his response, I flee the bathroom, the door clicking shut behind me. I don't stop until I'm in my bedroom.

As I lean against the wall, I gasp for breath, overwhelmed by the chaotic swirl of emotions surging inside me. This is yet another layer of complexity added to our already tangled relationship.

CHAPTER TWENTY-FOUR

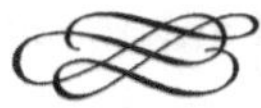

ROSE

nxiety gnaws at my core, a relentless and oppressive force that slowly erodes away my sanity. I feverishly scrub my skin until it's raw, desperate to remove the scent of Kieran from me.

My four mates may be newly consummated, but at least three of their primal beasts are still eager predators, constantly on the lookout for any potential challengers to the status quo. I can almost hear their roars reverberating in my head as thoughts of them coming home rushes through me.

When they walk through the bedroom door, I'm huddled beneath the window, shaking with anxiety, tears brimming in my eyes, ready to succumb to the wave of nausea rising in my throat. The urgency in which they move toward me only serves to heighten my fear.

"Holy shit, Rose," Theo hoists my trembling, still naked form into his arms. "Are you okay? What the fuck happened?"

The guys crowd around me, all speaking at the same time as the calming scent of their sweat-drenched skin reaches my nose.

Tears pour down my cheeks in sheets as I suck in heaving breaths, trying to speak, but losing the words before they can pass my lips.

"Baby," Deakan croons, his hands gently brushing the tangled locks from my face. "Who do we need to kill? Was it Dean Fallgren who hurt you?"

Mekhi takes my hand and brings it to his lips, murmuring words of comfort into my trembling fingers.

Jax pulls Theo over to the bed, forcing him to sit, bringing me into his lap.

"We've got you," he whispers, his hands coming up to caress my back. "We're here, we won't let anyone hurt you ever again."

Theo presses my head against his chest, rocking me back and forth like a child. "I'm sorry for leaving you," he whispers, his voice choking with emotion. "Someone needs to check the security cameras, see who hurt—"

I shake my head, tears coming faster now. "I cheated," I wail.

My mates go preternaturally still, and only the sound of Theo's racing heart against my ear can be heard.

"What?" Theo asks for clarification after a moment.

"Who?" Jax growls, and there's an edge to it I've never heard directed toward me before, which only makes me cry harder.

I meet their eyes, an agony greater than I've ever seen flashing across their faces. The bond in my chest squeezes in grief.

My voice comes out ragged as I explain in detail what happened. "Kieran thought I was trying to kill him, but I was just trying to surprise one of you jacking off in the shower."

"So then what, you fucked him?" Jax asks cautiously. He glances at Deakan.

"What?" I sit back. "No. I jumped out of the shower, he helped me clean his jizz off my stomach and then I fled the bathroom."

"And that's when you slept with him?" Mekhi whispers.

"What?" I rear back. "No. I didn't sleep with Kieran."

The four of them stare at me, confusion etched into their features, shoulders relaxing marginally.

"But you jacked him off?" Deakan asks, brows pinched.

"I didn't touch him, I whisper. "And I didn't sleep with him."

"Then why did you say you cheated?" Theo's voice is low, his eyes searching mine for understanding.

"Because I showered with another man, and he came all over me?" I explain, nearly on the edge of hysteria.

"You showered together? He bathed you? You bathed him? You're talking in pieces, baby." Theo's palm cups my cheek as I try my best to explain the situation to him. When I do, he sighs. "Rose, it was an honest mistake."

"If one of you did that? I'd probably kill the bitch before offing myself." Just the idea of that transpiring sends a wave of nausea through me.

"Rose," Deakan says, his voice gentle. "We don't blame you for it."

Jax and Mekhi nod in agreement.

"But," I whisper, "I still feel like I cheated."

Theo pulls me close and kisses the top of my head. "You didn't. That's the point. You didn't do anything wrong."

I nod and close my eyes, grateful for the support of my mates, but still reeling from the guilt.

Kieran

SHE WAS RIGHT THERE in front of me. Naked and stunning. Her arousal perfumed the air, and I thought it'd been my fantasy, but no, she was in the shower with me. The memory of Rose walking in on me still lingers, her presence like an open wound that won't stop throbbing. It's like a cruel joke, a reminder that she's within reach, but never truly mine. With a heavy sigh, I find myself back in the chaotic, dangerous, and unforgiving streets of Occasus, seeking refuge from the tormenting thoughts of her.

As I retrace my steps through the city, I seek the same toothless witch I'd encountered before. I lock eyes with her and approach, my expression as hard and unreadable as stone. "Is it done?"

The witch leans in, eyes shifting side to side. "We need more," she rasps.

She places the jar in my outstretched palm as I hand her coin. I bring it to my lips and feign interest in her wares—charms and potions and incantations—as I sink my fangs into the rubber seal.

Once my poison has collected in the jar, I fix my sight behind her as I brush past her, dropping it into her open bag.

Pulling the crumpled sheet of paper out of my pocket with the high queen's handwriting, I re-read the ingredient list:

Heart of a siren, fang of a basilisk, Occasus ruby, Sundahlian sand, bones of a traitor, moon fire ashes, Sea of Triune salt, ground gnome treasure, wood from a shipwreck, a compass, muscle of a berserker, sustai bird excrement, eye of a cyclops, and petal from a moon flower.

We have everything we need for the locator spell except for the bones of a traitor. That's not so hard to come by in Espero, as this is the underbelly of the realm. If I stumble across any bodies decomposing in the alley, I'm likely to find exactly what I need without having to check who they belong to.

To be on the safe side, I pick up several near a dumpster in a dark alley, slipping the sun-bleached bones into my bag.

As I continue through the market, I come across a stall that exudes a dark, foreboding aura. The vendor, a hooded figure whose face is hidden in shadow, stands before an array of vials, jars, and mysterious containers. I knew there were other dealers in the market who peddled dangerous and powerful substances—far more dangerous than those I've already indulged in—and it seems I've stumbled upon one of them.

I glance back toward the witch, still tending to her own stall, and then approach the shadowy vendor. As I draw closer, the air around me grows colder and I feel a heavy, oppressive presence bearing down on me.

"What can I do for you?" the vendor asks, their voice raspy and hollow, neither male, nor female.

"I'm looking for something stronger than Aeris Luminis," I confess, my tone laced with a mix of desperation and frustration.

Everything serpent fae takes needs to be potent.

They eye me with a mix of curiosity and amusement, sizing me up as though they know the reason for my desperation. "Looking for a stronger hit, are you?" They cackle, their laughter grating and filled with malice.

"I don't need your judgment, just give me what I want," I demand, the edge in my voice making it clear that I have no patience for their games.

"All right, all right," they concede, rummaging through the various containers on their makeshift stall. After a moment, the fae produces a vial filled with a dark, viscous liquid. They hold it out to me, their gloved hand steady and deliberate. "This is what you're looking for. It's called Abyssal's Embrace. It'll take you to the darkest corners of your mind, strip away all pretenses, and force you to confront the truth, no matter how painful."

"What do I do with it?" I ask, my heart pounding with a mix of fear and anticipation.

"Just drink it," they reply, their voice devoid of emotion. "But be warned, it's not for the faint of heart and it can be fatal for some."

As I take the vial, the vendor's words echo through my mind, making me question whether this is the path I truly want to take. And yet, with Rose's image haunting me, and the poison I have to give the witch, I have little choice. I hand over the coins, my fingers trembling as I clutch the vial of Abyssal's Embrace.

"Thanks," I murmur, my voice barely audible. The hooded figure simply nods, their face still hidden in the shadows.

My heart pounds in my chest as I walk away, the cold glass of the vial pressed against my palm. The weight of my decision bears down on me, but the prospect of escape, however fleeting or dark it may be, suffocates me.

I fucking love her, and the fact I can't have her is killing me. I feel it in my bones, the yearning in my soul that begs me to do something, to be with her. For a long time, I hated her, but now, I hate myself.

Am I destined to ruin things for her? For them all? Are they better off without me?

As I continue through the market, I come across a group of men huddled in a corner, their eyes bloodshot and filled with a twisted mixture of euphoria and anguish. It's clear they've taken something, and I can't help but be fascinated by the power of the substance I now possess.

Wandering further through the market, I find a secluded alley, far from prying eyes. The unbearable pain of wanting Rose, of knowing that she's beyond my reach, leaves me feeling hollow and desperate.

The darkness envelops me, making it easier to focus on my task. I unscrew the cap of the vial, staring at the viscous liquid as it catches the scant light filtering through the murky air.

My chest aches as I stare down at it, just wanting it all to stop. I don't want to be a burden anymore. But as I raise the glass jar to my lips, shouts from the flesh market reach my ears, reminding me that if I'm gone, they will be, too.

Or worse.

By last count, there are forty-two fae children, twelve adults, sixteen teen witches, and one human held captive in the underground dungeon running below these streets. The toothless witches' words come back to me now. *"You're their only hope."*

Three more full vials of my poison and they'll have enough to kill all ninety of the guards keeping them prisoner. Serpent fae venom is the most potent of all poisons, but it has a weakness: I can only generate a few drops at a time, making this a tedious process. It's why I keep coming back. I've got to save them before they're scheduled to be transported to the realm of Romarie.

I can't be reckless.

I put the cap back on the vial and slide it into my pocket. I need to get out of here.

CHAPTER TWENTY-FIVE

ROSE

It's the morning of our third and final part of the Arcane Scholar competition. The sun streams through the windows, bathing us in its gentle light. My mates and I are all nestled together in the spacious bed, our limbs intertwined, the warmth and intimacy of the moment drawing us closer than ever. A lazy Saturday morning, with no Spar Games on the horizon now that the season is over, allows us the luxury to indulge in each other's presence before all hell breaks loose tonight. The dean had insisted this final stage took place in the evening, and I keep wondering why.

Deakan runs his fingers through my hair as he peppers my body with his lips. Soft laughter and tender kisses fill the air as we savor the rare opportunity to simply be together without any pressing obligations. Our hands roam, lips brush, and we lose ourselves in the love that binds us so tightly.

My body tingles with anticipation as I feel the weight of Mekhi's hand on my thigh, his fingers teasing circles over my skin.

Jax's lips hover over mine, his warm breath tickling my skin as he turns and murmurs sweet nothings in my ear.

Theo pulls me into his lap, spreading my thighs for Deakan to settle between them. While we all went to bed in various states of dress, we're all naked now. This is the first time they're all planning on sharing me fully, and the thought of it has my breath ragged.

"Can I have you here?" Theo's erection nudges my ass.

Pleasure sears through me like a wildfire and I can't help but nod. Deakan leans over me reaching into the nightstand drawer and pulls out a bottle of lube, sending another wave of heat through my body.

Theo's hands roam over my breasts, kneading and caressing them as Deakan prepares me. I gasp as he slides a finger inside, stretching me so I can take Theo.

Mekhi's hand moves higher up my thigh, his fingers teasing the sensitive skin near the apex of my legs. Jax is kissing my neck, his tongue tracing patterns over my pulse point.

I'm completely lost in the sensations, my body humming with bliss as my mates touch me. Theo lines himself up, pressing the head of his cock against my ass. I inhale sharply as he pushes inside, the sensation of being filled by him making me moan.

"You take my cock so good." Theo's groan in my ear nearly undoes me.

The sensation of being filled by two of my mates sends shivers of pleasure racing through me. Theo moves his hips, pushing deeper with every stroke. His rhythm is gentle and tender, each thrust like a loving kiss.

Deakan takes his place at my front, pushing his hard length at my entrance. I arch my back, giving him better access as his hands grip my hips tightly. He slides inside me, a guttural groan escaping the three of us as just a thin wall separates the two inside me.

I'm consumed by pleasure as the sensations wash over me. The pressure builds until I'm trembling on the brink of ecstasy, all too aware of the heat radiating off both men surrounding me and filling me up completely.

Mekhi's hand inches further up my thigh and his fingers find their way to my clit, teasing and pleasing it as he watches us move together. Theo holds onto me tightly from behind, whispering words of encouragement to push me closer to the edge.

My breath hitches in anticipation until finally, I tumble over into an intense orgasm that ripples through all three of us with deep satisfaction. Slowly I come back to reality, wrapped in our embrace, before I'm passed off to Mekhi and Jax.

They take their turn, showering me with more passionate lovemaking until I'm spent and exhausted. I collapse between my mates, content and happy in the knowledge that I'm loved and cherished by the four of them.

We lay there in post-coital bliss, our heartbeats slowing and our bodies slick with sweat.

Mekhi's fingers brush against the delicate silver chain around my neck. He gazes at the small, sparkling diamond caught in the beak of the giant, black crow pendant, his eyes lighting up with admiration. "This necklace is beautiful, Rose. Where did you get it?"

My stomach lurches, and a sudden chill courses through me. I'd assumed Mekhi had given me the necklace, especially considering his past in crafting fine jewelry. "I . . . I thought you got it for me, or that you'd made it," I stammer, my voice tinged with uncertainty.

Mekhi shakes his head, his brow furrowing. "No, I didn't make that for you. I've never seen it before."

A hush falls over us as Theo, Jax, and Deakan all chime in, denying any involvement in the necklace's appearance. The sudden realization that none of my mates are responsible for the gift leaves me feeling exposed and vulnerable.

My thoughts race, and a name sends a shudder down my spine—Dean Fallgren. Could she have placed it in our bathroom back at the dorm? Or is someone else is watching me, leaving this mysterious gift to unnerve me?

The once gentle atmosphere now feels tense and uneasy, our intimate moment fractured by the unexplained presence of the necklace. Our entwined bodies shift as the concern for our safety and the lingering threat of an unknown observer weighs heavily on us.

The necklace, once a symbol of beauty and intrigue, now seems to carry a sinister message.

～

Rose

THE GUYS and I are in the living room when the sound of the front door slamming open sends a shockwave through the house, immediately drawing my attention. Footsteps echo through the hallway as Kieran rushes toward me, his eyes wide with a mix of excitement and urgency.

Guess we're not talking about the shower incident then.

"Rose, I've got the rest of the ingredients we need for the locator spell," he exclaims, slightly out of breath. He places a small bag on the coffee table, the contents making a few gentle clinks. "Your parents already had lots of the items, but there's one last thing we need—the blood of a mate."

My heart skips a beat, understanding the weight of his request. Finally, we're going to know where his grandma is. I'm mated to Mekhi, Deakan, Jax, and Theo, which means my blood is the final key to unlocking the spell. Knowing the importance of this spell and the closure it will bring, I don't hesitate. "I'll help you, Kieran."

His face breaks into a relieved smile, his gratitude radiating from him. "Thank you, Rose. This means everything to me."

"Do you need any of our help?" Theo places a hand on my thigh, giving it a gentle squeeze. "I don't think so. We'll take this outside in case there are fumes."

"Just let us know." Bennett glances up from the book he's reading.

Together, Kieran and I head to the courtyard and set about preparing the spell. Under the morning sun, already sweltering, I marvel at the wide array of ingredients that this involves: the heart of a siren, fang of a basilisk, an Occasus ruby, and Sundahlian sand. There's also the bones of a traitor, moon fire ashes, and Sea of Triune salt.

The collection continues with ground gnome treasure, wood from a shipwreck, a compass, and the muscle of a berserker. The final ingredients include sustai bird excrement, eye of a cyclops, and a delicate petal from a moon flower.

Together, Kieran and I head to a secluded spot in the courtyard where the ground is flat and free of debris. We arrange the ingredients in a specific order, creating a circle with a small indentation in the center to hold the final element. The air around us hums with anticipation, the energy of the spell beginning to take shape as my crow makes an appearance again. It circles the air, always flying sentry above. I return my attention to the spell because I can sense Kieran's desperation, his need for answers, and it only fuels my determination to see this through.

"Okay, the last thing we need is the blood of a mate," Kieran says, his voice slightly shaky. He hands me a small, sterilized blade, his eyes meeting mine as he adds, "You don't have to do this if you're not comfortable."

I take the blade, studying the gleaming edge for a moment before meeting his gaze. "I promised to help you, Kieran. And that's what I'm going to do."

As I carefully draw the blade across my palm, a thin line of crimson wells up, and I hold my hand over the collection of ingredients. The blood drips down, mingling with the other components, and the energy in the room intensifies. Kieran watches intently, his eyes filled with hope and fear as the spell begins to take shape before us.

As the spell continues to build, Kieran carefully places a map on the table before us. The map is old, its edges worn and slightly frayed, but it still clearly shows the layout of the island of Academia and the surrounding areas. The magical energies surrounding us seem to be drawn towards the map, as though they recognize it as the focal point of their purpose.

When the spell reaches its crescendo, the combined energies suddenly shoot toward the map, tracing glowing lines and symbols across its surface. Our eyes widen as we watch the spell's power come to fruition. There, on the map, is a tiny, glowing dot—the exact location of Kieran's grandmother.

I glance at Kieran, my excitement tempered by a sudden wave of fear. The dot on the map shows that Kieran's grandmother is much closer than either of us had anticipated, and the thought of facing her fills me with dread. As I reach out and place a hand on Kieran's arm, I try to steady myself and offer what comfort I can, but my own fear is impossible to ignore.

"Do you want me to come with you?" I ask hesitantly, not wanting to intrude on what will no doubt be an incredibly personal and difficult encounter. Especially knowing I'll have to call the guard to bring her in.

Kieran takes a deep breath and shakes his head. "No, I think it's better if I go alone," he says quietly. "I want to try and convince her that your family isn't to blame for her pain, and that there's a better way forward. I think I'll have a better chance of getting through to her if I go on my own."

I nod, understanding his reasoning, though it's hard to let him face this daunting task alone.

CHAPTER TWENTY-SIX

KIERAN

s I sift to the sand dunes, the world around me dissolves and reforms in the blink of an eye. Suddenly, I find myself standing amidst a vast expanse of golden sand. The early morning sun has barely risen, yet it already casts its blazing heat upon the landscape. I squint against the light, taking a deep breath to steady myself before I begin my search.

I call out for my grandmother, my voice hoarse and desperate. "Grandma! Where are you? Please, I need to talk to you!" The words echo through the dunes, disappearing into the empty, vast expanse. There's no response, no sign of her. My heart races in my chest, fueled by a mixture of hope and anxiety.

The sun continues its relentless ascent, and the sand beneath my feet grows hotter with each passing minute. Despite the heat, I push forward, focusing my thoughts on finding my grandmother and reconciling with her.

As I trudge through the sand, I notice how the dunes seem to stretch on forever. Every step feels heavier, and beads of sweat form on my brow as the sun bears down on me.

Minutes turn into hours, and I begin to feel the weight of my fear for the only person left in my life who shares my blood. I worry that I may be too late to reach her, but I can't let that thought take hold of me. I need to keep going.

And then, just as I crest the top of a particularly high dune, I see her. My heart lurches in my chest as I take in the sight of my grandmother lying unconscious on the sand. Her body is battered and almost unrecognizable, her onyx hair matted with blood and dirt.

Trepidation fills me as I approach her, my footsteps muffled by the sand. I force myself to take slow, deep breaths, trying to remain as calm as possible.

"Grandma," I whisper, my voice choked with emotion as I reach out to touch her gently, trying to determine the extent of her injuries. The thought that I might be too late to save her is unbearable, but I try to stay hopeful. My heart shatters in my chest as the full realization of what's happening strikes me. Grandma, my only living relative, who I love despite her mistakes, lies near death. Paralyzing pain reverberates through my body and brings me to my knees, the idea of losing her, unfathomable.

I notice her chest rising and falling ever so slightly, and relief washes over me. She's alive, though unconscious. I take a moment to process this, my mind racing with a thousand questions and worries, but I know I need to act quickly if I want to help her.

Despite the hope I feel upon seeing my grandmother still breathing, I know that she's in a critical state, and I need to do something to help her. Ignoring the heat and exhaustion, I focus my attention on using my healing magic. With every ounce of energy I have, I channel my power through my fingertips, trying to will her wounds to heal.

Nothing happens.

Panic begins to set in. My magic is failing me. Desperation gnaws at the edges of my thoughts, and I know I need help. I swallow my pride and pull out my cell phone, dialing Rose's number.

She answers after just two rings, her voice filled with concern. "Kieran? What's going on? Did you find her?"

"I found her," I say, my voice trembling. "But she's in bad shape, Rose. I tried using my healing magic, but it's not working. I . . . I don't know what else to do."

I hear Rose take a sharp breath; the weight of the situation apparent in the silence that follows. I can only imagine what she must be feeling, knowing the danger my grandmother poses to her family.

"Please, Rose," I plead, my voice barely audible. "I need your help. I don't know who else to turn to."

There's a brief pause, and then she speaks, her voice firm and resolute. "I'll call my parents. We'll figure something out, Kieran. Just hang in there."

"Thank you," I murmur, grateful beyond words.

As I end the call, I gaze down at my unconscious grandmother, her frost-speckled lips and bloodied hair a stark contrast to the golden sand beneath her. In that moment, I realize that my pride and my resentment must take a backseat to what truly matters: family. Even if it means asking for help from those I least want to involve, I must do whatever it takes to save her.

Rose's parents arrive with help, and all attempts to wake her fail. My knees crash to the sand, and despair clings to me just like it had the day I found my father dead.

The royal guard takes Grandma to the healing clinic at Bedlam Penitentiary, located at the northernmost point of Bedlam on Penn Island. They're going to try to treat her and then question her about her role in the threats against Rose's family.

"I need to be with her," I say, my voice shaking slightly as my hands dig into the ground, trying to find an outlet for the agony.

Rose kneels in the sand in front of me, cupping my cheeks in her hands. "My parents are arranging transportation to Penn Island now. They'll get you the necessary permissions since only people with certain authority can sift there."

"Thank you," I choke.

"I'm sorry, Kieran." She wraps her arms around me as tears fall in sheets down my cheeks.

As I wait for the arrangements to be made, I can't help but feel a knot of anxiety tightening in my chest. My memories of my grand-mother are a mix of warm, familial moments and the icy, calculating woman she became after we lost my parents. The image of her with onyx hair pulled tight into a bun and her frost-speckled lips uttering harsh words flashes through my mind.

She was different before the war took everything from us.

ONCE THE TRANSPORTATION permission is ready, I'm escorted to Penn Island, where Bedlam Penitentiary is located. As I step onto the island, I'm struck by the oppressive atmosphere created by the powerful and dangerous fae imprisoned here. The sterile smell of the clinic hangs in the air, a stark contrast to the rich, earthy scents of Sanctuary.

As I approach the prison, my chest tightens, and a knot of unease forms in my gut. The sky is an oppressive gray, the waves crash violently against the shore, and the scent of saltwater and old copper lingers in the air. The place has an eerie, haunting atmosphere.

I'm led inside by a guard wearing a blue uniform marked with an X over the breast pocket. The hallway stretches ahead of us, dimly lit with a flickering, cold light. The sound of our footsteps echoes off the stone walls, accompanied by the distant wails and murmurs of the prisoners.

As we walk, I can't help but glance into the cells we pass, each one holding a dangerous and powerful fae. Some stare back with expres-sions ranging from curiosity to pure malice, while others hide in the shadows or simply don't care to look up. Their gazes weigh heavily on me, heightening the unease that coils in my chest.

Is this where I'll end up if my crimes catch up to me? While the thought is unsettling, I'd do it again in a heartbeat.

We reach the clinic, and the antiseptic smell is a stark contrast to the damp and earthy scent of the prison. A nurse, clad in crisp white, greets us at the door. She glances at me with a mix of sympathy and caution, but I'm too focused on my grandmother to take any offense.

Inside the clinic, the sterile, white walls and harsh lighting add to the unwelcoming atmosphere. The hum of medical equipment fills the room, creating a monotonous backdrop to the urgent whispering of the staff as they go about their tasks.

I'm led to a private room where my grandma lies on a bed, hooked up to numerous machines that monitor her vital signs. Her once-imposing figure looks small and frail, her face drawn and pale beneath the patterns of ice-blue snowflakes on her skin. Her onyx hair is clean now, framing her face in a way that emphasizes her vulnerability.

A lump forms in my throat as I step closer. "Grandma," I whisper, reaching out to touch her hand. Her skin feels cold, and I wonder if this is a sign of her waning strength or simply the chill of the room.

The door to the room opens, and a healer enters, carrying a tray with various vials and instruments. They give me a curt nod before turning their attention to my grandmother. As they begin their work, I can't tear my eyes away from the sight of her, and fear grips my heart.

With every passing moment, I feel the gravity of the situation bearing down on me. The consequences of my grandmother's actions, the threat she posed to Rose and her family, and the overwhelming uncertainty of what's to come. All of it swirls in a storm of emotion that robs the breath from my lungs, and I don't know how to cope.

I stand in a solemn vigil beside my grandmother's bed, unable to tear my gaze away from her still form. I try desperately to cling onto the memories of her warmth and kindness before the war swallowed us into its dark abyss; yet the weight of her misdeeds hangs like a heavy cloud above us, suffocating any hope we have for peace.

In this cold and unforgiving place, despair continues to cling to me, strangling me and refusing to let go.

I'm tired of feeling like this.

As I continue to watch over my grandmother, lost in my grief, I hear the door open once more. This time, it's Bellamy who steps into the room, his sun-bronzed skin, blond hair, and lilac eyes immediately drawing my attention. As head of the guard and a member of the dragon order, he's a formidable figure, but Rose knows him to be a kind man, so I feel a little at ease that he's the one overseeing things.

"Kieran," he says, acknowledging me with a nod before glancing at my grandmother, his expression grim.

I stand straighter, bracing myself for whatever news he has to share. "Have you found any leads on who might've hurt her?"

Bellamy shakes his head, his deep-set dimples momentarily disappearing as he frowns. "Not yet. They've been scouring the area where she was found, but there's no clear evidence pointing to any specific individual."

A sense of helplessness courses through me, but I try to remain composed despite the cavern widening in my chest. "What about her condition? Have the healers discovered anything?"

"We're thinking magical interference." Bellamy hesitates, running a hand through his hair. "There seems to be an enchantment at work, making it difficult for her to be healed or to wake up from her coma. Our best magic wielders have been trying to break through it, but it's been a challenge. All signs point to magic, but there is no magical signature."

I stare at my grandmother, the worry intensifying as I consider the implications of this enchantment. Who could have placed it on her, and for what purpose?

"What can we do?" I ask, desperation seeping into my voice.

"We'll keep investigating and doing our best to counter the enchantment," Bellamy reassures me. "We won't give up on her, Kieran. They're going to run some more tests on her now, so we'll need you to head home, and we'll call with any news."

I nod mechanically, clutching my hair before burying my head in my hands. I stand, not bothering to hide the tears streaking my cheeks as I allow him to usher me out and toward the beach where I need to sift.

He doesn't need to know home isn't where I'm headed. At least not yet. There's only one thing that'll make me feel better right now.

CHAPTER TWENTY-SEVEN

ROSE

Nausea, exhaustion, and guilt fight for top spot inside me as I take a minute alone in the grounds near to where we're due to meet for the final phase of the competition. It doesn't feel right to be getting on with life in any normal way while Kieran is hurting so much. But the rest of my family need me too, and I've never been one to give up on something I've committed to.

I take three breaths, trying to cleanse my mind of the day's discoveries and focus it on what's ahead. My concentration falters when I notice a massive crow alight on a nearby branch, its ebony feathers shimmering in the sunlight. A familiar knot of unease twists in my stomach, as it's the same crow that always seems to be watching me. I study the bird, its dark eyes meeting mine, as if it can see through me, deep into my soul.

The sudden crunch of footsteps on the grass startles me, and I glance up to find Bella strolling toward me. Her shock-white hair catches the sunlight, and her almond-shaped silver eyes hold a mixture of curiosity and amusement. She casually squats beside me, leaning back against the tree trunk with an air of nonchalance.

"Hey there, Rose," she greets, her eyes flicking towards the crow before settling back on me. "You seem to have quite the admirer."

I frown, unsure of how to respond. Bella's presence always puts me on edge, but this time, she appears to know something I don't. "Yeah, it's . . . it's been following me around for a while now. I don't know why."

Bella tilts her head to the side, studying the crow with an unreadable expression. "Hmm. Crows are interesting creatures, you know. They're intelligent and perceptive. Some believe they hold a deep connection to the supernatural."

A shiver runs down my spine at her words. The way she talks about the crow implies she knows more than she's letting on. But Bella remains elusive, her lips curling into a knowing smile. "Maybe it's here for a reason, Rose. Maybe there's something it wants you to see, or to understand."

The enigmatic statement only deepens my unease. "And what reason would that be, Bella? What am I supposed to see?"

She looks at me with a cryptic smile, her silver eyes glinting. "Well, that's the question, isn't it? Maybe it's just waiting for the right moment to reveal itself."

As if on cue, the crow lets out a raucous caw and takes flight, its dark wings cutting through the air as it disappears into the distance. I watch it go, feeling both relieved and more unsettled than ever.

Bella rises gracefully to her feet, brushing stray grass from her black leather pants. "Anyway, I should get going. It was nice chatting with you, Rose. Good luck for this evening." She gives me a parting smile, leaving me to wonder about her true motives and the mysterious crow that continues to haunt my thoughts.

Bella seems to have a fondness for appearing when I least expect it. She's a paradox, always leaving me feeling like there's something more to her than meets the eye. I glance over at the spot where she had been squatting just moments ago, her cryptic words still ringing in my ears.

As I ponder the situation, the gentle rustling of leaves in the breeze captures my attention. I notice a small, delicate flower blooming near the base of the tree, its petals an iridescent shade of violet. A sense of calm washes over me as I take in the beauty of the flower, the vibrant color providing a striking contrast against the muted tones of the grass and fallen leaves.

Feeling drawn to it, I reach out to touch the flower's silky petals, their coolness soothing against my fingertips. As I do, a soft melody fills the air, like the distant tinkling of wind chimes. Startled, I pull my hand back, looking around to find the source of the sound, but there's no one there.

A sudden gust of wind stirs the air, sending the scent of the flower wafting towards me. It's a sweet, heady aroma, both captivating and otherworldly. For a moment, I forget about the crow, about Bella and her cryptic words, lost in the intoxicating fragrance that envelops me.

I blink, shaken from my reverie, and find that the sun has sunk lower in the sky, casting elongated shadows across the courtyard. Time seems to have slipped away from me, a sense of disorientation settling in. How long have I been sitting here, lost in thought?

The image of the crow comes back to me, its dark eyes holding secrets I can't begin to fathom. I can't help but wonder if Bella's words were a clue to something greater, something that ties everything together. What could the crow be trying to reveal to me, and how does Bella fit into the puzzle?

Determined to uncover the truth, I tuck the flower carefully into my pocket, a tangible reminder of the mysteries that seem to surround me. With each step I take, I can't shake the feeling that I'm on the cusp of discovering something extraordinary, something that could change my life forever.

But will it be a good change or a bad one?

CHAPTER TWENTY-EIGHT

ROSE

The Bedlam Moon bathes the grounds in crimson, lending an ominous tone to our final competition. As if today hasn't been terrible enough. I glance around for Kieran, my heart aching when I don't find him. Meeting my mates' eyes, they all shake their heads, confirming that they, too, haven't seen him.

I didn't think he'd show, but I was hopeful he would. I debated not even participating now that Dean Fallgren has been found and is no longer a threat to our family, but I don't want to let anyone down. Just because one threat has been eliminated, doesn't mean there won't be others in the future.

Grief saws through my chest as Dean Corvus projects his voice, explaining the course. There are considerably less contestants now. He explains that we're running a marathon, but instead of being on a track or a flat surface, we'll have to run through sand, dodging winged beasts and sand worms.

I steal another glance at my mates again, trying to draw strength from their presence. Their determined expressions bring a small measure of comfort, and I know that we'll face this challenge together, as we always have.

As we prepare to begin, I can't help but feel a mix of excitement and dread. The sand underfoot shifts and slides, making it difficult to find solid footing. I take a deep breath and mentally prepare myself for the grueling race ahead.

The starting signal pierces the air, and we take off, our feet sinking into the soft sand as we push ourselves forward. The first few steps are the hardest, our muscles straining against the resistance of the unstable terrain. But we quickly adapt, finding a rhythm as we race through the crimson-lit landscape.

As the marathon continues, sweat pours down my face, the sand sticks to my skin and clothes.

As we navigate the treacherous terrain, the cries of the winged beasts pierce the air, their sharp claws slashing as they swoop and dive toward us. My mates and I work together, relying on our collective strength to ward off their attacks. The sand worms, however, require quick reflexes to evade their surprise emergence from the ground and their gaping jaws.

The other contestants impress me with their adaptability and clever tactics, using their unique abilities to counter the challenges thrown at them.

My breathing becomes labored, each inhale a struggle as my eyes scan the crowd for any glimpse of Kieran. But with each passing second, hope dwindles, and the void left by his absence grows heavier. Despite the emotional turmoil, I steel myself and focus on the path ahead, knowing that I must persevere not only for my family. Winning Arcane Scholar will keep them safe, and that's all that matters to me.

It's all that's *ever* mattered to me.

My pulse pounds in my ears, determined to prove my worth. Each obstacle requires a combination of physical prowess and magical ingenuity, pushing me to my limits. My body aches and my lungs burn as I push forward, my mind racing as I strategize and adapt on the fly. Competitors stumble and fall behind as the course takes its toll, but I notice that Deakan, Jax, and Bennett are still going strong, a testament to our bond and the strength we draw from one another.

As we reach the halfway point of the course, I find myself running side by side with Deakan. Our eyes meet for a brief moment, and we exchange an encouraging nod, pushing each other to keep going. A particularly tricky magical barrier requires us to work together, combining our spells to create a force strong enough to shatter the obstruction. Deakan casts a spell, and I follow suit, our magic weaving together in perfect harmony. The barrier crumbles, and we continue on our way.

Jax isn't far behind, showcasing his incredible agility as he leaps and ducks through the obstacles with ease. His fierce determination is evident in the intensity of his gaze, and I feel a swell of pride seeing him excel in this challenge. I shoot him a cheeky grin.

"You know, you're looking pretty good out here," I tease, trying to lighten the somber mood that's taken over my psyche. "But I hope you can keep up with me."

Jax's eyes sparkle with mischief as he returns the smile. "Oh, I have no doubt I can keep up with you, Rose. The question is, can you handle it?"

Bennett, always the strategist, approaches each obstacle with careful thought and calculation. As he reaches a difficult section of the course, he pauses briefly to assess the situation before employing a brilliant combination of spells to bypass the hazard. His intelligence and resourcefulness never cease to amaze me.

Mekhi, ever the charming one, sidles up to me during a brief pause in the obstacles. "You're really in your element like this," he says, his smooth voice filled with admiration.

I playfully elbow him. "Don't think flattery will distract me from beating you in this challenge." He's struggling a little more than the rest of us, as he's a witch and the rest of us are fae.

Deakan, who's been focused intently on the competition, finally joins in on the teasing. "I think you're forgetting that I'm the one you should be worried about," he remarks, a hint of a smirk playing on his lips.

I roll my eyes playfully. "I'm not going down without a fight."

Together, we navigate the treacherous course, our camaraderie and shared determination propelling us forward.

Finally, the end of the obstacle course comes into view, and we push ourselves to the limit, our bodies and minds straining with exertion. The finish line is just ahead, and with one last burst of energy, we surge across it, breathless and exhilarated.

Dean Corvus waits on the other side, his eyes appraising us. His gaze lingers on me, and for a fleeting moment, I feel a shiver of yearning, quickly suppressed by my determination to remain focused on the competition as I drag my eyes away from him.

Only a handful of competitors make it across, including myself, Deakan, Jax, Bennett, and Mekhi. The next step of the challenge is a magic combat trial, pitting us against one another in a test of our magical and physical prowess. The matches are determined at random, and as I watch the pairings being drawn, I feel a knot of tension form in my stomach. Our names are called, and I find myself facing off against Jax in the first round.

"I guess there's no escaping this," Jax says with a wry grin, though his eyes hold a flicker of uncertainty.

"No, but we've sparred countless times before. We'll just treat this like another training session," I reply, trying to ease the tension between us.

As the battle commences, our familiarity with each other's techniques becomes evident. Jax opens with a swift lunge, but I counter his strike easily, having anticipated his move. We exchange a series of swift blows, our magic crackling in the air as we parry and dodge each other's attacks.

I manage to land a hit, and the pain and adrenaline cause my healing magic to flare. Jax's eyes widen as he registers the advantage my abilities give me, but he doesn't let it discourage him. "You're not the only one with tricks up your sleeve," he taunts, a glint of mischief in his eyes.

We continue to duel, evenly matched in skill and determination. The tension between us gradually gives way to the familiar rhythm of our sparring sessions, and I find myself enjoying the challenge. I can see the pride in Jax's eyes as we push each other to our limits, our connection as mates only deepening our understanding of one another's abilities.

"You know, this is the first time I've actually enjoyed fighting someone I love," Jax admits between strikes, his voice laced with affection.

"Me too," I reply, a fierce smile playing on my lips as we lock blades once more. "But don't think I'll go easy on you just because of that."

Our battle continues, and eventually, I manage to land a decisive blow that sends Jax stumbling back.

As Jax regains his footing, he looks up at me with a mix of pride and admiration. "You've gotten even better since we last sparred," he admits, clearly impressed. "But don't think I'm down for the count just yet."

We resume our battle, neither of us willing to concede defeat. However, with each passing moment, the line between our roles as competitors and mates begins to blur. The sparks of our magic meld with the electricity of our chemistry, and I can feel the healing energy coursing through me, both as a result of the pain and the desire I can't quite suppress.

Finally, with a well-executed feint, I manage to disarm Jax and force him to yield. He grins ruefully, panting from the exertion. "I never stood a chance, did I?" he asks with a chuckle, his eyes full of love and admiration.

"You gave me one hell of a fight," I reply, helping him to his feet. "Now, let's see how I fare against the others."

Next up is Deakan, his eyes filled with more adoration than determination as we square off. I brace myself for another intense match, well aware of his magical prowess and resourcefulness.

Deakan proves to be a formidable opponent, his command of magic and quick reflexes keeping me on my toes. As we exchange powerful blows, our eyes lock, and I'm reminded of the deep connection we share. Deakan's devotion only serves to fuel me, pushing me to greater heights as we fight.

Our duel is fierce, but the intensity of our combat is tempered by the underlying affection between us. I can see the pride in Deakan's eyes as we push one another to the limit, the bond between us only growing stronger.

After an intense struggle, I finally manage to outmaneuver Deakan and secure my victory. He smiles warmly at me; his eyes reflecting the pride and love he feels. "Well done, Rose."

As we embrace briefly, I prepare myself for the next match, this time against Corson, another teammate from Spar Games. I know better than to underestimate him; his magical expertise and adaptability make him a dangerous opponent.

Our match begins, and it's immediately clear that he isn't holding back. He comes at me with a ferocity that takes me by surprise, his movements quick and precise. Our battle is a dance of clashing magic, the tension between us igniting with every exchange.

"You've improved," he grudgingly admits, though I can sense the respect behind his words. "But don't think that means you've got me beat."

With renewed determination, we continue our battle, each of us pushing the other to their limits. Corson's expertise with magic is truly a sight to behold, and I find myself equal parts awed and infuriated by his abilities.

Eventually, I manage to land a decisive blow, forcing Corson to yield. Despite our unspoken rivalry, there's a sense of mutual respect that passes between us as we exchange weary smiles.

"Well fought, Rose," he concedes, his voice laced with admiration. "Might even be in line for captain next year."

As we recover from our duel, I steel myself for the final match—against Mekhi. Though he may be a witch and not naturally as gifted with magic as the rest of us, I know better than to underestimate his cunning and resourcefulness.

Our duel begins with Mekhi demonstrating an impressive mastery of his witch magic, his focus unwavering as we clash. Our connection as mates is apparent even in combat, our shared experiences and understanding giving us a unique insight into one another's tactics, as though we know precisely what the other is about to do before it happens.

With each move, I feel the pull of our bond, the desire to protect and heal him almost overpowering. And yet, Mekhi's own determination spurs me on, reminding me that we're both here to win. It's got to be any of our family members, doesn't matter who.

The battle rages on, neither of us willing to back down. Eventually, I manage to outmaneuver Mekhi and claim victory. As he concedes, his eyes are filled with love and pride.

"I knew you'd come out on top," he admits, his voice warm and genuine. "Now give him hell."

The air is charged with anticipation as Bennett and I square off for the final match. Our eyes meet, a shared understanding passing between us. Though we are twins, and our bond is unbreakable, we know that in this competition we must give it our all, because anything less means that our family will continue to be at risk. We're the last two standing, and the crowd has gathered around us, eager to witness this final clash of the high prince and princess of the fae.

As our battle begins, it becomes immediately apparent that we're evenly matched. Our shared upbringing, training, and understanding of each other's strengths and weaknesses create a fierce duel unlike any other. We trade blows with an intensity that should be reserved for sworn enemies, but we know that we can take it, and that we'll emerge stronger for it.

With a burst of speed, Bennett launches another attack, a powerful air spell that sends a shockwave rippling toward me. I narrowly avoid the impact, using my own magic to deflect the force, feeling the rush of adrenaline course through my veins.

As the battle intensifies, blood is drawn, but our Luna fae heritage immediately mends the wounds with a bright glow. The sight of our shared blood only serves to remind us of our bond, fueling our determination to give this fight everything we have.

Bennett and I exchange a series of powerful blows, our physical strength and magical prowess on full display. I narrowly dodge a spell that would have sent me sprawling, the force of the attack leaving a crater in the sand where I once stood.

I return with a spell of my own, my magic surging through the air, seeking its target. Bennett counters with a barrier of his own creation, the energy of our spells colliding in a brilliant explosion that illuminates the night sky.

Our breaths come in ragged gasps as we continue to trade blows, the intensity of the fight taking its toll. Sweat glistens on our foreheads, and despite the near-instant healing of our Luna fae blood, the pain and exhaustion begin to creep in.

"Come on, sis," Bennett taunts with a grin, his voice strained but filled with admiration. "You can do better than that."

I flash a wicked grin back at him. "You asked for it, brother."

The air around us crackles with the sheer force of our magic as we simultaneously unleash our spells. The powerful energies collide, casting an eruption of light and sound that engulfs the entire arena. The crowd gasps, instinctively stepping back from the intensity of our battle.

Our respective spells meet in the center, pushing against each other with a force that threatens to tear the very fabric of the air apart. We grit our teeth, sweat pouring down our faces, as we pour every last ounce of our energy into this final showdown.

I can see the strain on Bennett's face, the unspoken challenge in his eyes. Our connection as twins has always been our greatest strength, and even now, we know each other's limits better than anyone else. It's a test of our resolve, a battle of wills as much as it is a contest of magical prowess.

As we continue to force our spells against one another, I feel a surge of pride for my brother. We've fought side by side countless times, but it's in this moment, against each other, that I truly see the strength and determination that have shaped him into the formidable warrior he is today.

With a final push, our spells explode in a brilliant display of magic, and the arena is filled with the roar of applause and cheers from the crowd. We stand there, breathing heavily, our bodies aching, and our magic nearly drained as our order struggles to replenish it. Yet, there is a fire in our eyes, a fierce pride and respect for one another that cannot be extinguished.

Dean Corvus steps forward, his expression a mixture of awe and admiration as he surveys the aftermath of our battle. He turns to the crowd, raising his voice to announce the results. But for a moment, I don't care about the outcome. In this instant, it's not about winning or losing. It's about the unbreakable bond between a brother and a sister, forged in battle and tempered by love.

We're both a sweaty mess, but we stand together, arms around each other as we wait for the news.

The crowd falls silent as Dean Corvus begins to speak, and I take a deep breath, ready to face whatever fate has in store for me.

He clears his throat, and the anticipation in the air is palpable. "The winner of the final combat trial, and the one who will become the Arcane Scholar, is . . ." He pauses for dramatic effect, and I exchange a glance with Bennett, both of us equally tense. "High Princess Rose Drake!"

The crowd erupts in applause, and I feel a mixture of shock and elation wash over me. Bennett reaches out to embrace me, his grin broad and genuine. "I knew you could do it, sis," he whispers into my ear. "I'm so proud of you."

As my mates and fellow competitors gather around to offer their congratulations, I feel my heart swell with gratitude and love for these extraordinary people. Jax, Deakan, and Mekhi each take their turn to hug me tightly, their pride in me evident in their smiles.

Dean Corvus steps closer, his eyes fixed on me with an intensity that unnerves me. He extends his hand, and I take it hesitantly, feeling the electric connection that courses between us. "Well done, Rose," he says, his voice smooth and laced with an emotion I can't quite place. "I look forward to working closely with you as the Arcane Scholar. Come with me."

I glance at my mates, and they each give me an encouraging nod as I take the dean's hand.

CHAPTER TWENTY-NINE

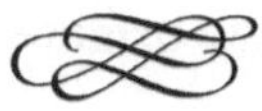

ROSE

*I*n an instant, we sift away from the cheering crowd, and I find myself somewhere beyond anything I've ever experienced. The colors and shapes shift and change around us, the air alive with an energy that seems to pulsate through my veins. I feel a strange and magnetic attraction to this place and to Dean Corvus, which leaves me bewildered, considering the love I have for my mates.

I startle when I see Bella standing amongst the giant stones which have been carved into chairs. "What the hell are you doing here?"

She tried to sabotage me during my second trials.

Her laugh titters through the air, and Dean Corvus rolls his eyes, gesturing to the fae who's been borderline stalking me since I started at Bedlam Academy. "Belladonna is a demigod."

"A what now?" I furrow my brows.

"Part god, part fae." He turns to face her. "Your half-aunt."

"Wait. What?" I cock my head, studying her. "How is that . . . Oh. OH. Oh, my gods." I rush toward her. "You're my grandma's child," I breathe.

She grins. "Surprise."

"And Rune's child?"

She nods.

"But you tried to kill me!"

"You wouldn't have actually died, and I had to make sure you were made of tougher stuff." She shrugs. "You were."

My mouth hanging open, I spin on Dean Corvus. "Then who the hell are you?"

He drops his glamor that suppressed much of his power. It hits me like I've run into a wall of heat, and I stagger back, my magic flaring in reaction to his. My skin glows bright, far brighter than it ever has, nearly blinding me.

"Guess it is her," Bella casts a conspiratorial grin at him. "Finally. After all this time."

Dean Corvus regards me with an intensity that makes my heart race. "It's time you learn who I am. I am Chaos, the first God, the one who granted the original Luna Goddess her magic. And now, I have chosen you."

I stare at him in disbelief, my mind reeling. Of course, I'd heard of Chaos in our legends, but never in my wildest dreams did I think I would stand before him. I feel a strange attraction to this god, a pull that goes beyond reason.

"Are you telling me that I was always going to win?" I ask, my voice barely a whisper.

Chaos' expression is enigmatic, and I can't help but notice the way his eyes seem to drink me in. "You possess qualities that are rare, even among the divine," he replies. "You are strong, compassionate, and wise beyond your years. The realms need someone like you, Rose. You'll be a god."

"I'm still a student," I whisper. "I'm no one."

He tsks. "That's where you're wrong." He leisurely strolls toward me, and I'm caught in his orbit, unable to turn away as he cups my cheek, his touch not frightening me in its intensity, but allowing me to bathe in it. "Hundreds of thousands of years I've waited for you."

"Why?"

"A story for another time, perhaps," he smiles down at me, his features so intense I want to weep from the beauty of him. "After you graduate, you'll come here. Along with anyone you want to bring with you."

Chaos studies me for a moment before continuing, his voice sincere. "As a god, you will have the power to protect your entire family. They will live like gods themselves, free from the threats and dangers that have plagued your lives. I know how important they are to you, Rose. This is a chance for you to ensure their safety and happiness."

I swallow hard, my thoughts racing. The idea of becoming a god and having the power to protect my loved ones is both thrilling and daunting. My family has always been my world, and the thought of being able to keep them safe is more than tempting.

"I understand that this is a lot to take in," Chaos says, his voice soft and understanding. "You don't have to make a decision right now. I'll give you time to consider my offer and to discuss it with your family and mates."

The weight of his words settles on my shoulders like a mantle, a responsibility I never imagined. The thought of joining the pantheon of gods both terrifies and excites me, and as I stand before Chaos, I realize I'll have several years to get used to the idea.

I never really wanted to be high queen, anyway. But to be a goddess?

"I'll bring you back now. Give you some time to process this."

"Are you coming back to campus as dean?" I study him.

He grins. "Someone has to keep an eye on you."

My mind spins with questions. "Were you keeping an eye on me—before? Before you came here as Dean?"

His face darkens. "That was the plan. I'm a god, right? It should have been a walk in the park to keep you safe."

"And Dean Fallgren?" I venture. "Did you know where she was the whole time?"

He stays silent for so long; I wonder if he has heard me at all.

"She was going to hurt you, Rose. You and your family. I couldn't let that happen."

"What did you do?" I whisper.

"I had her—taken care of. At least that was the plan. Have you ever heard the saying, 'you want something done properly, do it yourself?' Let's just say I learned my lesson on that one. She's still alive—barely—but she shouldn't be. And I should have known it in my bones. That's what should be expected of a god. Especially one as powerful as me."

I swallow hard. "Then how come you didn't—"

"My powers are waning, Rose. It's one of the many reasons I need to be with my soul-bond. I was fine without her for millennia; but it's different when one actually finds them, sees them." His voice softens. "Knows them." Toying with my crow jewelry—that I forgot to take off during the competition—a melancholy smile graces his lips before his eyes meet mine. He looks into my soul for several seconds, and then makes me jump when he speaks. "Until next time."

He presses his lips to my forehead, and warmth seeps into my skin. The next thing I know, I'm standing in the center of Sanctuary, staring at a crow taking flight.

Has that been him this *whole* time? The crow caws, almost as if he could read my mind. I shake my head, picking up my backpack that's suddenly at my feet. It's still dark out, or maybe it's the next day, I don't know. It's much colder, so it's clear that hours have passed while I was gone. All my mates have disappeared; no doubt they're searching every corner of Academia in search of me. I don't think any of us expected I'd be gone so long.

But being back here feels like coming home to a friend who's missed me. The jungle around me is teeming with life, and I can hear the squawking of birds and the rustle of leaves.

I walk through the house, and the place feels odd as I drop my things by the door. There's something different in the way it breathes, as though a deep sense of wrongness has seeped into its walls, and it's calling on me to do something. My attention catches on a spilled backpack near the cave entrance, and I approach it cautiously.

It's Kieran's.

The sound of my footsteps echo off the damp stone walls as I step into the tunnel. The air is thick with a musty scent, but there's something else in the air, something that makes my nose wrinkle.

As I make my way deeper into the cave, the scent grows stronger, until it becomes overpowering. It's a pungent odor, like compost mixed with ash. I can feel my stomach turn, and I wonder what could be causing it.

A chill creeps through my veins the moment I turn the corner and spot Kieran, sprawled on the ground like a broken doll. His skin is deathly pale, and his lips are tinged an icy blue. There's no movement except for his shallow breaths that fill the air with a rasping sound, cutting through me like a blade of cold steel. Fear clamps down hard on my chest as I let out a startled cry.

My heart races as I dart toward him, my feet pounding against the cave floor as if it could make a difference. His forehead burns with fever and his skin is slick to the touch. Desperately, I shake him, pleading for a response that never comes. He lies still underneath my hands, and I'm overcome with terror at the thought of losing him.

I never should've let him go see his grandma alone.

The smell assails my nostrils with a force that nearly knocks me over. It's a putrid, noxious stench, candied and pungent at the same time, like rotting sweetness and scorched earth. I can taste it in my throat, the bile rising up like acid in my mouth. My vision blurs and I feel myself shaking involuntarily, my stomach heaving as I fully comprehend the danger Kieran is in. Fear, dread, and despair wash through me like an overwhelming wave as my trembling hand picks up a glass vial lying on the ground next to him.

Abyssal's Embrace.

I try to remember everything I've learned about drug overdoses, about what to do in an emergency. But my mind is a blur, and I can't focus on anything except Kieran's labored breathing. As a serpent fae, I didn't think drugs could hurt him—at least, not like they can any other type of fae. The very blood in his veins is like poison.

"Why?" I wail. "Why did you do this to yourself?"

But even as I ask, I know.

I already fucking know why he did this to himself.

The fear gripping my chest tightens its icy clutch, threatening to choke the life out of me. I can feel it clawing at my throat, ready to take control.

He'd told me he loved me. And how did I repay him? By not knowing the depth of his addiction? By putting this competition above him?

By abandoning him when he needed me most?

Why didn't I tell him? Why couldn't I utter the words he was so desperate to hear? I felt them as sure as I feel Luna's beams on my skin, or the magic that flows through my veins. He just wanted to love and be loved.

Ready to burn the fucking world for you, he'd told me, arms wide, just waiting for me to admit to him I can't live without him.

But I'm a coward.

I pull him into my lap, sobbing as I draw on every ounce of strength I have and knowledge I possess, frantically throwing myself into action. My body trembles with exertion as I focus my energy, calling on the power that lies within me. My eyes close as I fight against the terror, desperately trying to save the person I've come to care about more than I ought to.

A bright glow emanates from my body, illuminating the dark cave. The magic courses through my veins, and I place my hands on Kieran's chest. I can feel the power of the magic as it flows into him, trying to heal him.

It's not enough. Theo's feather should work, but I don't know if Kieran has used it already. I don't know because I haven't been paying close enough attention when he'd been begging for a lifeline.

For anyone to save him from himself.

A scream tears from my throat, the sound more animal than fae as I bare my teeth and sink them into my wrist like a blade, drawing forth the warm, crimson liquid. With a trembling hand I press it to Kieran's parched lips, summoning every ounce of hope that it will somehow deliver a portion of my supernatural power to heal him.

If I'm supposed to be a god, there's got to be some kind of power in it.

I tear open my other wrist, giving him all of me as the blood pours from my wrists into his mouth.

"Please, please, please," I sob. "I love you. I love you. I love you. Open your eyes, gods damnit, so I know you can hear me!" My words end on a wail.

But it's no use. His body doesn't respond, and I can feel his life slip away. My screams don't sound like my own in this dank cave, the pitch of them too high and strangled with emotion, echoing off the walls like a haunting melody. I shelter his head in my lap, keens turning me inside out.

Cradling Kieran's lifeless body in my arms, the reality of his mortality crashes down upon me. Tears blur my vision as a searing pain surges through my chest. The thought of losing Kieran, of never hearing his voice again or seeing the mischievous glint in his seafoam green eyes, is unbearable. It's a wound that I know will never fully heal if I don't act now.

A desperate plan begins to form in my mind. I know the potential consequences, the possible repercussions of my actions. But the thought of a world without Kieran is infinitely worse than any price I might have to pay.

As I cushion his body closer to mine, I make a silent vow. I will bring him to Chaos, promising to join him if he'll save this man, this fae who has burrowed his way into my heart against all odds. My voice, when it finally breaks through the numbness that has settled over me, is barely more than a whisper, more broken than my heart.

"I'm going to bring you back, Kieran, no matter the cost. I won't let you slip away from me forever." Then the air zaps with power as I add, "I promise."

WILL Chaos save Kieran for Rose? And if so, is the price a cost she's willing to pay? And what the hell did Chaos mean about a soul-bond? Rose already has one. She can't have two . . . can she? Find out in <u>Forbidden Rose.</u>

ACKNOWLEDGMENTS

Oofta (my Midwest roots are showing). That was a rough ending, wasn't it? I've always had a soft spot for the morally grey, so seeing Kieran die makes my world a little less bright. But if you're a fan of my work, you know how this goes. I might break your heart a bit (or a lot), but I promise I'll mend it. Eventually.

I write about heavy topics in my work because I believe in the power of storytelling to heal. As someone who has battled addiction, mental health issues, and domestic violence, I know firsthand the pain these experiences can cause. By borrowing from my own path, I hope to infuse my characters with genuine emotion and help others see that they are not alone.

Addiction is a beast that gnaws at our soul, that devours our spirit. It is a whisper that seduces us, a mirage that promises us everything and delivers nothing. But we must not be fooled by its lies. We must fight back, with all the strength and courage we possess. If you or someone you love is struggling, please don't be afraid to seek support. You're not weak for asking for help.

As I write these words, I'm reminded that my own path has been a long and winding one. It's been almost two decades since I started on the road to recovery, and I'm still learning and growing every day. Watching these struggles play out on the page has been both cathartic and humbling, a reminder that there is always more work to be done, both in ourselves and in the world around us.

So to all of you who have taken this journey with me, who have laughed and cried and felt the weight of these characters' struggles, I offer my heartfelt thanks. You are the reason I do what I do, and I hope that these stories have touched your heart in some small way. May we all continue to grow, to heal, and to find our way home.

With love and gratitude,

Kathy Haan

P.S.

This book wouldn't have been possible without an army of support:

To Kirk, my loving husband, inspiration, and encouraging supporter, who has always believed in me and told me to pursue my dreams. Your patience, understanding, and unwavering support have been the backbone of this journey.

To my children, especially **Leo**, whose creative illustrations and stunning book cover have added a special touch to my work. Your imagination, talent, and willingness to lend a hand have made this book all the more special.

To Jess, my incredible editor, who turned my messy manuscript into a polished gem. Your keen eye, patience, and insightful feedback have been invaluable in bringing this story to life.

To my readers, who have become as obsessed with my characters as I have. Your enthusiasm, feedback, and support have kept me going on this journey.

And to my writer's support groups and masterminds, who have shared their wisdom, encouragement, and support every step of the way. Your generosity and camaraderie have been a lifeline in this often solitary pursuit. Thank you all for keeping me [marginally] sane.

ABOUT THE AUTHOR

As a blood descendant of literary greats like Jane Austen and Emily Dickinson, and from a long line of artists and creators, #1 bestselling author Kathy Haan believes that the secret to telling a great story is living one. The second youngest, in a massive horde of children between her parents, she did her best to gain attention and kept everyone entertained with jokes and wild stories.

She lives a life of adventure with her hunky husband, three children, and Great Pyrenees in the Midwest, United States. While this is her second series, you might've seen her work in Forbes or US News, where she's a regular contributor. Or, in Notoriety Network's 12x international award-winning documentary, #SHEROproject.

ALSO BY KATHY HAAN

<u>Bedlam Moon Trilogy (Complete)</u>

Lana sets out to find the truth about her past, and when a hot vampire begins to unravel it for her, she's caught up in the web of an evil cult, prophecies, and curses. All while falling for the King of Vampires and his royal court. This is a why choose romance.

Bedlam Moon (Bedlam Moon Trilogy Book 1)

Tales of Bedlam (Bedlam Moon Trilogy Book 2)

Wicked Bedlam (Bedlam Moon Trilogy Book 3)

~

<u>Fae Academia Series (Incomplete, 9 planned)</u>

A spin-off of the Bedlam Moon Trilogy, we follow Lana's daughter, Rose, while she attends a magical university. The summer before college is perfect until the family begins to receive threats, and Rose ends up getting into a different college from her twin brother and her boyfriend. A male roommate, his hot friends, and a sexy professor all find themselves eager to win her affection. This is a why choose romance. Books 1-3 are Rose's story, books 4-6 are Nova's, and 7-9 will be Bee's story.

Bedlam Academy (Fae Academia Book 1)

Arcane Scholar (Fae Academia Book 2)

Forbidden Rose (Fae Academia Book 3)

Moonfire Academy (Fae Academia Book 4)

~

<u>Aggonid's Realm Series (Incomplete)</u>

A Realm of Fire and Ash (Aggonid's Realm Book 1)

A Realm of Dreams and Shadows (Aggonid's Realm Book 2)

A Realm of Grief and Sorrow (Aggonid's Realm Book 3)

When the commander of an elite group of phoenixes ends up dead for real, she tries to convince the fae devil there's been a huge mistake. Can she convince him to let her go before he snags her heart? This is an enemies to lovers why choose romance.

~

<u>Fae Gods (Incomplete)</u>

Fae Gods (April 2023)

Fae Guardians (TBA)

They watched their charge her entire life, completely invisible to her and only intervening when necessary. When they get fed up with her miserable marriage, Jocelyn's fae god watchers decide to help. After all, no fae of royal lineage deserves to be left to wilt away on Earth. They devise a plan to reveal their true selves to her, calling themselves the Marriage Doctors. But what happens when, during the course of their live-in lessons, the infallible gods fall for their off-limits charge? This is a why choose romance.

~

<u>Bedlam Penitentiary (Incomplete)</u>

Bedlam Penitentiary (TBA)

At the most ruthless prison in the fae realm, you're either at the top of the magical food chain, or you've got to form alliances with those with the most power. Because at a prison where you must expend your magic or you'll die, it's a no man's land full of dangerous criminals. This is a why choose romance.

CHAPTER ONE OF A REALM OF FIRE AND ASH

BOOK ONE, AGGONID'S REALM TRILOGY

Convectus

$\mathcal{A}$ phoenix rises from the ashes of her remains. A symbol of rebirth, and a promise of the return of the gods. I remember the myths, but I don't believe. Not anymore.

The first time I died, I was a toddler. Trapped underground in Castanea—our world below the realm of Bedlam—my mother didn't have access to the life-saving medicines of the surface, and I'd been struck with the same fae fever that had swept through our colony via the trees.

My mother had wept as she watched me writhe in sweat-drenched sheets in our one-room treehouse high atop a canopy. The sickness came on fast and strong, devouring my body until it withered to nothing. Two months later, long after they'd buried me beneath a willow, my name carved into its trunk, I'd crawled into her bed, asking for a cup of water.

It takes minutes to resurrect now.

The Tolden—the name of my people in Castanea—thought I was a child of the gods. A gift. The sickness could've kept me, but it didn't.

Instead, it left a mark on my soul, a sign that I was theirs. For hundreds of years, I lived in fear they would come for me as they did every other child. I'd embraced the nights and hated the days. In the shadows, I discovered a different kind of beauty, while the brightness of the sun revealed its own terrors. The sickly yellow light of day was the burning of my flesh. The cold, dark night offered me safety.

That'd been millennia ago. I no longer live in fear, having spent thousands of years rising from the ashes. And I no longer believe I belong to the gods. I am my own person, writing my own destiny.

As there was, and always should be, a new beginning. That's my battle cry. A promise I made to myself, to my friends, and to the realm. It was the reason I lived: to rise again, to protect the innocent, and to bring justice to the wicked.

As a fresh gust of wind blows against the windows of my treehouse, I slide my bed a little to the left and feel along the floorboards until I find one with raised corners. After unscrewing the flooring, I pull out a wrapped bundle of well-worn letters. I bring the stack to my face, inhaling its musty scent of ink and parchment that stirs the memory of a distant ocean. The smell overwhelms me, crashing against my senses like a raging tide, bringing with it the roar of waves, the salty tang of the foam and the far-off horizon of an endless sea.

But even beyond all of that, all these years later, I can still breathe in the scent of Wilder and all those days we spent together before he left. Our best days were spent far beneath the surface, exploring the depths of the ocean where the light never reaches. Days when we'd forget about the war that waged above us and just revel in each other's company. But those days were long gone.

And now, there are no more letters. No more visits. No more combing beaches for shells, making out under the stars, or sneaking in and out of Castanea.

I've only got a graveyard of memories and these scraps of dead trees tattooed with his sweet words to keep me company now. This morning, I'd needed a glimpse of them more than ever. No part of today is going to be easy, as it's an anniversary of sorts. Almost two hundred years since I've seen his face. Two thousand since the day he told me he loved me.

I take one last deep breath of the bundle's scent before tucking it away and standing up from the floorboards, just as my house begins to shudder.

I hurry to the doorway, peering out at my second-in-command. For a phoenix fae, Noct sure doesn't have a quiet tread. She rushes down the footbridge to my treehouse, shaking the entire structure with her bounding steps. Despite my annoyance at her quaking the whole place, I can't help but admire her beauty.

When she shifts, she becomes a two-headed phoenix. However, in her fae shape, Noct appears as a striking figure with one head—like the rest of us—and her maroon hair falls in gentle waves down her back. Despite her unnatural beauty, her strength and power are evident, emanating from her very being. Her silver eyes are bright and piercing, with a keen intelligence that marks her as a warrior, ready to defend her people at a moment's notice.

It's rare she and I have the same two days off in a row, and we plan on practicing shifting from our fae forms to our phoenix forms while in-flight. We're going to do it just below the cave walls to give us an even bigger challenge.

As I open the door, Noct greets me with an excited grin so wide it nearly touches her pointed ears. She's dangling a flask between two fingers. "Look what I brought!" She pushes her way inside. But as she turns around to get a better look at me, her smile fades, replaced by a look of concern etched deeply into her features. "You okay, Morte?" she asks, her voice laced with worry.

I can see the concern in her eyes; feel the warmth of her hand on my arm. But I can't find it in me to smile.

Not today.

"Yeah." I grab my bag by the door and sling it over my shoulder. "Just thinking about him."

No one knows the details. Just that the man I love is someone I can never be with.

I can still remember the first letter Wilder gave me. He'd been nervous all day, fidgeting and avoiding eye contact. But finally, as the sun was setting, he stopped me before I could fly away and handed me a small envelope with my name written in scrolling ink. I'd flown to the top of a nearby oak tree and read the letter, tears streaming down my face as he confessed the depth of his love for me, but how his kind can only be with their *anchor*.

It's their version of a soul-bonded mate, and I wasn't his.

It'd wrecked me, knowing we could never be lovers or anything more than best friends. Still does. Especially after what he did for me.

For us.

But the letters he sent me every week were something to look forward to, something to tide us over until we saw each other again on the weekends. I cherished each and every one, reading them over and over until the paper was worn thin. And even though we were only apart for a few days at a time, it was hard. It was always hard. But we made it work because that's what best friends do.

Even if I was his anchor, I made a huge mistake. One I've spent my life trying to correct.

I step out of my treehouse, the cool air ruffling through my hair, carrying with it the scent of ash and smoke from last night's bonfire we'd had by the river as a squadron.

We'd had fun.

As a phoenix, fire and ash are a part of my existence, a constant reminder of my rebirth.

But today, it's the memory of Wilder's letters that weighs heavy on my mind, tugging at my heartstrings. The thought of him, of what we could have been, fills me with a sense of longing.

Noct follows me out, her excitement for our training now subdued by my somber mood. We make our way to the nearby clearing, where we can practice our shifting without causing any damage to the surrounding trees. I watch as she takes a swig from her flask, the contents sloshing around with her movements. She offers me some.

"Unless that's absinthe, I don't want it." I shake my head. The memory of my first taste of the spiced liquor comes rushing back to me, the bitter sweetness of it filling my mouth. I had found a jug of it abandoned in the Wastelands when I'd been without water for days. It had been enough to help me get through a rough sandstorm that made the journey much longer than normal, and I'd been grateful for it.

I push the thought away and focus on Noct, who's staring at me curiously. 'What's up with you?' she asks.

"Nothing," I mutter, but even as the word leaves my mouth, I wonder if there's more to it than that.

Absinthe always seems to find me just when I need it, and it's about the only time I ever indulge. It's rare, and no one seems to know who makes it.

"Might not kill you to live a little." Noct grins.

I roll my eyes at her, even as a smile touches my cheeks. "That's all we ever do."

Live.

Releasing her wings, they glitter in the dim light of the underground ecosystem, her feathers catching what little illumination is provided by the glowing lichen that clings to the walls. Her wings are matte and ashy, as if she'd been rolling around in soot, but they still retain an otherworldly allure. Her feathers shimmer with a mix of dark blue and violet hues, and the tips of her wings are tinged with fiery orange.

Fae flies illuminate the path, and as we move towards the clearing, the distant sound of falling water grows louder, and the air is filled with the fresh scent of damp earth and mossy trees. The clearing is a small patch of soft grass surrounded by towering pines, willows, and glowbarks that reach up to the ceiling of the cavern. It's peaceful here, away from the hustle and bustle of our daily lives, and I feel a sense of calm wash over me. Noct takes another swig from her flask, and I can hear the sloshing of the liquid inside as she moves.

I stretch my wings, feeling the power within me. Shifting from my fae form to my phoenix form takes focus and control, but I'm confident in my abilities. Noct and I stand facing each other, ready to begin. I close my eyes, taking a deep breath and centering myself.

When I open them, my phoenix form bursts forth, flames flickering at my feathers. I take flight, soaring above the trees, feeling the rush of air beneath my wings.

My wings are a glossy crimson, like a bloodstain on white cotton. There are tiny bumps in the colors, as if they're filled with a network of miniscule, iridescent scales. Up close, they're not scales at all, but downy feathers that seem to glow red, like embers caught by candlelight. Or firelight, as it were.

Noct follows suit, her two heads streaking through the air with a fierce determination.

We fly in tandem, weaving around each other in a graceful dance. I can feel the thrill of the moment, the exhilaration of being alive. For an instant, I forget about everything else. It's just me, Noct, and the rush of flight. But as we come in for a landing, the weight of my thoughts crashes back down on me. The same thought that always sends me hurtling down to the floor.

My mistake.

Noct notices the change in my mood and lands gracefully beside me, shifting into her fae form. "You want to talk about it?" She toes the rock near her, kicking it into the trees.

I appreciate her offer, but I shake my head. "Nah, I'll be alright."

"Maybe you just need a good lay. Isn't the old saying that the best way to get over someone is to get under someone else?" She plops onto the grass, digging into her bag and pulls out her phone. "I can text Ronin's friend, Quinn? He thinks you're hot, and I heard he's got a big di—"

"No," I interrupt, falling beside her to steal her phone. "Isn't he dating what's-her-face?"

"They broke up," Noct sing-songs, winking at me suggestively. "Trust me, he's available."

I roll my eyes, tossing her phone back to her, the thought of being with someone else only making me feel worse. "I appreciate the offer, but I don't think a random hookup is going to solve my problems. Besides, I'm pretty sure I'd eat him alive."

She's my closest friend in Castanea, the only one who knows the shit storm brewing inside me.

My parents are long dead, lost in the war with the werewolves. Their hearts were used to cure two werewolves of their affliction long before I ever met Wilder. The pain of losing them is easily one of the worst things I've ever gone through, and knowing the Tolden no longer need to live in fear of werewolves helped solidify why I'd ever agreed to form a squadron in the first place.

Yet, I can't muster the courage to confide in Noct my deepest, darkest secret. The insurmountable guilt of my recklessness weighs heavily on my conscience, knowing that it landed the one person I love more than anything else in this godsforsaken world in prison.

A life sentence.

It suffocates me like a noose around my neck, and I can't shake it off no matter how hard I try.

Before she can respond, the sound of laughter echoes through the woods, and we turn our attention towards the path at the far end.

Ronin and Quinn appear, and I turn a scowl towards Noct. "You set me up!"

Noct just grins at me, showing off her dimples. "I didn't set you up. I only hinted we might be here." She stands and dusts grass from her shorts. "Besides, Ronin and Quinn are good company. And who knows, maybe Quinn will be able to take your mind off of things for a while."

I sigh, but eventually get up to join them. Ronin greets us with a smile and a wave, and Quinn grins when he sees me. I can't deny that he's attractive, with his messy blonde hair and bright green eyes, but I just don't *feel anything*.

"Hey, trouble." He pulls off his shirt, flashing me a smirk as he uses one hand to tug his belt free.

"I didn't realize you'd be joining us." I sigh, averting my eyes from where he's undressing.

Quinn is an eagle shifter, and always makes a point to undress before shifting, rather than buying clothes he can shift in. It's almost as if he expects me to be impressed with his skinny legs and oversized arms.

A loud chirp goes off, and I pull out my phone to see a message from the general.

EMERGENCY MEETING IN 5, MEET AT
CASTANEA COMMAND

I mutter a curse under my breath, then show the message to Noct. She nods at me gravely, her expression mirroring my own sense of dread.

"Sorry, boys," she says. "Duty calls."

It's not unusual for a top-secret mission to call us away. Work is about all I do anymore. Anything to keep my mind busy, away from my obsessive thoughts about Wilder.

We keep to our fae forms as we take air, flying towards command. The flight itself will take four minutes, and we could sift—or teleport —but Noct needs to get the alcohol out of her system before meeting with the boss.

If he's here, whatever it is—it's big.

I CALL MYSELF MORTE, but that's not my name. My name is lost, but my title is not. I am the First, the leader of the Great Company, commander of the last remnants of the God Wars. My people have forgotten the truth, and it's up to me to correct them, so I tell them stories of the old times. I tell them about the gods and the wars and the lands of the old. I tell them about the first war, when gods and mortals fought against each other, and when gods stood on the thrones of man.

I wasn't there, of course. I'm not that old. But while fae are immortal, they can be killed, and I cannot. So I tell their stories. They used to call me to battle. Not to fight, but to hold their hands as they're read their last rites. To ensure they're not forgotten when the sun sets, their bodies lie cold, and Luna's beams kiss their cheeks as she guides them beyond the veil.

That's a burden I no longer have to bear. It wasn't long before more of us were born, each bearing long, flowing manes of hair that glow in shades of fire: whites, blues, reds, oranges, and yellows. Most of us have hues of red hair, and we're all female. My crimson tresses mark me as leader, though all our beasts—beautiful birds with long wings—are fiery red.

Since High King Finian Drake retook his throne, my legion of eight phoenixes has joined the royal guard. We don't fight on the front lines. We're a special ops division, only sent to the worst conflicts. Suicide missions, where death is inevitable.

After decades of trying to get into the prison—to right the wrongs of my past—my new role might do just that one day.

In the Castanea command room, we stand before General Risç, who commands all the royal squadrons. He's a giant of a man, with muscles bulging out of his armor and his wingspan almost as wide as he is tall. But his eyes are bright and light yellow, like the sun has kissed his corneas and never left, setting them aglow.

The general's footsteps thud in the room, like a battering ram on a castle gate. The solid thunk of his footfall is a stark contrast to the quiet din of the cave walls. Each room at command is carved into bedrock, and though we're underground, flora and fauna flourish, showcasing the magic at work to keep this underground sanctuary running for all the Tolden. Vines have snaked their way up the walls, giving them a lush and verdant look. Wildflowers bloom in patches, a riot of color set against the dark stone.

Tiny points of luminescence reflect off the walls, as if stars filled up this cavernous space. A sweet scent fills the air, the subtle aroma of damp earth and petrichor that linger in the background, giving a sense of safety and home.

The cave walls emit a gentle hum, like chimes in the wind. A low rumbling can be heard in some places, presumably coming from the magic keeping the sanctuary alive and functioning.

The General's eyes hold a touch of pride as he surveys us. When the Great Company joined forces with the guard, their military casualties plummeted, though we've been busier than ever.

My heart stutters as I hear General Risç's words, the chill of dread freezing the blood in my veins. "Bedlam Penitentiary," he growls, "has a rogue inmate who's wreaking havoc on the island."

Terror grips me with icy claws. My deepest fear isn't that they'll uncover my secret connection to one of the inmates, but for his safety. My fear sharpens, taking hold of every nerve in my body, pulling it taut.

Those who say you quake with fright have never felt true dread before. It's a primordial force that seizes you, rendering you completely immobile as your body comes to terms with the magnitude of your impending danger.

Noct jabs me with her elbow, and it's then I realize the general is in front of me, trying to hand me something.

I blink hard, clearing my sight.

I take the thick manila folder from the General, infusing as much magic as I can into my hands to keep them from trembling, while flipping through the pages and photos inside.

The first page is a data sheet with inmate information.

CLASSIFIED
01 MAR 2023
NAME: Noah Tackwater
ALIAS: No-No
ORDER: Hydra
SEX: Male
INMATE NO: 00626
AGE: 2,072
HOMETOWN: Gala, Convectus
MATE: Cora Drashor [DECEASED 01 JAN 1704]
SENTENCE: Vita damnationem [12 JUN 1704]
CLASS: Extremely dangerous
CELL BLOCK: H
CELL NO: 16WL
CONVICTION: 42 counts, 1st degree murder; 3 counts,
     attempted murder; 16 counts, assault; tampering with

> *evidence, 19 counts; resisting arrest, 1 count; torture, 316*
> *counts; kidnapping, 45 counts; false imprisonment, 45*
> *counts; rape, 1 count*
> **CELLMATE:** *None*
> **PREVIOUS CELLMATES:** *Priscilla Musgrove [DECEASED*
> *FEMALE 28 FEB 2023]*
> **EYES:** *Hazel*
> **HAIR:** *Brown, shoulder length*
> **HEIGHT:** *6'9"*
> **WEIGHT:** *290 lbs.*
> **TATTOOS:** *Star on right cheekbone*
> **BACKGROUND:** *Inmate escaped holding cell while in beast*
> *form, no known accomplices, sixteen guards killed, 302*
> *inmates injured*

My breathing stalls, and it takes everything in me to remain standing. Three-hundred-and-two injured? Gods, let him be okay.

I flip the page, reading our assignment.

MISSION: *Contain or exterminate*

Attached is a mugshot of him, a picture of him in his fae form, and a photo of him as a hydra. He's one of the realm's most prolific serial killers and is said to be a master at manipulating his body. There's a grainy screen capture from a video of him ripping off the head of an inmate, his hydra form replacing his arms and neck.

"What can he do?" I glance at the General before returning to pages detailing the guards he killed.

Small mercies none of the inmates are dead.

"Besides kill?" He snorts. "He can manipulate his body in a variety of ways." The General paces. "He can tear himself apart into many small parts and reform nearly anywhere, or shape shift his fae form into a hydra. The target can be in many places at once, or singularly. He can be a serpent, a dragon, a demonic-looking thing, or even a mist."

Dread consumes me. Hydras need water. So do merfae. They're likely in the same sector, which means that either way, I'm likely about to see the man I've spent my life pining for today.

Whole or otherwise.

"The man is phenomenally dangerous." He stops pacing. "And as of twenty minutes ago, he's killed six more than what's listed on that sheet. All of you will die. Multiple times, and likely in painful ways. I recommend extermination."

"Permission to speak, sir," Bow calls from her formation behind me.

"Permission granted, private."

"Are the other inmates separated from the target?"

"The target is currently moving about within the prison, though we've confined most of the other inmates. And one more thing: you won't have the use of your magic, as they have to keep the suppressant deployed or the other inmates with revolt."

I nod, stepping out of formation to call the squadron over to a map the general lays out on a nearby table.

I point to the last marker, near the water. "He won't venture far from here, because he'll need to dip in and out of the pool to maintain his shifted form."

Noct regards me with a curious expression but refrains from commenting on my knowledge. I learned this information from Wilder's mother, who'd casually mentioned it ages ago. She spoke of how fortunate merfae were to possess the ability to exist both on land and in water, unlike some water-dwelling creatures who could only maintain their form on dry land for a brief period before reverting to their fae form.

"Should we sift to here, then?" Noct points to just outside the prison walls. "We'll have a better vantage point for the attack, and we'll be closer to the physical and magical wards that seal off the buildings from the sea."

Sabine quickly notes down an entry point on the parchment with a streak of blue ink. "Theoretically, if we can slip past the wards without being noticed, we can corner our target."

"If we can do that, it's a matter of eliminating him by use of fire." I roll up the map, barking off orders before turning back to the general. "Give us a portal stone and we'll be there in fifteen minutes."

CONTINUE READING A Realm of Fire and Ash, featuring Morte and Aggonid who both make their first appearances in the Bedlam Moon Trilogy, though you don't have to read that trilogy first to understand this.